Jane G. Austin

David Alden's Daughter

And Other Stories of Colonial Times

Jane G. Austin

David Alden's Daughter
And Other Stories of Colonial Times

ISBN/EAN: 9783337154622

Printed in Europe, USA, Canada, Australia, Japan

Cover: Foto ©Andreas Hilbeck / pixelio.de

More available books at **www.hansebooks.com**

DAVID ALDEN'S DAUGHTER

and Other Stories of
Colonial Times

BY

JANE G. AUSTIN

BOSTON AND NEW YORK
HOUGHTON MIFFLIN COMPANY
The Riverside Press Cambridge

"And if I have done well, and as is fitting the story, it is that which I desired: but if slenderly and meanly, it is that which I could attain unto. And here shall be an end."

PREFACE.

MOST of the stories collected in this volume were written some years ago and printed in various magazines, — as " Harper's Monthly," " The Atlantic Monthly," the late lamented " Putnam's Monthly," and others, to each of which thanks for the privilege of republication are hereby tendered.

At the period when some of them — notably " The Love Life of William Bradford " and " Barbara Standish " — were written, the author was in the first flush of delight and surprise at discovering the wealth of romance imbedded in that " Forefathers' Rock " which to many observers still appears a mere mass of granite, stern, cold, and sad.

Perhaps the joy of this discovery, working upon a youthful imagination and untried powers, may have induced a certain fermentation of fancy, suggesting rather what " might have been," than what is known to have been.

Certainly, the author recalls with rather rueful mirth the reproof received from an aged relative

who, after vainly inquiring for " the documents in
the case " of William Bradford, remarked : —

" You have no right to defraud people by pre-
tending to have what you have not."

The reproof bore fruit, as righteous reproofs always should, and in later and more extended nar-
ratives of the same events nothing is set down as
fact that has not been carefully determined to be
such.

In this connection it seems well to notice a
somewhat sturdy popular error, supported as it is
by what should be important evidence. The error
is that Governor Carver left children, and that
one of them, named Elizabeth, became the wife of
John Howland, the Mayflower Pilgrim.

The important but most erroneous evidence is
a stone upon Burying Hill in Plymouth, erected
some forty years ago to the memory of the Pilgrim, whereon it is stated that his wife was daughter of Governor Carver, a statement resting upon
tradition, both printed and oral. But this, like
many another tradition, was slain at the root in
1855 when the long-lost journal of Governor William Bradford, taken by the British soldiers from
the steeple of the Old South Church in Boston,
during the Revolution, was rediscovered in the
library of the Bishop of London, and by the cour-

tesy of that prelate accurately copied and printed
by the Massachusetts Historical Society. There the
governor, as if foreseeing the importance to posterity of such information, has set down not only the
names and relationships of every passenger of the
Mayflower, but thirty years later has continued the
record with memoranda of the subsequent fortunes
of these passengers. This is a statement at first-
hand and of the most incontrovertible character,
and from it we learn that John Howland, who
accompanied Governor Carver as some sort of
assistant, married Elizabeth, daughter of John
and Bridget Tillie, who with their brother Edward
Tillie and Ann his wife died in the first sickness.
Carver and his wife also died within three months
of landing, leaving no children, nor is there any
reason to suppose that they ever had any.

A certain Robert Carver appeared in Marshfield
in 1638, but he never claimed connection with the
governor, nor has the most careful research discovered any tie between them. From him have descended a numerous posterity, many of whom
proudly claim Governor Carver as an ancestor,
until the facts are set before them and they are
painfully convinced that a childless pair cannot
become anybody's ancestors.

It is much to be wished that the misleading

stone upon Burying Hill might be amended before another summer brings its thousands of True Believers to the Mecca of New England, and the authorities have promised that this shall be done.

Doubtless we who are proud to claim descent from John Howland should be glad to claim Carver as the father of his wife, but we may be sure that the man who even among the Pilgrims bore a reputation for probity and uprightness, would be the last to desire fictitious honors, or a deceitful record.

JANE G. AUSTIN.

PLYMOUTH, *October,* 1892.

CONTENTS.

DAVID ALDEN'S DAUGHTER

AND

MAJOR BRADFORD'S RED ROKELAY.

A DROVE of cattle, followed by a man on horseback, and surrounded by an active collie dog, came
slowly into Roxbury town in the afternoon of a
day in July, 1698, and paused at the Parting
Stone, or, to be more accurate, at the Parting, for
the Stone was not there then.

It is now, however, and if you like, you may go
to Roxbury and see and read, as people have been
doing for a century and a half, upon its honest
eastern face, —

THE PARTING STONE
1744
P. DUDLEY

while the northern side directs you "To Cambridge
and Watertown," and the southern one more gen-
erously gives you the route "To Dedham and
Rhode Island." It is only a curiosity now; but
when Paul Dudley set it at the junction of two
lonely country roads just behind his own house, it
was as much a convenience as the guide-boards we

hail with so much pleasure in our country drives this very summer.

"So this is Roxbury, is it?" said Samuel Cheeseboro, staring about him; "whoa, Lightfoot! Let be, Rover, let 'em graze a bit if they can find a bite. 'T is the last grass they 're like to see, poor beasts. Roxbury, eh?"

And Samuel pulled off his clumsy wool hat, took a bandanna handkerchief from the pocket of his riding coat, and proceeded to rub his head, face, and neck very much as a warm and dusty man does, after two hundred years of progress.

A comely and personable young bachelor was Samuel Cheeseboro, and so thought and declared not only most of the maids and widows of Stonington, Connecticut, where he lived, but nearly every woman encountered upon the long journey he was now completing from that place to Boston, measuring the distance by the footpace of his carefully driven cattle. Of course, he had been many nights upon the road, and at his last stopping place came near falling a victim to the determined overtures of a buxom widow, who plainly declared that the drover's cattle and her pasture suited each other so marvelously that it was a sin to divide them, and that she would give her eyes if her farm had so shrewd a master as Cheeseboro would be sure to prove.

"At any rate, you 'll be coming back this way when you 've made your market on the beasts, and you 'll tarry a day or two and rest, and look over

my acres, won't you, Samuel?" asked she, tenderly, when the young man persisted in pursuing
his journey; but Samuel pursed up his mouth,
and shook his head mysteriously.

"Not this way, dame," said he. "Not with the
load I'll be taking home. There's too many gen-
tlemen of the road between here and Stonington
for a man with a sack of silver on his nag's neck.
I have planned to ride home with neighbors of
mine who are visiting their kin somewhere nigh
hand to Boston, and we must take another road
altogether. Doubtless the loss is mine if we do
not meet again, but so it is."

"Well, and you're right, my lad," replied the
widow, good-naturedly. "And I'd as lief not
think of your riding these lonely roads with a bag
of coin jingling a call to evil-doers. What with
the Indians, and what with the swashbucklers that
pretend to hunt them, the roads are far from safe.
But when you ride Dedham way again, you'll
stop nowhere but at Joyce Patterson's, will you,
now, Samuel?"

"You'll have another goodman by then, and
he'll none of me," retorted Samuel, who, safely
mounted upon Lightfoot, with the herd already
under escort of the accomplished Rover, found himself enough at his ease for pleasantry.

And so, a few hours later, the drove and the
drover paced softly through the dust of the Dedham road, and coming to the Parting paused, the
drove to snatch a last mouthful of grass, — even as

at the same day the merry lads bound up Tyburn
Hill paused for a last deep, strong draught of
spiced ale or mighty spirits at the hostelrie known
as The Highwayman's Exchange, — and the drover
to look about him.

"Roxbury, eh ?" again remarked Samuel Cheeseboro, restoring the bandanna to his pocket and the
hat to his head. "Well, 't is a tidy little town
enough, but not a patch upon Stonington."

A verdict loyal and self-respecting upon the
part of the Stonington man, but liable to contro-
versy if a Roxbury man had heard it, for Roxburi-
ans at that date considered their settlement rather
as the Court End of Boston, the dignified retreat of
its wealthiest citizens, than as a village by itself.

Turning his back upon the Parting Stone, one
now faces a quaint old meeting-house, and sees the
Norfolk House at his right hand. Samuel Cheeseboro, standing where the Stone should be but was
not yet, faced the ancestor in the fourth degree of
that meeting-house, and saw at his right hand a
comfortable hostelrie called the Flower-de-Luce,
kept by Samuel Ruggles, a worthy citizen of Roxbury.

Grouped around the meeting-house were several
substantial mansions belonging to magnates of the
settlement. Chief of these was the great mansion
and the seven acres of merestead originally set off
for Governor Thomas Dudley, and in 1699 owned
by his son Joseph, and grandson Paul, who benevo-
lently placed the Stone. The house stood nearly

upon the site of the present Universalist church, and the garden joined the grounds of the meeting-house at what is now Putnam Street. In front of the mansion, along what we call Guild Row, flowed the bright waters of Smelt Brook, over which Paul Dudley later on threw a stone bridge. But we must not keep Samuel Cheeseboro, who is very thirsty, waiting any longer.

" They 'll have a tap of ale over yonder for sure," remarked he, considering the Flower-de-Luce, a large low-ceiled house, with gambrel-roof, swinging casement windows with roses and columbine twining around them, a sign painted with three fleur-de-lis, and a great oaken door set wide open, and giving entrance to a cavernous, low-browed chamber with sanded floor and wainscoted walls, one heavy oaken table in the midst, and others set in convenient nooks for customers needing only a " snack " and a draught. This, the principal room of the inn, served as dining-hall, bar, conversation room, and general exchange for the citizens who found themselves with an hour and a sixpence to spare for social intercourse and a glass of ale or Geneva bitters.

" You 're just in luck, young man, for the maid is putting supper on the table," cried the landlord heartily. " Or will you rather have a hack at a round of spiced beef and a home-baked loaf for a shilling, not counting your draught ? "

" My thanks to you, landlord, but I 'll tarry for neither, though I 've as good a stomach for it as

any man you ever saw; but I must get my beasts
on, and over The Neck before nightfall. To-morrow is Thursday, as you must know."

"Ay, market day, sure enough. Well, do you
know, drover, that the Boston folk will have no
more cattle pens, barring those nigh the Town
House, at the head of King Street? The yard
by the docks is closed, to make way for the growing
traffic in that quarter."

"All the more reason for me to hasten, then,"
replied Cheeseboro, blowing the foam from the
pewter tankard of ale with a roasted crab-apple
floating upon it, just handed him by one of the
drovers. "And I'd as lief pen my steers by the
Town House as farther a-field, for I shall put up
at the State Arms, in King Street, and that 'll be
handy by."

"Better stop at the Old Anchor, in the same
street, neighbor," said Ruggles, cheerily; "they've
a better strike of malt on tap just now."

"Give me the Dragon, the Green Dragon, 't is
nigh hand to the Mill Pond, — Union Street they're
taking to call it nowadays; set 'em up!" growled
a gray-bearded companion, who sat next to Cheeseboro, sipping a rummer of hot Hollands and water.

"The King's Head, close to Scarlett's Wharf, is
the best of all, says I," remarked another.

"Without you make your manners to the fe-
males, and say the Queen's Head, a little furder
up the street," amended another; and the next
man spoke a good word for the Red Lion, kept by

a kinsman of his own ; and his neighbor claimed
the palm for the Noah's Ark, in Ship Street, kept
by old John Viale ; until at last Cheeseboro, smiling
broadly on all around, tossed down the threepence
due for his ale, and said : —

" If but one man had spoke, I might have pon-
dered his counsel, but since there are so many and
so good ordinaries, I 'll e'en keep to my first choice
and get me to the State Arms, as I was bidden
before I left home. So a fair good e'en to ye all,
neighbors."

" Good e'en, drover," replied the landlord, carelessly ; " and since you will go, it is as well for you
to get on, for more than one wayfarer has been
swamped in the marshes either hand the roadway
across The Neck. One poor fellow got stuck there,
and froze to death, in a bitter night last winter."

" Yes, 't is a parlous place of a dark evening,
what with the trees and bushes, and the swamps
and flats," said the graybeard.

" They 've cut pretty nigh all the trees that were
fit for firing, but there 's a mort o' scrub left," remarked another ; and leaving them to their gossip,
Cheeseboro mounted his horse, whistled to Rover,
who at once began collecting and driving on the
cattle, and in a few moments the herd moved
briskly down Meeting-House Lane, which we now
call Roxbury Street, past the stately Dudley mansion, over the ford of Smelt Brook, and, leaving
the houses behind, entered upon the dreary stretch
of waste and broken land then lying between Rox-

bury and Boston, and called by everybody The Neck.

At what is now Dover Street, the narrowest part of the isthmus, a mud wall had been thrown up, with a pair of strong gates in the centre, and this fortification, with various improvements, remained for nearly two hundred years, until 1832, as a line of demarcation between city and country.

In good time to pass the gates, closed at sundown, Samuel Cheeseboro drove his weary cattle through, and, once within the city limits, looked curiously about him. I wish we could pause to tell just what he saw, and what are the changes two hundred years have made at the South End of the city some of us love so well. But space and time forbid, and we hasten on, until we find our hero penning his cattle just behind the Town House, a building then about forty years old, standing on the site of the Old State House of our day. Some fifty years later, the Town House was burned, and with it many valuable records never to be replaced. But, rising again and yet again from its ashes, the Town House held its original place, with King Street running past it at either hand, until the one became the State House, and the other State Street. The cattle pens lying just behind it have disappeared, however, and Thursday is no longer market day for all Boston. Between the Town House and the sea lay what might be called the South End of the Boston of that day, while the mass of the citizens lived at the North End, around Copp's Hill.

The cattle and Lightfoot safely bestowed for the night, Samuel Cheeseboro, having secured his bed at the State Arms, sallied forth to view the town, with a certain sense of Bohemian delight incident to the first visit of a countryman to the metropolis.

"Go look at the Province House, master," advised his new landlord. "'T is the finest house in town, as befits the dwelling of a real live lord."

"What! Sir William Stoughton?"

"No, but the Earl of Belmout, — my Lord Belmont, as he 's to be called. Have never you heard down in Connecticut of my lord's appointment?"

"Nay, we 've heard naught of the grandees since Sir William Phipps was sent home to England to answer for malpractice in office," replied Cheeseboro dryly, and the landlord laughed with a relish, for the imp of independence was already born in the American colonies, although it took some half century to bring it to maturity.

The next day was market day, and before noon Samuel Cheeseboro had sold his beasts to good advantage, refused more than one offer for Lightfoot, paid his score at the State Arms, and set out for Hingham, where he intended to pass a night with the Hobart family, and carry to the widow of the Rev. Peter Hobart his mother's love and a little pot of rose-conserve, which had been a great trouble to him upon the road, as his entire luggage consisted of a horseman's knapsack strapped to the back of his saddle. This knapsack, furthermore,

was now stuffed to repletion with gold and silver
pieces, amounting to between two and three hundred pounds, the price of the drove of cattle. The
principal purchaser had, indeed, offered to pay in
one of the new-fashioned letters of credit then beginning to be used after the manner of bankbills,
but Samuel Cheeseboro looked askance and shook
his head.

"I won't say they're not just as good as the
gold, neighbor," began he, "but" — And here the
other indignantly interrupted : —

"Why, surely they are, drover ! This one is
drawn on Jonathan Gibbs, the shipowner and merchant, whose warehouse you may see down King
Street this minute. If he's not good for a hundred
pounds, I'll give you my head for a China orange."

"Doubtless he's good for more thousands than
I ever saw hundreds," replied Cheeseboro, good-
humoredly. "Natheless, friend, I'd rather hold
the coin than a slip of paper in the stead of my
cattle. They are not all my own, and I know well
enow that those who trusted them to me would be
but ill-suited with a bill of exchange, or letter of
credit, whichever name I might give it, when they
look for gold and silver in hand."

"Say no more, man. Gold is scarce, but so
long as Neighbor Hull turns out his sixpences and
shillings at the rate he does, there's plenty of
silver. Didst hear that he dowered his daughter
t'other day, when she was wed to Justice Sewall,
with as many pine-tree shillings as would weigh

her down in his own scales? Thirty thousand
pound they footed up, I 'm told."

"I heard naught of that, but I 've seen a many
of Master Hull's shillings," replied Cheeseboro,
cautiously.

"Nay, I 'm not jesting with thee, man! 'T was
so in sober verity; and now I 'll be off to fetch
some of those same shillings to meet thy demand,
since thou 'lt have none of my bill of credit."

"I 'd liefer have guineas than shillings; they 're
less bulky," remonstrated Cheeseboro, but the
other retorted mockingly : —

"The Colony's silver is legal tender, and what
more is needed for a good citizen who lodges at
the State Arms rather than the King's Head?"

This business finished, and the noonday dinner eaten and paid for, Samuel Cheeseboro lei-
surely walked his horse over the desolate Neck and
through the gates into the open country, with a
heavy bag of coin strapped to his saddle-bow besides the knapsack at the croup.

"Better throw your coat over yon bag, friend,"
suggested the gate-warden, who with four men
kept watch over the safety of the town by day and
night. "It looks marvelously like a money pouch,
and there 's no lack of light-fingered gentry on the
road 'twixt here and Connecticut."

"Many thanks to you, friend," replied the young
man, gayly. "But I 've a comrade at either hand
that will have a word to say to any such gentry I
may meet withal." And, touching the butts of a

pair of pistols in the holsters of his saddle, he rode through, adding distinctly : —

"I shall hardly reach Wrentham to-night."

"Wrentham, says he ! " ejaculated a rough-look‑ ing horseman, who had dismounted at the gate a few moments before, and now hastily mounted again ; "why, it's a matter of five-and-twenty mile to Wrentham, and none too good a road. He'll never get beyond Dedham, sure."

"If that chap has his will, the drover'll never reach Wrentham with that bag o' coin at's saddle‑ bow," remarked the warder, gazing after the horse‑ man, and his subordinate slowly shook his head and filled his pipe, as who should say it was no affair of his.

But arriving at Roxbury Line, the canny drover suddenly put spurs to his horse, and turning to the left pushed down Eustis Street, as we now should say, a proceeding which so bewildered his follower that he drew rein, and sat staring stupidly after him, until, a brilliant idea penetrating his brain, he muttered an oath or two, and putting spurs to his horse galloped off down the Dedham Turnpike, to wait in ambush at a point where a cross-road con‑ nected the southern and southwestern highways.

"He thinks to cheat me by making a roundabout turn, does he? Well, he'll find I'm upsides with him, I fancy," muttered he.

Meanwhile Samuel Cheeseboro, unconscious that he was "wanted" by this knight of the road, passed quietly by the turning that would have led

him into the snare, and pushed gayly on through
Dorchester, Quincy, and Weymouth, reaching
Hingham in good time for supper at the hospita-
ble parsonage, where the aged widow of Peter
Hobart received his mother's message with that
pathetic gratitude for remembrance one finds
sometimes in very old persons.

The next morning, soon after breakfast, Cheeseboro was again in the saddle, and passing through
Scituate and Marshfield reached the confines of
Duxbury just about as the sun told him that it was
nearing midday.

" They 'll have eaten dinner at Master Alden's,
and I shall put them about if I go there fasting,"
muttered he, drawing rein at the top of a long,
sandy hill, and looking about him in search of some
house where he might apply for a dinner to be
duly paid for.

No house was in sight, but as he gazed behind
him another horseman suddenly appeared, rapidly
riding along the road he had just covered.

" Mayhap he 'll know," murmured Samuel; and
turning Lightfoot across the road he saluted the
stranger on his approach with, " Good-morrow,
friend ! Can you tell me of e'er a house nigh
hand where a man might find a crust and a cup ? "

" Oh, ay — surely — why not — why not ride
with me so far as my brother's, just past that little
wood ? They 'll be gay and glad to give you all you
want," stammered the stranger, who was in fact
none other than he who had accompanied our hero

out of Boston, and, having since then learned his
plans from the hostler at the State Arms, had
spurred after him, hoping that, owing to the
drover's delay in Hingham, he might overtake him,
as he in fact now had.

Something in the man's voice and looks and
strange embarrassment of manner touched the
vein of caution in the nature of the Connecticut
man, and it was very coldly that he presently
said : —

"Well — I 'm beholden to you, sir, and if your
brother truly lives nigh hand, and they will sell
a meal to a man " —

"Surely they will, friend, surely," replied the
robber, who had now recovered his presence of
mind. "They 'll give you of their best, and ask
naught but your good-will in return."

"Nay, then, that 's not my fashion," returned
Cheeseboro, stolidly. "I pay as I go, among
strangers, and ask no favors but of them to whom
I can give favors."

"A pest on your proud stomach! But come
along, come along, and sith you 're so particular,
I 'll promise you shall pay handsomely for all you
get."

"This way, do you say ? "

"Ay, 't is but a bridle path through the wood,
but 't is the shortest way."

"Well, go you first, and show the road."

Without reply the stranger pushed his horse
into an obscure path leading, very much as it does

to-day, into what has been called the Cathedral
Wood. Cheeseboro followed closely, and after a
few rods both horses emerged into a little clearing
with a spring welling up in the middle. Lightfoot, thirsty with her long journey, whinnied ap-
provingly, and, snatching the rein from her master's hand, made a push for the water and thrust
her muzzle into it.

"It's like your willfulness," exclaimed Cheeseboro, reaching far over his saddle for the bridle
just slipping into the water.

The defenseless posture was too great a tempta-
tion to the robber, and, pushing his own horse close
behind that of his victim, he aimed a terrific blow
at that lowered head with the loaded stock of his
riding whip. Some slight sound, some subtle instinct, warned Samuel Cheeseboro of a danger that
might well have been his last, and with a sudden
start he swerved from the blow, which fell, indeed,
but upon the shoulder of the mare, who, with a wild
cry of terror and pain, wheeled in her tracks and
flew again through the narrow path into the open
road, the bridle trailing around her knees.

With a furious oath the robber gathered up his
reins and started in pursuit, but as his horse flew
through the thicket bridle path, and emerged into
the main road, he came into violent collision with
the sober steed of an elderly gentleman, jogging
quietly along the road from Plymouth to Duxbury.

Now, this quiet, elderly gentleman was none
other than Major William Bradford, eldest son of

the late governor of the Colony, and a man of wealth and consideration in not only his native town of Plymouth, but in all the country round, even as far as Boston.

Invited to a festive occasion at the house of his step-brother, Constant Southworth, the major had donned holiday array, and especially adorned himself with his new scarlet roquelaure, embroidered in gold thread and fastened with a silver clasp.

Now, Major Bradford was not a fool, and unfortunately highway robbery was by no means an uncommon occurrence, even in the Old Colony, at that date ; so, seeing one man carrying a heavy saddle-portmanteau rush out of a wood, with flying reins and disordered air, and another pursuing him with a leveled pistol in his hand, the major understood the case as well as if he had been present throughout, — understood, but unfortunately had no means of interfering, except the slight dress sword he wore at his side, a weapon quite useless, unless the highwayman would consent to pause and meet it.

" Halt, you rascal ! " shouted the major, and as he shouted, the east wind, which that day tore madly in from sea, seized and filled out his scarlet roquelaure with such sudden fury as to drag one side of the great silver clasp from its fastening, and tear the whole garment from the major's shoulders, filling it out and lifting it for one moment like a great collapsed balloon, and then with a sharp gust, too much like elfish laughter, tossing it into the face of the highwayman and around

the head of his horse, who, already exasperated by
sharp and sudden spurring, neighed wildly, reared,
plunged, kicked, and finally set off at a mad gallop
on the road toward Plymouth.

Major Bradford turned in his saddle, and stared
after the fugitive for a long minute, then, raising
his cocked hat, bowed ceremoniously toward the
retreating figure, saying : —

" A pleasant ride to you, friend, and so soon as
I arrive at my brother Southworth's house I will
take care to send a swift messenger to Plymouth
with testimonials to your character. But glad am
I that you left my rokelay behind, albeit in the
dust."

So saying, the major dismounted, deliberately
picked up his cloak, examined the parted fastening,
and finally, throwing it loosely over his shoulders,
led his horse to a convenient stump and remounted.

" 'T is best to see whether Orlando Furioso gathered up his reins, or if the nag hampered himself
and flung his rider," muttered the major, resuming
his road and noting the deep imprint of the flying
horse's feet. Passing with only a reluctant glance
the road that led to Constant Southworth's and the
wedding feast, Master Bradford again soliloquized
a little : —

" Ah ! he 'll come to David Alden's by this
road, and they 'll care for him if he 's in straits.
David has two comely daughters left, though John
Seabury has carried off my sweetheart Bessie.
Well, well ! 't is the way of a man with a maid ;

they 'll aye crop the fairest flower and make off with it for themselves, caring little enough what lack they leave behind. Ay, old Solomon had the rights of it " —

But just here the major's philosophical mutterings were cut short by the sight of a riderless horse cropping the stunted native grass beside the road, with the reins dangling broken beside her head.

" Oh, you unmannerly brute ! " exclaimed he angrily ; " you 've flung your master, and now your only concern is to fill your own belly ! "

Lightfoot, thus adjured, raised her head, and, whinnying in an apologetic manner, trotted slowly back upon her tracks, and presently stopped beside a tangle of red-leaved blackberry vines and elder bushes half hiding the crumpled body of a motionless man.

" Here we are ! Hi, friend ! Art hurt ? " queried the major rather uselessly, as the man was obviously unconscious. Then, without waiting for a reply, he cautiously dismounted, tied Lightfoot's broken bridle to that of his own steady nag, and, stepping gingerly through the briers, stooped over the unconscious form of the drover and carefully moved the limbs, turned the face to the light, and laid an intelligent finger upon wrist and heart.

" Yes, yes ! poor fellow ! Grievously hurt, yet not unto death — yes " —

A curious sound compounded of a growl and a whine startled the major from his abstraction, and a footsore and bewildered dog, brushing past his legs, planted himself upon the other side of the prostrate body, and fixed a glance of stern inquiry upon the stranger.

" Hi, good dog ! 'T is your master, is it ? Well, now, that's well enough, for you shall stay and keep goold while I ride for help. Watch him, good dog ; watch him, sir ! "

To this superfluous charge Rover vouchsafed no reply save a somewhat contemptuous wave of his tail, but the expression of his face and attitude announced better than words his acceptance of the kind offices of this well-meaning if somewhat impertinent interloper, who evidently was not the person responsible for his master's misfortune.

" That's all as it should be, then, and I'll come to David Alden's in five minutes by the sun-dial," quoth the major, mounting briskly and stirring his fat cob to unusual speed, while Lightfoot, with the precious saddle-bags intact, trotted contentedly beside him.

Rover, a little uneasy at this proceeding, bounded from his master's side to the road, growled faintly, and, leaping against Lightfoot, made a feint of seizing her bridle, but yet in so tentative a fashion that, when the major stooped, and patting his head said, " 'T is all right, good dog ; all right ! I do but serve thy master, sirrah, and am his friend and helper," Rover accepted the assurance, and, standing in the road with faintly waving tail, watched the horses out of sight before he slowly resumed his position beside his master.

Half an hour later, Major Bradford returned, and with him an ox-sled driven by Samuel and Benjamin, sons of David, and grandsons of the Pilgrim John Alden, but lately gone to his rest. The sled had been hastily provided with a straw bed and some rugs, and the major, still on horseback, bore a flask of mingled spirit and water, a generous dose of which he at once proceeded to pour down the throat of the young man, now slowly returning to consciousness.

"His arm is broken for sure," remarked Samuel, as he and his brother carefully raised the helpless body.

"And Comfort Starr gone, and no other leech nearer than Boston!" suggested Benjamin, gloomily.

"Nay, father and I can set it as well as ever a doctor of 'em all," replied Samuel, and the major added: —

"Ay, that you can, Sam. David Alden and I dressed many a broken arm, and leg too, in the Pequod time."

"The womenfolk are all agog to have the care of him," suggested Benjamin with a grin. "Mother and Betty (you know, major, our Betty and John Seabury, her goodman, are on a visit to the old homestead) and Prissy and Elsie are just gay at thought of such matter of wonder and amaze."

"Ay — they 're women," returned the major briefly, and the oxen started on, Rover trotting sedately at his master's side.

A week later, Samuel Cheeseboro, paler and thinner than when he drove his cattle over Boston Neck, but otherwise very nearly his own man, lay upon a broad wooden bench beneath the balm o' Gilead trees that shaded David Alden's doorstep.

Near him sat David himself, comfortably smoking his evening pipe, and chatting with John Seabury, the husband of Elizabeth Alden, while that young matron, crouching upon the doorstep, held a half-whispered conversation with her mother sitting just inside the house. Priscilla, a comely, fair haired maid of eighteen, and Alithea, her younger sister, strolled up and down just out of earshot, and laughed and murmured little confidences, and laughed again in the sweet foolishness of untired youth, and made so fair a picture in the summer gloaming that Samuel Cheeseboro answered more than once at random to the wise remarks his host was making upon the result of Andros's maladministration.

Suddenly his reverie was interrupted by a question from John Seabury.

"Shall you be able to ride by then, Cheeseboro?"

"Ride by — when? where?"

"For the where, to thy own home, man, and to mine, to Stonington," returned the other, laughing. "And for the when, it is just what I was asking of thee. My wife and I would set forward to-morrow, or on Wednesday by farthest, but I am doubting if you can ride all day, and for more than one

day, so soon.   What think you yourself, young
man ?"

"If 't were not for this arm" — murmured
Cheeseboro, casting a rueful look at the wounded
member as it lay in a sling of red silk handkerchief.   The others laughed good-naturedly, and
David Alden said : —

" Why, if 't were not for that arm there would be
no question at all.   But as it is, we must not have
the kindly intention of its healing disturbed more
than can be helped, and I fear me the jar of riding may do it no good.   If, now, we had some sober
lad to ride behind you and support the bent arm
just as it lies " —

"Ay, to hold it in his own arm, as it were,"
suggested Mistress Seabury eagerly.   "If it were
not that I have the baby to carry, I would do it
myself."

" Why might not I do it?" cried a fresh young
voice, and hastily looking around, Cheeseboro saw
that Priscilla and Alithea had halted close beside
the group and were listening to the conversation.

"If you only would, mistress!" exclaimed he
ardently, so ardently, indeed, that Betty Seabury's
eyes sought her husband's with a many-volumed
romance in their depths.

" Why should you not, Pris?" cried she hurriedly, before her mother could utter the slow re-
buke upon her lips.   "Father and mother said but
yester eve that you might go home with me for a
visit, and father was to spare Ben to carry you and

fetch the horse again; so now, if you can ride behind Sam Cheeseboro, father 'll have to spare
neither Ben nor horse, and you can hold up the
broken arm to pay for the accommodation."

"There's no pay wanted " — began Cheeseboro,
but stopped short, struck dumb by the merry warning glance of the young matron's eyes, and David
Alden, dear old soul, helped on the matter with the
prosaic statement : —

"I shall be glad enough to keep Ben and Dobbin
at home to haul kelp."

"Of course you will, father, and I 'll be thankful
enough if I may have Pris to spell me with the
baby on the road and at home."

"You 'll take turns riding behind Master Cheeseboro, then ? " suggested the careful mother, looking
from one daughter to the other, and although Priscilla's dainty color was deeper than its wont, her
eyes were placid as the summer sea shining in the
distance, while Betty answered for both : —

"Of course we shall, mother, and I 'll warrant
me Pris shall do her full share of jogging behind
my John with little Molly on her lap;" and Mistress Seabury in the twilight ventured to give a
reassuring little push to her mother's foot close beside her.

"How could you do it, Pris?" said Alithea, as
the two girls prepared for bed in the fragrant dusk
of their unlighted attic bedroom, an hour later.

"Why, did n't Parson Holmes tell us no longer
agone than yesterday that we were every one of us

to play Good Samaritan so often as we got the chance? And wasn't this a rare good chance, Mistress Alice?"

"Rare and good, Mistress Pris. I only wish Judah Paddock might break his arm at our gate."

"Nay, that's not a Good Samaritan at all, Elsie!"

Then with a delicious little giggle the two maids fell on their knees, and the sweet summer night was still.

"'T is too good to be true; they'll think better of it by morning," confided Samuel Cheeseboro to his pillow in the next room; but although David Alden, after a talk with his wife, looked upon the proposed arrangement as more serious than he had as first considered it, he did not withdraw his consent, and Priscilla made her preparations for the journey with a heart beating in some strange, new excitement, which she chose to attribute to her first visit so far from home.

The next morning but one, when the sun still dripped glory from his morning sea-bath, two horses, a frantic dog, two men, two women, and a baby grouped themselves about the flat boulder serving as horse-block in front of David Alden's cottage, and with all the bustle and chatter and running back and forth incident to such occasions, the husband, wife, baby, and a bag of varied provisions for man, woman, and child were packed upon Rufus, John Seabury's strong roadster, and moved forward to leave room for Lightfoot, to whose saddle a thick pillion had been attached at the rear, while the money bags were elaborately fastened in front, forming a fortification almost amounting to breastworks for the rider.

" Now, then, fair and easy, my son," said David Alden, beckoning Cheeseboro to step upon the boulder. " Come up hither and slide into the saddle 'twixt bags and pillion as gently as a gouty old man might do. There, then, that's clever! You 're saddle-fast, and now, Priscilla, — wow, then, my lass, thou dost need no more help than a bird to reach thy perch! Settle thyself well, seize Samuel's belt with thy left hand and put the right under his elbow, so — nay, 't will not bite thee, foolish lass! Put out thine arm, so that his may rest upon it as a shelf. There! That's better. Now, Cheeseboro, how does it seem? As if 't would do?"

" As if 't would do for life, sir," replied the young man, with a vigor that reminded David Alden of his wife's hints and suggestions so forcibly that he remained speechless. Perhaps the reflex of those suggestions reached the heart and conscience of the younger man; for after that startled pause, a deep red surged up even to the back of the neck Priscilla was shyly contemplating, and pulling off his hat he said in a low voice : —

" I heard you bless Seabury and his wife, — won't you bless us, too?"

" Indeed I will, my son, for he who craves a blessing surely means to deserve a blessing."

"God so deal with me, father, as I shall deal with thee and thine," murmured Samuel Cheeseboro; and as the patriarch blessed them and sent them forth into the world together, a new day began in their lives as well as over that quiet, pastoral landscape; a fair summer day, with sunshine and flowers and song of birds, and delicious fragrance of moist woodland and herbage, and the sweet, strong breath of the incoming tide. What a journey that was! Spite of all her stout-hearted promises, Elizabeth Seabury trusted no one but herself with the care of her precious baby, or the privilege of clinging to her husband's belt, nor did Priscilla weary of tenderly supporting the broken arm, whose breaking Samuel Cheeseboro counted as the most fortunate incident of his life.

Day after day of that wonderful journey they rode along through the enchanted country which most of us have visited, yet never might abide in; that fairyland whose experiences lead us up from earth into the misty mountain regions where our ideals dwell forever, safe because we never reach them.

Yet day after day Samuel Cheeseboro forbore to touch the little hand upholding his wounded arm, or to speak one word of all those trembling upon his lips and shining in his eyes.

"She shall be safe in John Seabury's home before I tell her how I love her, or so much as put that dear hand to my lips," said the brave fellow to himself, and kept his word so well that, as she slipped from her pillion at her sister's door, Priscilla's beautiful eyes were too heavy with tears to rise to her lover's face, and when he eagerly asked, " May I come to see you to-night, Mistress Priscilla ? " she dared not assure herself for what he wished to come.

That was in July, and on the old records of Stonington Church one little sentence tells the story of the next six months : —

" 1699 January. Samuel Cheeseboro to Priscilla Alden," and some later hand has added, " granddaughter of Pilgrim John."

THE WIFE OF JOHN CARVER.

I.

"A FAIR wind and a strong! Shame it were that it should be wasted as those before have been! Sit you here, Dame Kate, while I go up to the change-house and speak again to Master Jones, who of a truth is treating us but scurvily in thus delaying. You do not fear to tarry here a short half hour, with Roger Wilder for guard and Elizabeth Tillie for company, — eh, Kate?"

"Surely not, John. Go your ways, and we will spend the time in walking up and down the pier. This same fair wind blows somewhat shrewdly for sitting still."

"Nay, if it is cold to thee, sweetheart," replied the husband, a grave man already in middle life, and dressed in the sombre garb of the Separatists, turning back and looking somewhat anxiously into the face of his wife, a young and lovely woman, whose blonde beauty proclaimed her English birth, as her somewhat sad-colored and demure garments did her adhesion to the strait sect of which her husband was a prominent member. And yet, had Dame Katherine Carver allowed herself the aid of all the coquettish appliances distinguishing the toilet of the gayest beauty among the cavaliers, she

could hardly have selected head-gear so becoming
as the hood of dark purple velvet shaped around her
face in the fashion first introduced by Mary the unhappy Queen of Scots, and followed at intervals by
the whole female world for almost three hundred
years. Against the background of this hood the
pale, pure face, with its delicate features, faint col-
oring, and sweet, calm expression, showed in almost
angelic loveliness ; while the glimpse of a throat
whiter than ivory vouchsafed by the handkerchief
modestly crossed upon the bosom, and the delicate
hand, foot, and ankle displayed at intervals by the
" shrewd wind " of which the lady complained,
were, if not so angelic, perhaps equally admirable
points of beauty.

Fair and winsome as she was, who can wonder
that John Carver's thoughtful and somewhat anxious gaze softened as it rested upon her face, and
that a loving smile stirred the gravity of his expression ? But to the tender expostulation, sec-
onded by a movement to lead her away from the
pier, Dame Katherine hastily replied : —

" I said not it was too cold, goodman, and I am
overweary of staying within-doors. We two, Elizabeth and I, can walk or rest here in all safety until
your return, and Roger Wilder shall guard us if
you will. Come, Bess."

And putting her hand within the arm of her
companion, a sweet English lass, not yet past her
seventeenth summer, and fresh and blooming as an
English spring, Mistress Carver led her down the

pier, while John Carver, the smile still lingering
upon his lips, walked rapidly back toward the
town.

" There he is again, dame," said Elizabeth, suddenly, as the two women approached the end of the
pier.

" He ?   And what he, my girl?" asked the elder
lady, a little coldly.

" Why, the young man of whom I was speaking
yester-eve. I said that he looked in desperate case,
and as if but little more were wanting to send him
off the end of the pier, where he sits to-day as he
sat then, gazing now into the water at his feet,
now at our vessel riding there at anchor. I marvel
if he may be wishing to join himself to us."

" If he does, he should make his petition to
Master Bradford, or Master Carver, or Captain
Standish. Of a truth he does look in evil case;
and what is worst of all, he seems too downcast to
bestir himself to the mending of his condition. I
would that my goodman were here, that I might
ask him to give the poor soul opportunity to speak
with him."

Even as she spoke, chance and the wind presented the coveted opportunity to the object of this
conversation ; for, as Mistress Carver drew from
her pocket a handkerchief somewhat heretically
embroidered, the breeze snatched it from her hand,
and would have whirled it into the water, had not
the young man sitting at the end of the pier caught
it as it flew past him, and, rising, come toward the

two ladies with an eagerness of manner immediately noted by the younger.

" Beshrew me, mistress, but he is glad enough of the chance to speak with us," said she, softly.

" Hush, Bess," replied the other, and the next moment returned the obeisance of the young man, with a gesture courteous, but full of dignity and reserve, while she said : —

" Truly, sir, I am beholden to you, and render you my thanks."

" It is nothing, madam. If I might venture to say it, I am myself your debtor in being permitted even so simple a service."

" You have my thanks, sir, and good-even to you."

" Pardon, madam, if my foolish words have offended you. I spoke only as I felt."

" I am not offended, young man, but I and my husband, and this young gentlewoman my friend, are of the adventurers in yonder vessel, and, as perhaps you know, we of that sort hold not to compliments and courtly phrases, such as you seem to have been bred in."

And the young woman could not or did not restrain a swift, scrutinizing glance at the soiled and disorderly dress which might have placed this stranger very low in the social scale, had not his manner, words, and expression been unmistakably those of a gentleman. The object of this look caught and read it as rapidly as it was given.

" I have, indeed, been bred to other things than

I have attained, madam," said he, gloomily; "and, although not yet past my seven-and-twentieth birthday, have come to the end both of my patrimony and my friends. Poor as this suit may be, it will last my life out, and serve for grave-clothes, too."

The last words, muttered to himself as he turned away, and not intended for the lady's ear, reached it, nevertheless, and she exclaimed : —

"What is that? A full-grown man, hale and sound of limb, and not untaught, and speak after that fashion! Nay, sir, you shall give me warrant for your words, and if I have not skill or means to help your hurt myself, it may chance that I know those who can. What is this deadly trouble which has turned your brain, as it seems to me ? "

As the sweet, somewhat imperious, but kindly and womanly tones fell upon the young man's ear, he turned suddenly, and, raising his haggard eyes to the lady's face, exclaimed : —

"You are the first woman, madam, who has spoken to me for mine own good since my mother died."

"Poor lad! And will it help you to tell me something of your case? I would not intrude, but it may be I or mine can help you."

"What there is to tell, madam, I will gladly narrate ; but there is not much chance of help."

"Say not so. Had we, whom you call Separatists, been thus easily daunted and dismayed, I had not been here to-day to listen to you," said Mistress Carver, seating herself upon a bench beside a pile

of merchandise, and motioning Elizabeth to sit beside her. "Know you not, young man, that we
sailed out of the Low Countries nigh upon two
months by-gone, and that since we finally bade
farewell to home and friends we have twice been
turned back from the unknown road we are bound
to travel, putting in once at Dartmouth, and now
here at Plymouth, where we have been forced to
give up one of our ships and part of our company,
but yet are steadfast to proceed with what is left,
although we journey whither we know not, and to
what ending no man can tell? And of our company are many aged and infirm, many little children, and women to whom God has denied such
strength as they earnestly desire, but yet are none
afraid, or willing to turn back. Is this spirit yours
as well? But come, get thee to thy story, for my
husband will be here anon to take us on ship-
board."

"First, then, madam, my name it is John Howland, and I come of a good family in Essex; but
my father and mother being dead, and my elder
brother in possession of their estate, I, with my
younger son's portion, have long been a stranger
to the house where I was born; and it is now three
years since the last sixpence of that portion left
my pocket. How it went it would be shame for
me to tell, and unfitting for you to hear; but my
brother, who looked coldly upon me while I was
wasting my patrimony in riotous living, turned his
back outright when I went to tell him that I would

fain adopt some honest course, and be put in the
way of earning a decent livelihood; so, being turned
off by frowning Virtue, I e'en returned to smiling
Vice, and danced to the Devil's piping until I had
no longer a groat to pay the piper; since when I
have lived I know not how, save that I have never
begged or stolen, or done aught of which I need
to be ashamed. For this week past I have watched
your vessel there at anchor, and wondered if by
any chance it might befall that those holy adventurers would receive among them an unholy adven-
turer desperate as myself; but I have no money,
and no recommendation; and now that the Speedwell is condemned, and her passengers crowded
upon the Mayflower, I should never dare to ask to
be taken."

"I said, Dame Carver, that he fain would go,"
murmured Elizabeth Tillie; and John Howland
turned his hollow, hungry eyes upon her for the
first time.

"Said you so, mistress?" asked he, kindly;
and the girl, blushing scarlet, murmured assent,
while the elder lady slowly said : —

"Of a truth, we are crowded overmuch, but it
seems a question of saving a man body and soul,
and — Ah! here is my husband. Elizabeth, take
Roger and walk down the pier, and Master Howland may accompany you if he will, while I speak
to Master Carver."

Rising as she spoke, with a delicate flush upon
her cheek, Katherine Carver went to meet her hus-

band, who received her wonderingly, and listened
to her story, at first with some distrust, but finally
with grave sympathy.

" And, John, if you would take him for your
servant, and bear his charges until we come to Virginia, he will repay you amply with his service. I
am sure of it," said the young wife, in conclusion,
and so earnestly that Carver smiled.

" Why, dame, if he was thy brother thou couldst
not plead more earnestly," said he. " How can
you be so sure of a stranger all at once ? "

" I know not, but I am ; and I have set my
heart upon snatching this goodly brand from the
burning ; and you will not refuse me your aid,
goodman ? " replied the wife, with so subtle a smile
that it was reflected upon the grave face of her
husband as he replied : —

" Why, no, Kate, I will not refuse thee ; for
thou art such a shrew that indeed I dare not."

" That is well, and as it should be," replied Mistress Carver, merrily ; " and now call John Howland and settle matters with him, while I speak
with Elizabeth Tillie."

So then it fell out that when, in the course of
the next day, Captain Jones was prevailed upon
to set sail from Plymouth in England toward
what was to be the Plymouth of New England,
John Howland was enrolled among the passengers of the Mayflower as " servant to Mr. John
Carver."

II.

The annals of that voyage have descended to us; and, simple and unconscious as they are, every page is filled with a story of sublime faith, heroic endurance, and indomitable resolution such as never in the world's history has been excelled, and is only equaled by the inspired voyage of Columbus toward these same shores.

In the story of the Mayflower's winter passage occurs one mention of our hero not to be omitted here. William Bradford says : —

" In sundrie of these storms the winds were so feirce and yᵉ seas so high as they could not beare a knote of saile, but were forced to lie at hull for diverce days together. And in one of them, as they thus lay at hull in a mighty storme, a lustie yonge man called John Howland, coming upon some occasion above the gratings, was with a lurch of yᵉ ship throwne into yᵉ sea; but it pleased God yᵗ he caught hold of yᵉ tope-saile halliards which hunge overboarde and ran out at lengthe; yet he held his houlde, though he was sundrie fadomes under water, till he was haled up by yᵉ same rope to yᵉ brime of yᵉ water, and then with a boate-hook and other meanes got into yᵉ ship againe, and his life saved; and though he was something ill with it, yet he lived many years after, and became a profitable member both in church and commone-wealthe."

Before the Pilgrims landed upon the famous rock, now become the Mecca of the New World, Master John Carver was formally chosen governor of the

colony about to be founded, and accepted the office
in the primitive spirit which ordained that he who
would rule should also serve, and that the chief
among a people should be he who labored most
anxiously and untiringly for its good. No man,
accordingly, wrought more laboriously than the
new-made governor at the arduous tasks of unload-
ing the ship, landing the passengers and their ef-
fects, felling trees, hewing timber, and building first
the common-house, to serve as a temporary refuge
for those who first landed, and then smaller cabins
for the accommodation of separate families. When
these families were small, it was adjudged that
they should receive the addition of two or three
single men, of whom there were quite a number,
and in this manner the hundred and one persons
comprising the colony were divided into nineteen
households. The governor, partly out of deference to his position, partly because his family already numbered eight, — namely, himself, his wife,
Desire Minter, and another maid-servant, John
Howland, Roger Wilder, a servant lad named William, and a little adopted boy called Jasper More, —
was allowed to occupy his cabin alone ; and it was
hardly completed before it began to assume a certain air of refinement and delicate care hardly to
be accounted for by the few articles of handsome
furniture John Carver had indulged his wife by
saving from the wreck of their household plenishing
in Leyden. Chief among these *meubles* was a great
arm-chair, richly carved and quaintly fashioned,

which may to-day be seen preserved in the Pilgrim
Hall of Plymouth, Massachusetts, where the memory of this her earliest governor and faithful servant still is venerated, although he left no descendant, and the Carvers of the present day come from
another stock. But it was not the chair, the table,
or even Katherine Carver's dainty sewing-stand and
carved footstool which gave to the unfinished sitting-room of this cabin its air of taste and elegance:
it was the presence of the woman herself; it was
the gentle and refined atmosphere which surrounded
her, — the impress of her own pure and womanly
delight in all that was graceful, beautiful, and fitting. Elizabeth Tillie, coming often hither for
refuge from her own noisy and utilitarian home,
more than once asked, not without a sigh : —

"What is it, dear Mistress Carver, that makes
this house so different from the rest ? Certain it is
that my mother and I toil more than enough to
bring our own home into order, and we, too, have
some little furniture from over-seas, but our place
is forever in a hurly, or else so cold and formal
and forbidding. What is the secret, mistress ? "

"Truly I know not, except that John Carver
dwells here, and not there," the wife would sometimes reply; but Elizabeth only shook her head,
until at last one day John Howland, waiting until
Katherine had left the room, said to the despondent
girl : —

"Do not be cast down, Elizabeth, because you
cannot be like the governor's dame, or make your

home like that which takes its hue from her. Do the flowers droop and die because they are not the moon, who shines over all, and whom all may love and admire, even though they never may come anear her, or even imitate her?"

"And you hold the governor's wife even thus above all other women?" asked Elizabeth, sharply.

"Even as the Papists hold their saints," replied the young man, gravely. "A being to be loved, venerated, followed humbly and awfully, — a light set above the path of sinful man, even as a lamp unto his feet and a guiding beacon to his weary eyes."

"It is well that Elder Brewster hears you not, young man," said Elizabeth, dryly. "He would surely deal with you somewhat straitly for giving that adoration to a fellow-creature which is only fitly placed above."

"I did think, Elizabeth, that you, too, loved Mistress Carver heartily and singularly," replied Howland, a little severely.

"Well so I do. Who dares say I do not? But — but — that is another matter. Good-even to you, John Howland."

And as Elizabeth quickly left the house. her face flushed, her eyes brimming with tears, the young man looked after her in astonishment, muttering:

"Truly the ways of women pass a man's understanding. How have I angered her by praising our lady and mistress!"

Hardly were the Pilgrims disembarked when

came the pestilence, which in three terrible months carried off half of their little band, leaving barely fifty alive when it passed away. Day after day, as Carver and his two assistants returned from laboring with or in the service of the sick, they had a new story of death or disease to relate, and Dame Katherine, her sweet eyes overbrimming with tears, would hasten from her own household duties to such offices at the bedside of her neighbors as she could with her slender strength perform, until she herself was stricken down; and Carver, returning home at night, found her and Desire Minter stretched upon their beds and groaning with pain, while in the next room Roger Wilder and the little Jasper lay dead, the boy William and the maid-servant being in almost as bad case in the loft above.

" Here is work enow for us at home, John," said the governor, sadly. " And if we could but have a woman's help " —

" John Tillie and his wife died yesterday, and Edward, his brother, and his wife are dead to-day, and Henerie Sampson and Humility Coper are better, so that Elizabeth Tillie has naught to do at home but mourn, and might come hither, if Mistress Carver wills it," suggested John Howland, his hand upon the door-latch.

"Go and ask her to come, John," replied the governor, his wistful gaze fixed upon the flushed face of his darling.

And Elizabeth, wiping the tears of orphanhood from her eyes, came at John Howland's bidding;

and they two nursed not only Katherine and the others, but the governor himself, who shortly after fell sick, more of weariness and over-effort than of the disease, which at last left only seven persons able to perform the offices for all the sick and dying and dead about them.

But with the sharp spring winds came a change. The pestilence passed, and its victims crept out into the pale sunshine, and, finding some uncertain strength returning to their gaunt frames, applied it to the great task, still scarce begun, of building a home in this wilderness for themselves and their children.

Among these laborers was Carver, who, still feeble from long illness and anxious attendance upon his wife, now in a measure restored to health, daily led forth the laborers, under the direction of Squanto, an Indian, who, alone surviving the pestilence which had some years before desolated this region, still lingered about his birthplace, and became very serviceable to its new inhabitants. Squanto it was who taught his pale-faced friends how and when to sow their scanty crop of corn, where to catch fish, how to net the abundant shoals of herring with which to dress the poor and exhausted soil, and many another savage art, known and practiced by his fathers upon this very spot for centuries before the Pilgrims, or even Columbus, saw the shores of the New World.

Squanto, too, it was who brought his adopted chief, Massasoit, to make a treaty with the white men, and later on warned them of hostilities meditated against them by the Narragansetts, and other hostile tribes and factions, proving himself from first to last their firm and faithful friend. And it was Squanto who, opening the door of the governor's cabin while the family sat at breakfast, stepped lightly inside, and said, in the broken English he had acquired during a captivity in England some years before : —

"Good-morning, master. Want plant corn again to-day ?"

"Yes, Squanto, yes. We must be up and doing, — must labor while it is yet day, for the night cometh " —

And, not finishing his sentence, the governor stood still in the middle of the floor, fastening a strange look upon his wife, who felt it, and rising came toward him, inquiring tenderly : —

"John, must you work so hard again to-day ? You are not yet strong from that terrible illness, and you overwrought yesterday."

"Dear heart, be not alarmed. It is my place to set a good example to my brothers, and the Lord will uphold his servants. Come, John Howland, Squanto is already gone."

But John lingered until he could say to Katherine, unobserved by her husband : —

"I will stay by his side, dame, and lighten his burdens if I may, and though he look something pale and meagre he has the strength and spirit of two yet in him."

" I thank you, John, and I trust him to you for
so much as he will allow you to do; but it is this
very spirit that leads him on emprises beyond even
his strength."

" I will do my best, dame," repeated John,
mournfully, and hastened to follow his master to
the field; while Elizabeth Tillie, watching the private conference, bit her lip, turned red and pale by
turns, and finally left the room, muttering: —

" I know not what to think of this saint-worship.
No, not I."

III.

The April day rose soft and sweet, but, rapidly
increasing in heat as the hours marched on, arrived
near noon at the sultry fervor of July; such another day as that famous 19th of April, a hundred
and fifty years later, when the British, retreating
beneath the fire of every stone wall from Concord
and Lexington, dropped exhausted in their march,
overcome as much by the intense heat as by their
enemies or their own panic.

" Truly, if this is the spring, what shall we
expect of summer weather? " panted the choleric
captain, as he vigorously broke the matted sod with
his heavy hoe. Beside him toiled Winslow and Carver, side by side, John Howland close at the governor's right hand. All three, all four indeed, had
been gently nurtured; all were of the class whose
habits inure to luxury rather than to toil; but no
four men among the twenty or thirty laboring be-

neath that scorching sun kept even pace with these that day. It is not the large-boned, heavy-limbed draught-horse who bursts his heart in voluntary emulation or endeavor, but the fiery thoroughbred, whose superb muscle and sensitive nerve are but the electric wires between his noble spirit and his wonderful deeds ; and among men, the heroes and martyrs are not they who simply do their duty, but those who see in duty the broad foundation of aspiration and endeavor.

The sun had reached its meridian, and already some of the toilers straightened their bowed backs, and glanced at their cumbrous watches, when John Howland, about to request his master to follow their example, saw his face turn deadly white, then flush of a dark red, while his eyes glared wildly, and one trembling hand wavered uncertainly toward his head, then grasped wildly at the air. The arms of the young man were already about him, and Master Winslow, seeing his comrade's case, threw off the sick dizziness besetting him also, and came to Howland's help.

" It is a return of the sickness," said one.

" Nay, it is a flow of blood upon the brain," cried another.

" It is a sunstroke. The great heat hath been too much for his weakened condition," said John, tremulously. " But let us get him home to — nay, who shall warn the poor wife of the terrible calamity that hath befallen her and us? You, Master Winslow? Where is the Elder ? "

" He went home with a bitter pain in his head an hour or more agone," said one of the men ; while Winslow, kneeling beside the insensible body of his comrade and chiefest friend, groaned aloud : —

" I cannot, John ; no, I cannot. This new cross is bitterer than all the rest, and I lie crushed beneath it. Oh, my friend, my friend, my more than brother! The hand of the Lord is very sore upon us this day ! "

"Then it is I who must bear the tidings ! " exclaimed Howland, in a voice of anguish. " Tarry for yet a few moments, friends, then bear him home, and I will hasten forward to prepare " —

The next words were smothered in the great sob that all unconsciously rose in the young man's throat, and then he sped away, running as fast toward the scene he dreaded scarcely less than death, as ever hastened guest to joyous festival.

The frugal dinner was already upon the board as Howland entered the house, and Elizabeth Tillie was putting the last touches to the little decorations with which she had learned to embellish these simple feasts. She turned as she heard the familiar step, but stopped short in the cheerful greeting that first rose to her lips, and stood staring into the ghastly face of the messenger, the rich color slowly fading out of her own.

" What is it? Oh, John, what has happened ? " gasped she.

" Where is the mistress? I must see her this moment."

"She went to lie down, quite worn out, but now. What is it? Hath aught befallen " —

At this moment the door from the inner room suddenly opened, and Katherine Carver stood before them, a smile upon her lips.

"Truly, dear Bess, I am but a loiterer " — began she, yet paused panic-stricken as John Howland, stepping forward, took her passive hand in his, and, leading her to the great arm-chair, seated her therein, saying sadly : —

"Dear mistress, I am the bearer of ill-tidings; but I beseech you not to be utterly dismayed, for the Lord yet reigneth, and He will guide his own."

"My husband! Is he " —

"No, dear lady, he yet lives ; but he is very, very ill, — stricken down but now, even at my side."

"And you promised to guard, to save him! Oh, false friend and careless servant, who did not see that this was coming upon him, — did not warn him, save him!"

"Nay, dame, what man can foresee the hand of the Almighty, or guard against his decree " — began Elizabeth, half indignantly. But Howland silenced her with a look, and turned again to the bereaved and almost desperate woman, who was rising from the chair, casting an indignant and contemptuous look upon him, and moving toward the door ; but Howland threw himself in her path, crying : —

"Dear lady, go not forth to meet them! The feet of them who bear him hither are already at the

door. Dear, dear mistress, be strong, be steadfast;
arm thy soul with courage such as it hath already
shown among us. Oh, beloved mistress, he is sorely,
sorely ill ! "

" He is dead — tell me the truth ! " demanded
Katherine, hoarsely, but still she tottered toward
the door.

" Not dead, but smitten very sorely. They are
here. Elizabeth, where shall he be laid ? Rest
upon this chair, mistress ; cover thine eyes, and
pray for strength ; for verily thy need is at the
greatest."

" Lay him upon his own bed, his marriage-bed,
the bed where I, his widow, will lay me down to
die," whispered Katherine, shuddering from head
to foot, yet suffering herself to be put gently back
into the deep chair as the shadow of those who
bore her husband home fell across the sunny room.

Then came the solemn, heavy footfalls, the suppressed question and answer, the passage of that
mournful group ; and then they laid him down, a
dying man, upon the bed his death should widow.
But Katherine, pushing aside the trembling hands
that would have detained her, arose and followed,
saying, in a voice no longer like her own : —

" It is my right. Let be ; I am his wife."

So she and Elizabeth ministered to him as best
they might, the maid weeping and shivering, but
the wife, with a rigid calm of face and manner
awful to those who looked upon her.

" He will never speak again, — he will scarce out-

live the day," murmured Standish, who was reputed
to have more knowledge of leech-craft than the rest.
And John Howland, listening, shook his head, and
looked with eyes of anguish at the wife, who, pale
and cold as marble, stood holding one of the icy
hands, her stony gaze fixed upon the deathly face.
The brave and gentle soldier caught the glance and
followed it, then moved toward Dame Katherine's
side, and took her other hand.

"Sister," said he, "you spoke words of marvel-
ous comfort to me when Rose Standish died, three
months agone. Think upon them now, for I can
speak none half so sweet or wise."

She heard, yet never moved her eyes from their
set gaze, nor changed her frozen calm, although she
muttered: —

"Let be; I am his wife."

"As Rose was mine; but God took her, and you
bade me bow before his judgment. You told me
she was safe and happy now"—

"I prithee peace, friend! Vex not mine ears
with words whose meaning I cannot guess. Oh,
leave me, all of you, — leave me with my husband —
my husband!"

And with a wild sob she flung herself upon her
knees, and buried her face one moment; but as a
faint moan broke from the lips of the dying man
she rose, and, stooping toward him, seemed to still
even her own breathing, lest by emotion she should
shake ever so lightly those last few grains not yet
run out of Death's hourglass.

But it was not until three more days had passed
that the noble and heroic Carver drew his last painful breath, and passed from beneath the cross to
receive the crown he so well had earned.

" Our brother sleepeth in the Lord," solemnly announced the reverend Elder Brewster, who watched
beside the bedside of the dying man ; and then he
turned to Katherine and laid a hand upon her arm,
saying : —

" Come away, daughter ; thy work is ended here.
Come and pray for comfort to Him who alone can
give it."

But breaking from his hold the bereaved and
stricken woman, with one cry of such agony as few
are called to endure, fell prostrate upon the bed,
her head upon that heart which had pillowed it so
tenderly and so faithfully through the bright brief
years of her wifehood, and never, never had met
her with coldness or with silence until now.

" My husband ; oh, my own ; my treasure ; my
darling ; my life !   My husband, my husband ! "
And clinging there, she swooned so utterly, and so
long, that they thought she too had died.   But after
weary hours of waiting, and of unceasing effort,
those who watched beside her saw her eyes open
slowly, at first with only a heavy, unconscious sadness in their depths, across which presently shot a
gleam of sharpest anguish, and then the dull apathy
of hopeless suffering.   It was John Howland who
first ventured to address her, and he said : —

" God be praised, dear mistress, that you have

come back to us, else had we been like lost children indeed, lacking both a father's guidance and
a mother's love."

But Katherine only moaned, and turned her face
upon the pillow, where it lay for hours cold and
white and still as that of the husband sleeping
his last sleep upon his marriage-bed in the room
beyond.

IV.

The funeral over, William Bradford, upon whom,
as men already whispered, should devolve the gov-
ernorship of the little colony, and the personal su-
pervision of its private as well as public interests,
came to see the widow ; and after certain wise and
kindly sayings, mingled with exhortations to resignation, or at least submission, whose only fault was
that they were somewhat hard and strong for the
nature to which he would adapt them, the governor-
elect inquired : —

"And how will it suit you to live, Mistress Carver? Will you continue here, with Desire Minter
and John Howland and Elizabeth Tillie for company, or would it be easier for you to conjoin yourself with the fragments of some other broken family, as hath been done already in several cases ? "

"I will stay here in the home which my husband
made, and where he died ; and if these will tarry
with me " —

"I, for one, will tarry with you, mistress, until
you send me from you," said John Howland, his

eyes fixed upon the delicate face of the young
widow, and his own cheeks glowing with eagerness.

William Bradford looked scrutinizingly at the
young man, and drew his eyebrows deeper above
his keen eyes, as if to shield the thought suddenly
arising behind them. In the Mayflower, which some
two weeks before this date had sailed for home,
went a letter from William Bradford to Alice
Southworth, his early love, telling her that he was
a widower, and beseeching her to come out to him
as his second wife, and not yet four months had
rolled over the watery grave of poor Dorothy May,
so that the mind of him who had been her husband
would naturally not be startled overmuch at thought
of second nuptials somewhat speedily arranged.

"Thank you, friend," said Katherine, gently; "I
shall not long keep you from gayer company."

"I pray thee, mistress " — began John, and
stopped. Bradford took up the word: —

"Nay, dame, such intimations are but rebellious,
or, at the least, weak and cowardly. You will
doubtless live out the days appointed for you, and
it may be that the affliction which to-day seems to
touch your very life will in time become but a
chastened memory, above which may be built the
structure of a fair, new life."

Neither of his hearers replied, and after a few
more words Bradford arose to go. Howland left
the house with him, and as the two walked down the
steep street toward the water-side the elder said : —

"We who are men, friend Howland, are bound

to protect and guide the weaker vessels that are conjoined with us, and it has become your especial duty, it would seem, to have a care for this sad and weeping sister of ours. Should it even seem as if this end could best be reached by a marriage between you two, I for one should consider such marriage a wise and advisable step. It is much for the interests of the colony that every man should rear a family to succeed to his work and his possessions ; and also that women, bereaved of their natural protectors, should receive others as soon as may be. It is needless to say more at present upon these matters. You apprehend my meaning and my object in speaking to you at this time ? "

"Yes, sir. You thought I should have considered such a hope too wild and too high, and should have crushed rather than encouraged any yearning I might find in my heart toward a lady so far above me " —

" No man in this wilderness is above another ! " sternly interposed Bradford. " Did not we leave all that was easy and comfortable and dear, all save our own souls and those of our wives and children, and brave a thousand deaths, that we might also leave behind us the vanities and godless rule of the Old World ? Each man, and each woman too, stands here to-day, as he shall one day stand before God, answering only for himself, founded only upon himself, worthy of respect or love only from his own deeds and efforts."

So spake the governor of the infant republic

dropped like an acorn upon the shores of the New World, and destined one day to develop into the oak whose roots grapple the round earth, and whose crest rises free and glorious in the light of the rising and the setting sun.

Returning homeward, John Howland met Elizabeth Tillie, who had been present, although silent, during Bradford's visit to her friend and mistress, Dame Carver. She paused as John was about to pass her, compelling him to do the same.

" You staid not long at the water-side," began she.

" No ; we did but go to look at the fare of fish the men took this morning. It is a goodly one."

" Ah ! And did you hear news of the marriage that is to be ? "

Howland started, and turned pale. Elizabeth, watching him narrowly, tossed her head and bit her lip, and, before he could reply, continued : —

" Nay ; I know not why it should go so near your heart, seeing the bride is to be the widow Susannah White, whose goodman died but two months since ; while Master Edward Winslow, who is to marry her, buried his wife Elizabeth seven weeks agone come Monday. It is the fashion of the colony, you see, to bury a man's memory along with his bones ; and the first decays sooner than the last. I think not overmuch of widows like that, even though Master Bradford lend himself to make the match."

" It is not well to judge too hardly of our brethren, Elizabeth" — began the young man, in a troubled voice; but the girl snatched the word from his lips.

"Lest we make for ourselves a law against our own inclinations," said she, sharply; and, without waiting for reply, kept on her way, leaving Howland to slowly and thoughtfully climb the hill and enter the house, where he found Katherine still seated, as he had left her, in the governor's great chair, her pale face laid against the back, and the great tears slowly gathering upon her lashes and rolling over her thin white check. The young man stood looking at her for a moment, then slowly approached, and stood close beside, but without touching her.

"Dear mistress, your sorrow breaks my heart. If I could soothe it in any fashion, — if the knowledge that one man at least would give all else to pleasure you and bring you comfort" —

"Thanks, good friend, and more than thanks. I know that you would think any trouble light, if by it you could ease mine; but, oh, John, it is my life that is crushed, my heart that is broken; and for that trouble what balm can even your kind and brotherly affection devise? Stay with me until the end, John, and soothe my dying bed as you did his; no more is possible."

"I will never leave you while we two live, Dame Katherine," said the young man, solemnly; and between those two full hearts fell a silence, broken only by the sound of the stormy waves lashing the shore hard by, and the solemn voice of the clock telling of Time speeding momently toward Eternity.

V.

Another month passed over, and May was softening into June, when Governor Bradford, meeting Howland a little way from the town, abruptly inquired : —

" How is Mistress Carver now, and how comes on thy wooing, man ? "

" My mistress is but poorly, sir ; and I have never dared intrude such a thought as that of another marriage upon her sorrow," replied John, with such a change of color that the elder shrewdly remarked : —

" But you have thought upon it yourself, and the idea is a marvelously sweet one to your mind."

" I cannot deny so much, sir, but " —

" Leave ' but ' to keep company with ' peradventure,' and go home and speak your mind to the widow. You are but a young man, and know not women as your elders do, John. They love to be importuned, and persuaded, and urged even against their own commands. Many a man has lost his chance from too great a modesty and distrust of his own worth, like our gallant Captain with Priscilla Molines. Go you home and ask Dame Carver to promise to become Dame Howland by and by, and you shall see that the roses will bloom again upon her cheek, and the tears dry from her eyes. I fain would see that matter settled."

And the governor, assuming a little more than his usual dignity, as if to compensate for the frivolous nature of the discourse in which he had just indulged, strode up the Burying Hill to search the offing for the ship of supplies then anxiously expected, and Howland meditatively pursued his way.

" It is all but hopeless, and yet — it might give a change to her gloomy thoughts at least," said he ; and finding Katherine alone, sitting, as was her wont, in the great chair, her hands locked upon her lap, her sad eyes fixed upon them, and an air of abstraction and melancholy veiling her from head to foot like a garment, he seated himself beside her and gently said : —

" Dear lady, I wish that I might see you less sad."

Katherine looked up with a wan smile.

" I am not so sad as I have been, John."

" God be praised if your sorrow is lightened."

" God be praised that He is answering my prayer."

" Your prayer for resignation ? "

" Nay, but to be allowed to follow him who hath gone before."

" You do not mean that you would die ! " exclaimed the young man, turning pale. A gentle smile alone replied to him, and, covering his face with his hands, he groaned aloud.

" Nay, John, why grieve that I am at last to be happy once more, after so many days of suffering and well-nigh despair ? "

"Because — oh, mistress of my heart and my life — because I love you with all the strength that is in me, and have loved you since first you spoke to me that black day long since, when I did but wait until you should be gone before I drowned myself; and you it was who saved me and made a man of me, and brought me hither, and I worshiped you saint-wise, nor thought of earthly love until now that you are all alone in the world, and I at least might stand between you and suffering and want; and, oh, Katherine! if all the love and all the worship that are possible from man to woman would move you, — if the thought that you were leading me heavenward day by day, if " —

"Oh, stop — stop! Cruel, false, unfaithful that you are, how dare you thus insult my wifehood! How dare you think of me or speak to me as other than John Carver's faithful wife, whom God hath for her sins divided from him for a while, and after will bring into his presence for an eternity of bliss? Oh, John Howland! you have bitterly disappointed me, for I did think that in you I had a true and trusty friend and brother; and now " —

"And now you hate and despise me, and will withdraw even the liking and the confidence that you have entertained for me so far," broke in the young man, bitterly.

"But how could you, John, — how should you even dream of such a matter? And I had thought to see you wedded to Elizabeth before I died."

"Elizabeth?"

"Yes, Elizabeth Tillie, who loves you, and has loved you for all these weary months; and you never saw it?"

"Nay, dame, I thought not of her, at any rate," replied Howland, sadly and abstractedly. Mistress Carver, her short-lived indignation changing to milder feelings, sat looking at him for a while, then said, kindly:—

"Think not overmuch of my reproaches but now. I might as well have answered you more kindly; for you did not mean to wound me, and I am not so rich in love that I should trample upon an honest heart, though it may be that I could not so much as think of accepting it; but, John, it is true that I am soon to leave you, and I fain would see the two I love best happy together before I die. John, you said you would do much for my pleasure."

"God knows I would, dame," groaned the young man.

"Then will you marry Elizabeth?"

"Oh, mistress, will no less satisfy you?"

"Naught else would give me half the pleasure, or add to the delight I have in following my husband."

A long silence followed, and then John Howland laid his cold and trembling hand upon his mistress' knee.

"I am all yours, lady," said he. "Do with me as will best pleasure yourself."

"Thank you, dear friend. Shall I speak for you to Elizabeth?"

" An you will. But profess not that I love her other than as a kind friend and sister. Let her not mistake."

" I shall ask her, as I have asked you, to do this for the love and satisfaction of a dying woman who holds you two dearer than any now on earth."

Then forth into the chill and damp spring night the young man rushed, and wandered for hours, wrestling with a man's strength against his own rebellious heart and disappointed hope.

Four weeks later Elizabeth called her betrothed to the bedside of the beloved mistress, whom now all confessed to be a dying woman. Dame Katherine held out her thin, hot hand, and looked into his face with a tender smile.

" Faithful friend, be not so sad and downcast in seeing the day of my deliverance at hand. Would you weep if you saw a dear sister wedded to the man she loved ? — and I go to rejoin the husband dearer than any bridegroom. But first — for still will the cares of this life follow us even to the gates of the next — first I fain would see my poor Bessie happier than she is. John, you do not love her overmuch."

" I strive to be kind to her, dear mistress ; and I did ask you to tell her at the first that I was no lover," replied the youth, struggling for composure.

" But, John, that is but keeping the word and breaking the spirit of your promise to pleasure me in this matter. I would see you love her as well as be kind to her."

"Oh, dame, you are very hard, very cruel with me! You know that your word is as a law to me, and you are pitiless as the grave!"

"John!"

"Nay, pardon me! I am but a savage to speak thus, and you lying there; but oh, if you had bid me die for you, it had been easier."

"Yes, dear friend, for it is easiest of all to die when one is called to prove a great love; and so, because your love was yet greater than enough for that test, I have put it to a sharper one, and asked you to live for me, — yes, and to be happy, and to make another happy, and all for love of your poor heart-broken sister, who can do naught for you. John, did I count too far upon that love of yours?"

"Dear lady, if it may be that the blessed spirits look down from heaven upon this sad earth of ours, you, so looking down, shall see your friend Elizabeth a happy and an honored wife, — yes, and a beloved one in time, if love will grow by care and will."

"I would fain see the beginning now, if it might be. Will not you wed her here at my bedside this very night, for I doubt me if I see to-morrow's sun?"

John Howland reverently raised the wasted hand he held to his lips. It was the first approach to a caress he had ever offered to the woman he so passionately loved, and it was also the seal of the abnegation he had made of that forbidden love. Then he said : —

" I will speak to Elizabeth and to the magistrate,
and all shall be appointed as you wish. I will go
this moment; but" —

" I will not depart before you return, dear John,"
murmured the dying woman, reading his thought;
and with one glance of anguish this man, whose
love, as Katherine herself had said, was greater
than that of him who dieth for his friend, went out
to do her bidding.

When he returned, Elizabeth, pale and silent, sat
beside the bed. Katherine lay with her eyes closed,
yet not asleep, and, as he entered, gently asked: —

" Has Master Bradford come? "

" Yes, mistress; he is waiting in the outer room."

" And is all in readiness, Elizabeth? "

" All, dear mistress, so far as I am in question."

" And you, John? "

" I am ready, mistress."

" Then hasten, for the time grows short."

Howland, without replying, summoned the magistrate, and in a few minutes more he had become
the husband of Elizabeth Tillie, who, pale and
silent, looked as little like a bride as he like a
bridegroom. The ceremony over, and the governor
gone, Katherine called the two to her bedside, and,
giving a hand to each, whispered a few words of
thanks and love; then, closing her eyes, lay still
and silent, until, as the beautiful light of the pure
morning broke over sea and sky, touching the
sombre forest and the rugged hills with glory, and
transforming the wilderness of waters to a golden

highway leading straight from earth to heaven,
Katherine Carver's faithful soul went gently forth,
seeking reunion with its mate, and entering, as
who shall doubt, into that eternal joy of which the
purest and the happiest earthly love is but a dim
reflection.

John Howland and his wife lingered beside her
grave when all else were gone, — she weeping, he
still and self-contained. All at once she said : —

" You loved her better than me, John, and you
married me to pleasure her."

The husband was silent for a while, then passing
his arm around his wife's waist he softly said : —

" And as we both of us loved her, and she loved
both of us, that love shall be a holy tie between us,
Elizabeth, and out of it shall grow a happy and a
loving life, if you will help me to cultivate it."

" But all for love of her ? " persisted Elizabeth.

" She is now an angel in heaven, and you are my
wife, and all that I have on earth to love me or to
love.   Elizabeth, will you love me, and help me try
to make a happy life out of this our great sorrow ? "

Silently the young wife laid her hand in his, and
they two went home to the lonely house to begin
what was in the end a life as fair and sweet as its
beginning was sad.[1]

---

[1] In grading Cole's Hill, which was the first burial place of the
Pilgrims, a grave was found, containing the skeletons of a man
and a woman. The male skull was of fine development, and it is
very possible that this was the grave of Governor Carver and his
faithful wife.

BARBARA STANDISH.

THE pale sunset of a New England winter day was fading from sea and shore, although it lingered in the tops of the melancholy pines sparsely clothing the sides of Burying Hill in the town of New Plymouth, when a young woman painfully climbed its steep acclivity, and, drawing her cloak of fine gray duffle closely about her, sank upon one of the tree-trunks lying all about, waiting to be squared and fashioned into beams for the fort not yet erected.

A fair, young girl she looked, with lovely rose-tints on cheek and lips, mild blue eyes, a wealth of golden hair, and a sweet mouth, just now piteously down-curved. Gentle and timid and loving she looked and was, none more so, and yet the strongest man, the most robust woman of the hundred, who had borne her company across the stormy winter sea, — not one had shown more of the high courage and brave endurance that were their glory than this frail girl, Rose, wife of Myles Standish, already military leader of the colony.

Through the discomforts and privations of the voyage, with its mishaps, delays, and constant disappointments; through the sickness and death already rife among the doomed company; through the lonely terrors that must have beset her while

her husband led his little band of explorers into
the unknown fastnesses of the forest, and was absent from her days and nights that might mean
forever; through the fatigue and annoyances of
debarkation, and the necessity of putting her
dainty hands to uses they had never known before,
— through all and everything, this fair English
Rose had borne herself with a noble courage and
strength, the admiration of all who saw her, the
wonder of all except the husband, who knew her
for his fitting mate.

But now the end was drawing nigh, and she felt
it. Sitting upon that desolate hillside, with the
winter sky darkening above her, and the winter
wind moaning through the pine-trees at her back,
she looked across the sea, whose waves, leaden in
hue, and each tipped with an angry line of foam,
came hissing sharply in upon the sandy shore below, and thought of the fair home which she should
see no more forever. The deep lanes white and
odorous with hawthorn bloom, the sunny nooks
filled with violets and daisies, the meadows gay
with cowslips and blue with harebells, the trees
green with spring and filled with those blithe home
birds whose very songs were gayer and more
heart-free than these of the new, strange world
about her could possibly be, — all these she saw
and heard, sitting so motionless there in the pallid
twilight, and gazing across the bitter sea to the
line of palest blue, which, like a wall of ice, shut
her away from all these tender memories. Then

her eyes wandered slowly back to the encampment at her feet, the huts of hastily felled timber, some few complete, others in every stage of progress, and already arranged in the steep and formal street by which the pilgrim of to-day climbs from the shore to the level of the town. Among them stood the temporary common-house erected upon the first landing, and still occupied by most of the company; and nearer at hand the half-finished cabin which her husband and John Alden were building for her own future home.

In the offing lay the Mayflower, weather-beaten, insufficient, unreliable, and yet the one only link between home and the hundred brave or failing hearts who had abandoned that home and all its joys, all its security, devoting life and fortune, — nay, planting their very bodies as seed in this barren soil, whence was to spring the magnificent growth of a nation.

" Never, never, never again ! " whispered Rose Standish, drawing the warm cloak about her, and yet shivering through its ample folds. " Never shall I see home flowers bloom again, or hear the song of home birds, or kiss my little Barbara's lips; and I would that yon vessel were away, for its gray sails beckon me like hands, and tempt me to wish that my lord should carry me to lie among my kin, and beneath the old yew-trees where we cut our names " —

" What, dame, is 't thou ? " exclaimed a voice somewhat gruff and hoarse perchance, but powerful

and frank, as befitted the captain of the colony's
army, and the protector of its hundred lives.
Most vigilant, too, was he in its defense, and had
mounted the hill in the winter twilight to make
sure that all was safe and well about the embryo
fortress, whose chief architect and deviser he was.
And here among the timbers, and the tools, and
the black frost, and the glooming night he had
come suddenly upon his tender Rose, sitting so
fair and spirit-like, as if she were the guardian
angel of the little camp below.

"What, sweetheart!" repeated the captain, his
hand upon her shoulder. "How come you here,
and all alone?"

"I was so tired, Myles, of the noise and heat in
the common-room, and my head ached so sadly,
that I thought perhaps the cold, fresh air would
help it."

"Thy head, child? Yes, and those blue eyes
are over-bright, and thy little hands are scorching
hot even in this nipping cold. Rose, darling little
one, you are ill at last, and who can wonder?"

He threw his arm around her as he spoke, and,
raising her to her feet, pushed back the hood from
her face and perused it anxiously. The sweet face
smiled upon him bravely and tenderly, yet could
not hide the terrible story written so legibly upon
it. Full five minutes they stood thus, while the
waves sobbed heavily upon the shore, and the wind
moaned among the pine-trees in awful sympathy.
Then with a sudden movement the soldier, the man

who knew no fear in face of foe or sternest privation, clasped his wife close to his heart, and bending his head upon hers, cried aloud, in sudden
terror : —

"Rose, my Rose! What were I without thee!"

"Dearest, our God is good. I will not die if
He will let me stay," whispered the girl, and clinging to her husband's breast she shivered heavily,
like one who feels the cold blast from an open door
strike through his blood. Yes, and the door was
opened wide, the door that never opens in vain,
nor closes until one has passed through to return
no more forever.

Myles Standish bore his wife down from the hill
that night in his arms, her head lying heavily upon
his shoulder, and her quick breath scorching his
cheek. Ten days later he took her in his arms
again, while the fair head drooped yet more heavily
upon his shoulder, and the dim eyes vainly strove
to speak the love that neither pain nor death could
chill, and the cold, faint breath fluttered across the
pale lips, and died upon those that bent to meet
them.

"Good-by, dear love" — those were the words;
but whether they were spoken by the dying lips of
flesh, or the deathless spirit already exhaled from
its fair tenement, Myles Standish could not say.

One of the matrons standing weeping there took
the precious burden from his arms, softly saying : —

"Alack, dear heart, she is gone at last, and now

is free of all her pain and weariness. Thank God for that, at least, goodman! "

" Hold thy prating tongue, dame, nor bid me thank God for taking away more than mine own life ! " exclaimed the captain, sternly ; and so strode from the room, from the house, and away into the wilderness, leaving all who heard him aghast at such impious rebellion.

When he returned, hours later, mild Elder Brewster sought and labored with him long and zealously, yet at the close went away sadly, shaking his hoary head.

" It is a strong and stubborn heart ; yea, and a proud, unyielding neck," murmured he. " God must deal with him in his own way, for I am not strong enough."

They dug a grave for Rose Standish upon the hillside, — one of the earliest among the graves so soon opened in the virgin soil of that stern new home ; but before spring there were so many that the Pilgrims leveled and planted them with wheat, lest the savages, whom as yet they knew not and ignorantly dreaded, should perceive their ever-increasing number, and so take courage to fall upon and exterminate the feeble remnant that remained alive.

And ever as the pestilence spread, and one after another was stricken down, until the living scarce could bury the dead or attend upon the dying, Myles Standish held the foremost place, whether as laborer, as nurse, as counselor, — providing food for those who could eat, forcing the churlish ship-master to supply such things as were needed from his stores, ministering to the sick, burying the dead; ever strong and resolute as men should be, gentle and patient as women are; never shrinking, as his noble fellow-laborer, Bradford, has recorded, "from the meanest or most loathly services;" never yielding to fatigue, or infection, or despair; so that the Elder himself confessed at last: —

"Though he may not be godly, he is of a verity goodly; and though holy words are full seldom in his mouth, holy works are ever in his hands."

So passed the winter and the spring, until the day when the Mayflower set sail again for England, bearing among her other dispatches a letter from Captain Myles to the relatives of his late wife, recounting her death and the manner of it, and ending thus: —

But this heavy sorrow and loss makes no change in the purpose I expressed when last we met, with regard to relieving you of the charge of maintaining my late wife's cousin Barbara, and she may be forwarded to me by the first ship sailing hither. It was very near to my wife's heart that the child should come to us; and now that she is gone, I do but desire the more to fulfill her wishes, and in this case still the more that it has been told me Barbara is neither welcome nor happy under your roof; and although God knows it is little enough I have to offer here, such as it is is heartily at the service of Rose Standish's adopted sister or, for that matter, at the service of any of her kin who choose to come hither.

Lest there should be talk of unfitness in placing a little maid in the care of a gruff, middle-aged soldier, I will say in this place that I have thought of marrying again with a very modest as well as comely young woman of this place, whom the sickness of the last winter has bereft, even like myself, of all that belonged to her. And this I do, not through forgetfulness or carelessness of Rose, my wife, who has her own place in my heart, wherein no other can ever enter, but because in this new country it is well for every man to be the head of a household, and to rear up children to become fighting men for the defense of the colony, and sturdy mothers to increase it. In such a handful of struggling souls as this, every man is bound to act, not for himself, but as part of the whole, and has no more right to indulge a selfish and churlish grief than to burn up his own house because it no longer pleases him, and in so doing set the whole village in a low.

All this I say, not that I see need of setting up a defense against your judgment, but that you may know under mine own hand the deliberate reasons for the course I propose, and which may very likely be hardly judged by those of you at home who sought, and vainly, to divide Rose from me before that we were wed.

And so, with a father's greeting to the little maid, and such as are fitting to you and the rest, I remain,

MYLES STANDISH,

Captain of the Plymouth Colony.

"There they have the bitter and the sweet together," muttered the captain, laying his letter among those John Alden, his helper and housemate, was preparing to send by the Mayflower on the morrow. "They are rid of this poor little Bab, and they know that I shall marry again, and none of their blood shall ever sit in Standish Hall as heir of mine, should I come by my rights."

But before the gray sails of the Mayflower had sunk behind the Gurnet upon her homeward voyage, Standish had committed the fatal error of sending John Alden to do his wooing, instead of venturing himself, and Priscilla Molines had murmured that naïve sentence which comes down through the centuries as fresh and bright and girlish as any utterance of to-day : —

" Why don't you speak for yourself, John ? "

We all know how that ended, and how the captain, hardly pausing to hurl an angry reproach at his unfortunate and yet too fortunate envoy, rushed away to fight the savage Wituwamat and his band, who had hurled defiance at the little colony in the form of an imperious summons to depart as they had come, leaving the land already occupied and owned by the red men. This message was accompanied, so says the old chronicle, by the skin of a rattlesnake filled with arrows, — a symbol of deadly warfare ; but when this was laid upon the council table by the envoy of the Indians, Standish seized it, threw the arrows contemptuously upon the floor, and filled the snakeskin with bullets ; then he thrust it with a few stern words into the hands of the messenger, and pointed toward the door.

So there was war to the knife between the colo-

nists and the Indians; and in the early gray of the
next morning the captain led forth his little band
to fight — to die, if so God's will should be ; and in
the leader's breast lay rankling the bitter thought
that if it should indeed be death, he left no one
behind to shed so much as a single tear upon his
bloody grave.

Have you read the quaint old story? Do you
know how the stern little band of Christians put
to shame a whole tribe of savages, and slew their
leader in their very midst, hewing off his head to
bring back as a trophy to be set upon the roof of
their citadel as a warning to his fellows? If you
have not, get the old record and see for yourself
how the men of those days bore themselves, and
with what sublime arrogance they punished and
dispossessed these savage interlopers in " the land
which the Lord had given them."

But killing savages, and leading night-marches,
and wearying himself with all sorts of toil, proved
but a slow cure to the great hurt which not only
the captain's heart but his pride had received, and
it was about this time that he set up a temporary
shelter for himself on what is still called the Captain's Hill in Duxbury, the town itself named in
memory of a part of his ancestral domain. Here
with Hobomok, his faithful Indian friend, and one
or two of his fellow-colonists, he delighted to retire
as often as his duties would permit, although still
retaining his house on Burying Hill, and his cus-
tody of the fort.

In July of 1623, two years and a half after the landing of the Pilgrims, the ship Anne came sailing into Plymouth Harbor, and might well have dropped her anchor to the tune of "Sweethearts and Wives," so many of them were on board.

Myles Standish, stern and silent as was his wont, stood with the rest of the townfolk upon the beach, and watched the ship's boat as it left her side and rapidly drew near with its first load of passengers.

"There is — one for whom I looked," exclaimed William Bradford, breaking his sentence in the midst, and glancing with austere confusion into the face of his friend and comrade but not confidant, the silent captain. And then, as Mistress Southworth rose in the boat, and gave her little hand to the sailor who lifted her on shore, the governor went down, hat in hand, to meet and greet her ; and Myles Standish stood alone, fiercely tugging at his yellow beard, and looking beyond the boat to the gloomy offing and the ship already riding at anchor within the curving beach.

So he stood when Governor Bradford returned toward him, Mistress Southworth upon his arm, and beside them a fair and stately maiden, with bright northern eyes, golden hair, and a head regal as that of Editha, last of the Saxon queens. Standish made some slight obeisance, and would have moved aside, but Bradford, his noble face lighted with a sudden secret joy, and his bearing full of a tender exultation, detained him.

"Ho, there, thou valiant man of war. Wouldst

play the dastard for the first time, and run from
these fair ones who have braved the perils of the
seas and of the wilderness to visit us? Here then,
let me present the valiant captain of the Plymouth
Colony to Mistress Southworth, of whom he may
have heard me speak. And here, friend Myles,
here is another, a maiden who asked for thee or
ever she had stepped from the great rock to the
sands. This is thy late wife's cousin, Barbara, who
has journeyed hither under the protection of Mistress Southworth, who in very sooth looks to need
protection herself."

"Is this Barbara?" exclaimed the captain, staring into the bright, proud face so nearly upon a
level with his own; for the maiden was tall and
stately beyond the wont of women, and the gallant
soldier was low of stature.

"This Barbara!" repeated he. "Why, I thought
she was a child."

"I was twenty years old Sunday was a se'night,
cousin Myles," replied Barbara, in a clear, sonorous
voice, and meeting his scrutiny with fearless eyes.

"You do not look like Rose. She was little,
and " —

The captain did not finish his sentence, but
gravely taking the two hands of his cousin in
his, kissed her upon both cheeks; then following
the governor, who already was climbing the hill
with Alice Southworth by his side, he led her toward the irregular row of houses already named
Leyden Street, and said, somewhat confusedly: —

"You are welcome, Barbara; as welcome as though it had been the child I imagined. But a fair maiden like you will hardly brook the solitude and dullness of the lonely hut where I abide. You will fret for your gay home and young companions, I fear me."

"Do you not live in the village, then, cousin?" asked the girl, climbing the hill with firm, elastic tread, and examining everything with her bright blue eyes.

"Well, I do and I do not," replied the captain with some hesitation. "The home of my choice is over there." And pausing upon the brow of the hill, close to the edge of the wheatfield beneath whose waving green lay the dust of Rose his wife, Captain Myles pointed across the head of the bay to a promontory crowned by a stockade, with some roofs showing above it.

"There is my favorite dwelling-place," said he, briefly. "I call it Duxbury, after the place owned by my people in Lancashire. I reach it by water, and there you see my boat buoyed close beside the rock. Sometimes, indeed, I walk; but that would be a rough journey for you, and perhaps you had better abide here in my old house. I cannot tell" —

"I will, by your leave, speak to my friend Mistress Southworth first," said Barbara, gravely. "For she did charge me to make no disposition of myself until she saw whether we might not abide together, at least until her marriage."

"Aha! she will marry Bradford, then!" exclaimed Myles, with some show of interest.

"Surely. It was for that she came," replied Barbara, simply, and with no girlish flutter or giggle. Her kinsman looked at her attentively, and somewhat disapprovingly. In truth, he did not quite admire this frank and fearless bearing, this want of shyness and weakness, this self-reliance, which, as he thought, would have better befitted Rose Standish's brother than her adopted sister. And, in sooth, it was the contrast between the two which displeased him most of all; and still standing there upon the brow of the hill, with the wheat-field at his feet, and the tall, stately maiden at his side, he said again: —

"You are very unlike Rose, and still your features have a trick of hers. She was a marvel of sweet humility and patience, yet brave and untiring withal as any among us; a rare and admirable creature, a model among women, was Rose Standish."

And with eyes downcast and absent the soldier strode on toward the houses; while Barbara, keeping at his side with her quick, light steps, said somewhat bitterly: —

"And I know naught of sweet humility or patience; and though I may be brave and tireless, I am not gentle or admirable, and no man will ever call me a model among women. You see I take your meaning, cousin."

"Be not over quick at snatching the gage before

it is flung down to you, mistress," replied the captain, dryly. "To praise the dead is not to dispraise the living ; and there are men enow in this colony who, wooing you, will swear that you are the model of all that is loveliest in woman."

" I came not hither to be wooed, or to woo," began Barbara, hotly ; but with an imperious gesture the captain silenced her, and led the way into one of the rough yet comfortable cabins, which already had gathered about them the air of occupation and home comfort not to be obtained in the first months of residence either in cabin or palace.

" Here is the house where Mistress Southworth will abide, as I am told," said Standish, gravely ; and, in fact, it was Governor Bradford himself who opened the door of the inner room and met them upon the threshold.

" Your friend is asking for you, fair Mistress Barbara," said he, pleasantly ; and the captain, pushing his charge gently forward, said : —

" Go you in and find her, then, and I will see you presently. Master Bradford, a word or two with you."

And the military leader of the colony walked away beside its civil guardian, leaving his kinswoman standing upon the threshold and looking after them.

" I do not wonder my poor Rose died of disgust at finding herself chained to such a boor for life," said she aloud, and then went in to find Alice Southworth, who greeted her eagerly.

"You are to bide here with me, Barbara," said
she. "Master Bradford tells me that your father
— nay, your cousin, but indeed he looks more like
your father — has naught but men in his household,
and that he dwells for the most part in a savage
and even dangerous spot, far away from the town,
— (alack, that this should be called a town!) — so
even he saw how unfitting it were for a young
maid to take up her dwelling there at present; and
of course we must all heed what Master Bradford
says, for is not he the governor? And, Barbara,
what think you of his looks?"

Barbara stooped and kissed the laughing, blushing face of her friend, and answered gayly: —

"Methinks he looks wondrous happy; and, for
that matter, so do you, Alice!"

"I? Truly I am right happy in setting my feet
on shore once more, and off that filthy, crowded
ship. Think, girl, of finding water plenty enough
to bathe in, and to be able to wash and dry one's
linen without submitting each piece to the scrutiny
of a crew of bold, staring fellows, who seemed to
me always at hand when they should have been
away, and away when they might have been useful!
And how like you the captain?"

"He may be a very good captain, but hardly
much of a gentleman," replied Barbara, with a
little acrimony; and Alice Southworth laughed
gayly.

"Ah, he has begun to chasten that haughty
spirit and teach the beauty of obedience, has he

not?" asked she. "You will be none the worse
for a little training to prepare you for a husband's
yoke, Mistress Bab."

"I will never marry if I must bend my neck to
the yoke in doing so, and Captain Myles Standish
will never teach me obedience, kinsman though he
may be," said Barbara, proudly; and Alice Southworth, fluttering and joyous in her own great happiness, kissed her friend once more, and laughed,
while she ran away to look for her mails, she said,
but in truth to see if William Bradford were returning.

So Captain Standish went home alone to his
fortress upon the hill, and smoking his pipe beside
the roaring open fire, grimly smiled in remembering his mistake: —

"I thought to bring home a child to sit upon
my knee and play with her rag-puppets, and here
instead is a strapping wench as tall as I am, and
three good inches taller than any woman has a
right to be, and with a will and a pride as over-
grown as her stature. Mistress Priscilla Alden
may be thankful that she is not Mistress Standish,
with the charge of such an Amazon upon her hands.
Glad enow am I that Mistress Southworth found
it unseemly to let me fetch her home here, and I
will see that it becomes no easier. I must find
some stout fellow to take her off my hands, some
man of courage and spirit, and not easily cowed,
or, my faith, it will be the worse for him. To
think of her being close kin to Rose, my wife!"

And as that name and that memory rose freshly in the soldier's mind, he leaned back in his chair, his eyes fixed upon the fire, his face softening from the stern and somewhat sneering expression it had worn but now, and one idle hand beating a tattoo upon the arm of his wooden chair, while the other held the forgotten pipe. Then while the firelight played upon his grizzled hair, and bronzed face, and high, proud features, a strange dimness crept into the captain's keen blue eyes, and something dropped and shone upon his thick-set beard.

"There was never woman like her, there never will be, and she has spoiled me for the rest," muttered he at last, and with a long sigh roused himself, relighted the great pipe, and called upon his henchman, John Howard, to come in and give him an account of his day's work among the corn.

Three weeks later Alice Southworth was married to Governor Bradford, and Barbara removed with her to her new home, partly as guest, partly as assistant in the household labor ; for in those early days there were no servants among the colonists, but each man and woman did with all his might whatever his hands found to do, and he was the most considered who proved himself of most value to the whole.

Affairs of state, military necessities, and a mutual friendship drew the captain and the governor constantly together, either in public or at the Council Chamber on Burying Hill, or at Bradford's own house, where Standish was often hos-

pitably entreated to dine, sup, and take lodging for
the night. He had thus, without effort or indeed
thought of his own, ample opportunity to cultivate the acquaintance of his young kinswoman,
who, on her part, rather sought than shunned opportunities of meeting him, for the very purpose,
as Dame Bradford declared, of angering and shock-
ing him. For instance, one day when the talk at
the dinner-table was of Indians reported prowling
about the settlement, Barbara gravely turned to
Bradford and asked if she might borrow his musket that afternoon for a little while.

The governor, smiling, gave assent, adding, however, " But I will draw the charge, fair mistress,
lest thou do thyself an injury."

" Nay, that will not answer my turn," replied
Barbara, willfully. " I must have it loaded, and
that carefully."

" And what then? What will you do with a
loaded musket when you have it in your foolish
hands?" sternly inquired Myles Standish, turning
sharply toward her.

" What will I do with it! Marry, the same that
you would, cousin-in-law. I am going to walk in
the woods, and if I find an Indian I will shoot
him and bring in his scalp, or, at the very least,
his scalp-lock."

She spoke with a perfectly serious face, and the
captain, after looking at her a moment in deep
displeasure, replied : —

" Verily, I think no less than the scalp would

serve your turn. It is a pity you came hither,
mistress, for we had men enow already, and needed
some women."

" When the men are so stunted, the women have
to learn manly arts," replied Barbara, quickly.

And the captain : —

" It would be well, minion, if you might learn
the manly art of holding your tongue."

" I can hold my tongue when it pleases me, and
I can speak out when it pleases me, as Priscilla
Molines did, when she told John Alden she had
rather marry him than you."

But at this taunt the choleric captain lost patience altogether, and pushing back his chair from
the table, left the room and the house, his face
black with anger, and his step hasty and disordered.

" Now see there, thou naughty child ! " exclaimed
Mistress Bradford, half vexed and half amused ;
" thou hast angered our good captain so that I
doubt he will never forgive thee. Why needest
thou have thrown Priscilla in his face ? "

" She likes it, you know, for she threw herself at
John Alden's head ; and I must say I wonder at
her taste, for even my cousin-in-law is better than
that," replied Barbara, leaving the room almost as
hastily as Standish had done. The master of the
house looked after her and shook his head.

" The maiden is too froward, Alice," said he.
" She needs a master, and a sharp one."

" Spoken like a man," replied the wife, smiling

subtly. " No master but Love will quell our Barbara's spirit, and he has not come yet."

" Isaac Allerton was speaking to me this morning on her account," replied Bradford, hesitatingly.
" It is a secret, dame, but I trust it with you."

" Have you told her ? " asked Alice, quickly.

" I said something of it," admitted the husband.

" Before telling me, William ! Well, how did
Barbara receive it ? "

" But coldly. She said she had no mind to wed
at all, but when I urged her to consider the matter
further, she took until to-morrow morning to think
of it."

" Perhaps it is that makes her so waspish with
her cousin," suggested Alice, smiling. " It is irri-
tating to weak nerves to be in doubt and quan-
dary."

" I had not thought of Barbara's nerves being
weak," returned Bradford, smiling, and stooping
to kiss his wife before leaving the house.

Myles Standish meantime was striding along
through the town and into the woods at a prodi-
gious rate, his face flushed, his brows knitted, and
his blue eyes bright with anger.

" I would she were a lad, and under my command for but a month," muttered he. " Beshrew
me, but I 'd tame that spirit of hers. And she the
kinswoman of Rose, my wife ! "

A little way from the town the captain stopped
at the smithy to see if the iron braces he had that
morning bespoken for his boat were finished; but

Manasseh Kempton was only just beginning them, and in reply to the captain's impatient queries, replied that his wife lay ill in bed, and he had been nursing her all the morning, but if the captain would wait but a couple of hours —

"Not a couple of minutes, varlet," roared the captain, forgetting a little the social equality and brotherly love of the New World. " Do you think I have no other errand but cooling my heels in a smithy? Get the boat done as fast as may be, and to-night John Howard shall come and fetch it."

So saying, he strode away along the narrow footpath bordering the head of the bay, leaving the stalwart smith amazed and somewhat ill-pleased.

" What ails the captain now? " muttered he, throwing one arm above his eyes to shelter them from the sun, and watching the wiry, active figure of the soldier as it passed into the shadow of the pines, and so out of sight. " Has he been a-wooing again, or have the Council refused to let him pursue the savages to their haunts, as men were saying he was fain to do ? "

And shaking his head in solemn protest against such hastiness of speech, or temper, the smith went back to his work, humming a holy hymn between his teeth, and timing the cadences with blows of his heavy hammer upon the white-hot iron he was fashioning for the captain's boat.

Two good miles of sand and scrub and forest had Myles Standish put between himself and town when, on the crest of a little rocky hill, he threw

himself down to rest for a moment; and taking off
his steeple-crowned hat with its waving plume of
cock-feathers, worn partly as symbol of his calling,
partly in honor of his ancestral crest, the captain
wiped his brow, and suffering his eyes to rest upon
the lovely view of headland, bay, bright waters,
and brighter sunshine spread before them, felt the
anger of his mood dying within him, and a feeling
of amusement mingling with his annoyance.

"It is ill-befitting a man's dignity to quarrel
with a saucy girl," muttered he, and presently
laughed outright. "I would that I might see her
try to fire the musket that she begged! Ten
pounds to one that it would kick her over."

The smile was still upon his face, and the merry
fancy in his brain, when up from the woodland at
his feet, the woodland through which he but now
had passed, rang a wild, wild shriek, — the cry of
a woman in deadliest terror or pain.

"What now! Is it a tiger-cat again?" exclaimed Standish, starting to his feet, and hastily
resuming the musket and equipments he had
thrown aside on lying down, and without which no
man traveled in those days. Before he had them
adjusted the cry was repeated, this time a little
nearer. The soldier replied to it with a stirring
halloo, and darted down the hill in the direction
whence it sounded.

"Help! help! Oh, quick, for the Lord's sake!"
shrieked a voice that he knew; and striking off
from the path into the low growth of the pine

wood, he caught presently the glimpse of distant
figures, then the rustle of displaced branches, then
the flutter of a woman's clothes, and springing forward with an angry cry he cut off the retreat of
his flying foe, and stood face to face with a stalwart savage, who dropped his prey when thus fairly
overtaken, and, dodging behind a tree, threw his
tomahawk full at the head of his assailant, who
caught it upon the barrel of his piece, and at the
same moment fired at the outline of the Indian's
figure left exposed by the insufficient tree-trunk. A
derisive whoop spoke the ill-success of the shot,
and the next instant the twang of a bowstring
sent an arrow into the captain's shoulder.

With a shout of defiance he sprang forward,
grasping at the dusky arm of the savage and drawing his knife, but with another mocking laugh the
Indian slipped from his grasp, and would have
escaped, when the tomahawk he had thrown was
thrust into the captain's hand, with the hurried
injunction : —

" Hurl it at his head ! "

And hurl it Myles Standish did, so strongly and
so well that it bit deep into the brain of the flying
savage, and laid him convulsed, dying, dead, at
the foot of the great pine whose shelter he was
seeking.

Then the captain turned to his ally, who stood
pale and trembling, now that all was over, her
hands clasped, and her lips quivering with agitation and alarm.

Myles Standish looked at her for a moment with a grim smile upon his lips, then extending the knife he still held toward her, he said : —

" Now, mistress, go and take the scalp, if you will." But instead of blazing out in anger, as he had expected, Barbara only flushed crimson, raised her eyes appealingly to his, and softly said : —

" Oh, Myles ! That is not kind of you."

" Not kind ? Well " — and the captain walked away to the side of his fallen foe, looked at him for a moment, then returned. " The savage is dead," said he, quietly, " and I will take you back to the town, and tarry there to-night myself."

" Thank you, Myles," said the girl, now so pale again that her kinsman put his arm about her, asking anxiously : —

" Art going to swoon, child ? "

" No — there, I am better now — let me but rest a moment —not here, though — let us get from the sight of that horrid creature " —

" But you came out of purpose to find and slay him," insisted Standish, mockingly.

" Nay, Myles, I had not thought you could be so cruel." And the proud, bright head suddenly bent itself upon his shoulder, and Barbara sobbed, as she did all else, with her whole strength.

" Now, then, now, what is this ? What ! crying, girl, for a cross word or two, and that from me, whom you hate of all men ! " exclaimed the captain, putting his hand beneath the square white chin and raising the quivering lips to meet his own.

" Why, there, then, let us kiss and be friends, as the children say. I meant not to hurt thee, lass."

" But you did hurt me, and you are ever hurting me, with chiding and sneering at me and all my ways ; and when you say I hate you, you mean that it is you who hate me, and let slip no occasion of showing it, and I wish — I wish — I had never come out of England to be your mock and scorn."

Down went the head again, while the tears so long gathering gushed out like a summer tempest. The gallant captain, the man who knew no fear, stood for a moment appalled at this most unexpected attack ; then, seizing both the strong white hands with which the girl sought to hide her face, he held them in his own, saying, eagerly : —

" Here is some strange to-do. Tell me, Barbara, didst really think I hated thee, and mocked at thee ? "

" I did not think it, I knew it," said Barbara, softly.

" See there, now. While I was thinking that it was you who could not abide the sight of me, you were thinking that I hated thee, and so we went on plaguing each other, and turning the worst side instead of the best. Dost know, Barbara, I like thee all the better that thou wast so afeard but now ? "

" I was horribly afeard, in good sooth," murmured Barbara, clinging to his arm.

" Then thou didst not come out to seek the savage ?" asked the captain, smiling with grim playfulness.

"I forgot all about the savage when I came."

"Ay? And for what didst thou come, then?"

"I was trying to overtake thee, Myles."

"What! Why was that, child? What was thine errand?"

"I — I wanted to tell thee that I was sorry for the gibes and insults I so saucily put upon thee to-day. I did not mean all I said, Myles, and I take shame for my frowardness."

Myles Standish looked long and keenly at the fair and noble face, dyed in blushes, and drooping before his gaze with a proud shame he had never seen upon it before. Long he looked, and earnestly, and then he said : —

"Why, Barbara, thou art a very woman after all; a woman sweet, and tender, and modest as the most timid of thy sisters ; yes, as womanly as Rose my wife, and worthy to be her adopted sister, as she so often called thee. Barbara, seeing thee thus, I am filled with sudden wonder that I have not rightly seen and known thee before. Girl, take care, or instead of hating I shall come to loving thee outright. I, the gray, grim old soldier, with his stunted form, as thou didst say to-day, and his" —

"And his great heart and noble spirit, such as bigger men never yet dreamed of possessing!" broke in the girl, her eyes rising brightly upon his, then falling in a sudden terror at their own temerity.

"Barbara! Can it be, Barbara, that I might

win thee to love me, and to look upon me always
with those sweet and gentle eyes, instead of the
scornful regard with which thou hast met me hitherto?　Can it be, Barbara?"

"Thou shouldst have seen what a poor pretense
the scorning was, Myles."

"Then, maiden, thus I make thee mine."

And the captain, taking his betrothed in his
arms, pressed his stern and bearded lips upon her
pure and fresh ones, then led her tenderly on toward the place so soon to be her home.

For they were married within the month, and
they lived at Duxbury, at the foot of Captain's
Hill, where you may trace the foundations and
stand upon the hearthstone of their house to-day,
and in the Pilgrim Hall of Plymouth you may see
the captain's mighty sword, some household relics
of his home, and a sampler wrought by his only
daughter, bearing a legend beginning with the
words,

"Lorea Standish is my name," etc.

Not only one fair maid, but sons, brave as their
father, tall and comely as their mother, sprang
from this union, and the eldest of them, Alexander
by name, wooed, won, and wedded Sarah, eldest
daughter of John and Priscilla Alden, thus uniting
the two families in one common bond at last.

WILLIAM BRADFORD'S LOVE LIFE.

I. — ALICE CARPENTER.

"ALICE, will you give me your answer? I have traveled many leagues and run no little risk to ask this question."

"And after all may get no answer at all," retorted Alice Carpenter, pouting her pretty lips, and glancing mutinously into the grave face bent toward her.

"Nay, child, be not froward, nor trifle with what is or should be solemn earnest to both of us. I have already told you that this is the only hour I can call mine own while we remain in England. It is true, I accepted the mission with the full intention of seeing you while here; but, having accepted, I must fulfill it, and to-night's sunset should see me far on the road to London."

"Why wait for sunset, Master Bradford? If your London business is so pressing, I marvel that you should delay it for the sake of a silly maiden, who in truth knows not her own mind as yet."

And the spoiled little beauty turned to chase the greyhound who leaped in sport upon her.

William Bradford stood moodily watching the game of play which followed, making for himself, all unconsciously, a picture of the scene never to

be forgotten amidst all the vicissitudes of a stormy
life.

It was the garden of an English manor house in
Somersetshire, built in the reign of Elizabeth, then
but just closed, and bearing the sign manual of that
era in the formal architecture of the great rambling
buildings, and the quaint ordering of the garden,
with its yew-trees sedulously clipped in shape of
towers and ships, falcons, peacocks, and rampant
lions; with its great beds of roses, cultivated not
only for their beauty, but as material for conserves,
rose-water, and scent-jars; with its trailing honey-
suckles and sweet-brier running riot among clumps
of heart's-ease, garden lilies, love-lies-bleeding,
prince's feather, marigolds, and hollyhocks. The
northern limit of the garden, near which William
Bradford stood, was defined by a high wall built of
the same hard, red bricks as the house, and upon
the southern face of this was nailed a long range
of espalier fruit — black-heart cherries, peaches,
pears, and great golden plums, celebrated throughout the country for their size and flavor. They
were ripe just now, and the hot sun brought out a
musky odor from their rich clusters, filling the air,
and mingling forever in William Bradford's memory with the hum of the bees, the ringing laughter
of the girl, and the glowing crimson of the roses at
his feet.

Many and many a day, in the dark years that
were to come, that garden bloomed and ripened,
those rich scents filled the air, and the hum of bees

and peals of laughter filled his ears, among the black solitudes of the New England forests, or the cold desolation of the rock-bound coast; and yet, looking upon the scene to-day, he saw it not, heeded it not, — thought only of the merry girl, who, suddenly deserting her playmate, stood beside him, and mockingly exclaimed : " What! not gone yet, Master Bradford ? Truly the elders of your church did ill to intrust their mission to such a dreamer and laggard as yourself."

But her jesting drew no responsive smile to the face of the young man, as, laying a hand lightly upon her arm, he gravely answered : —

" You have had your jest, fair Mistress Alice, and you have taken your time. Now I will pray you to give me a serious answer to my most serious petition. Will you be my wife, and fare with me to Holland, or it may be farther still — for our people are minded to remove thence to some country over seas where shall be room for all and opportunity for all to thrive by honest labor ? It is no life of luxury, no certain prospect of any sort, that I can offer, Alice; and yet I dare to urge you, for I know that the great love I bear toward you, and the earnest will that I find growing within my heart, will give me power to make you happy, and shield you from all suffering but such as God appoints. Alice, will you be my wife ? "

For a moment the girl stood with downcast eyes and blushing cheeks, her answer trembling upon her smiling lips, and shining from beneath her drooping lids. The lover read it, and suddenly clasped her to his breast.

"Yes, sweet one, you confess it at last, — you confess even without a word; and thus I take the answer you have been so long in giving."

He pressed his lips upon her own, but hardly had tasted their honey when he was startled by a smart blow upon the cheek, while Alice, tearing herself from his embrace, cried, angrily : —

"Not so fast, good sir. I never have said that I would even give you any answer, and here you pretend to read it in my face, and proceed to take it unspoken from my lips. I 'll give you no answer at all to-night, no, nor to-morrow morning neither, unless the humor takes me to do so."

"Then, Alice, you will never give it," replied the young man, not angrily but resolutely. "When that sun, now lost in the fir-tops, sinks behind the horizon, I shall say good-by; what comes between now and then it is for you to decide. The petulant blow and the froward words I forgive, but further trifling with an honest heart and a man's life I shall find it hard to pass over. Your answer, Alice."

"I have told you once, fair sir, that I have no answer for you before to-morrow morning. I have a will as well as you, and if you do not care enough for me to abide my pleasure, why, good-by, good Master Bradford."

"Good-by, Alice, since you so will it, and yet, I pray you, pause once more. This is no idle play,

Alice, but saddest earnest. I solemnly asure you that I must be gone at sunset, and I cannot leave London again before we return to Leyden. If you are my betrothed your father will bring you to me, and we will be married " —

" Again not so fast, good master," interposed Alice. " Suppose I refuse to be brought to you in London. Suppose I demand a longer wooing and somewhat more ceremony in my wedding? And, in good sooth, I fancy that your style is altogether too masterful for me already. I know not what might chance if you were indeed my lord, so I think I will say you nay — for to-night at least ; it may be that in the morning I shall have changed my mind, but now — fare you well, sir."

" And fare you well, Alice. I have your answer, and I have told you more than once that I can wait for no other. And yet — Alice, I shall be three days longer in London — if you will come to me, you and your father " —

" Marry come up ! I go after you to London, saying, ' Kind sir, will you of your goodness take me to wife ? ' A long day it will be before I seek you, Master Bradford, a very, very long day."

And half in anger, half in mockery, she flung her handful of roses full into the grave face of him whom she addressed, and ran, light and swift as a fawn, up the path toward the house.

One of the roses lodged upon the young man's folded arms, and, smiling bitterly, he caught it, looked for a moment into its glowing heart, then put it inside his doublet.

"A fair ensample of her love, — as sweet, as short-lived, and as thorny," muttered he ; and leaving the garden by the postern gate, he mounted the sturdy horse awaiting him in the green lane beyond, and rode away just as the sinking sun touched the horizon.

"He will come to-morrow," whispered Alice Carpenter, watching the sunset, and listening to the horse's retreating feet, while her bright cheek grew pale and her eyes filled with tears.

But the morrow came, and brought neither lover nor message, and still another and another morrow, until a grave friend of her father's, down from London for a day, set the girl's mind at rest by mentioning that the deputies from the dissenting folk at Leyden had returned thither, having met but ill success in their attempt to obtain a patent from the Virginia Company.

"Fool! Fool! Fool!" muttered Alice between her set teeth, as she stormed up and down the garden path, where now the rose-petals lay a-dying. "Fool that I was, and more fool that he was, not to know that a maiden's no-say does not always mean blank no! And yet I care not; who shall say that I care overmuch?"

In this mood her father found her, and placing her hand within his arm restrained her hurrrying steps to his own pace, while he said : —

"Daughter Alice, I have received a proposition of marriage for you from a worthy gentleman, not as I think quite disagreeable to you. Indeed, it is the son of our friend within there."

" Master Southworth ! " exclaimed Alice.

" Yes. His son Edward asks your hand, dear child. What is your answer ? "

" Yes."

The father turned in some surprise, and looked into his daughter's face. It was white and rigid almost as death.

" My daughter, there is no need for such instant consent unless you are quite sure of your own mind. I had thought that Master Bradford " —

" Do not mention that person, if it please you, sir. I like Edward Southworth passing well. He is a brave gentleman, and a courteous ; and, please you, dear father, go and tell your friend that I say yes, and excuse me for to-night. Good-e'en, father."

" Good-e'en, little maid ; and yet, wait one moment before you run away. It is but right that you should know that I have nearly settled my mind to sell all that I have, and cast in my fortunes with our brethren in Holland. It was for that I went to London so often in the last month, while worshipful Elder Brewster and his associates were there. If I do this, and you wed with Edward Southworth, who abides in London, we must be parted, my little girl, — we two who have never been parted yet."

" Oh, father ! " and Alice, clinging about her father's neck, wept piteously ; wept for the approaching separation, and wept for the death of her young love-dream, yet never wavered in her desperate determination.

" Oh, father, father!" sobbed she, and then —
" but you will have all my sisters left, and I could
never abide in Holland."

" It will not be like this, truly ; " and the man
looked round upon the pleasant garden where he
had played in childhood, where he had wooed his
sweet young wife, where he had wandered seeking
comfort for her early death, and where he had
thought to watch his own day draw to its close.

" Not like this, but ' whoso loveth house or
lands better than me ' — it is daily borne in upon
my mind that I must go, Alice ; and for myself I
grudge not the sacrifice ; nor for your sisters who
are ready to go ; but if you shrink from the toil
and privation, or if your conscience does not bid
you go, sweet one, here is an opening for honorable
escape.   What say you ? "

" I will never go to Holland, father.   And if
Edward Southworth cares to marry me, he may."

She was gone, and her father, looking after her
in wonder and some doubt, could only say : —

" What man so wise as to read a woman's heart!
But yet it was consent, and as such I must repeat
it."

Six months later, Alexander Carpenter, with his
daughters Agnes, Juliana, Mary, and Priscilla, arrived at Leyden, and among his first guests was
William Bradford, who, with pale lips and a high-
throbbing heart, inquired of him for news of his
daughter Alice.

" Alice ?   She wedded with Edward Southworth

the morning that I sailed from Southampton," replied the father, carelessly, for already he had forgotten a dim suspicion formed by the strange manner of the girl at the time of her betrothal, and
Bradford had never opened his mind to him.

II. — DOROTHY MAY.

From the house of Father Robinson, the pastor
of the struggling community at Leyden, and with
whom Master Carpenter was at present lodged,
William Bradford returned to his own abode in
a family of the name of May. In the little par-
lor sat a young girl spinning flax upon a small
wheel, who at his entrance glanced up, blushing
brightly.

" So soon returned, William!" said she, shyly.
" Did not you find your friends?"

" Yes — and no," replied the young man, tossing his hat upon the table, and throwing himself
upon the high-backed settle beside the fire.

" ' Yes and no!' You speak in riddles, friend,"
said the girl, her bright color fading as quickly as
it had come. " Have you ill news from home?"

" No, Dorothy, no ill news ; no news at all to a
man who knows what women are ; only tidings
that one whom I thought mine own has given herself to another man, and I dare to say, were
the whole truth known, cares naught for either of
us."

And as he spoke he folded his arms upon the
end of the settle, and bowed his face upon them,

careless whether she who watched perceived the emotion he could no longer conceal.

A few moments passed in utter silence, and then a light foot crossed the floor, a hesitating hand was laid upon his head, and a girlish form sank upon its knees beside him.

" William, dear William ! " said Dorothy May's soft voice ; " all women are not like that."

" What care I whether they be or not ? " And the young man ground something worse than a sob between his clenched teeth.

Another pause, and then again the timid voice :

" Nay, William, do not scorn all because one is false, for that is neither just nor kind to yourself."

" I do not scorn you, Dorothy. You are good and kind, and will, I doubt not, some day be true to the man who wins your love ; but she " —

" Indeed I would be true, did the man I love love me," sighed the girl, her head sinking so low as to hide the glowing color of her cheeks.

William Bradford listened ; took counsel of his own heart : nay, then, of his wounded pride and love, if you will have the truth ; finally sat upright, and placed a hand beneath the chin of that rosy face, raising it to a level with his own.

" And you love a man who loves not you, fair Mistress Dorothy ? " asked he at length.

" To my shame be it spoken."

" Nay, to the honor of thy tender, humble heart. And wouldst thou wed that man, knowing that he

had loved another woman passing well, and that
the wound was not wholly healed ? "

" I would wed him, and try to heal the wound
with my own love," whispered the girl.

" Dorothy, am I that man ? "

" None other."

" And thou wilt be my wife ? "

" A true and loving one, so surely as God gives
me strength and life."

" So be it." And again the young man raised
the blushing face, and kissed the trembling lips.
It was a strange betrothal, — a most unwise one ;
for human love is at best but a feeble staff to support one over life's rough places ; and, weakened
as this was, ah, who could not have foreseen the
end ?

But Dorothy May's parents saw only comfort
and satisfaction in the gaining a husband for their
child of so well-esteemed a character and so fair
worldly prospects, not to mention the setting at
rest a suspicion which had for some time haunted
the good mother's mind, connecting Dorothy's pale
cheeks, lagging step, and tearful eyes with William
Bradford's attention or neglect.

So all was arranged without difficulty on the
one side or the other ; and the second letter that
Master Carpenter sent home to his daughter
Alice announced the marriage of her " sometime
playmate, William Bradford, to a very worthy
and also comely young woman, Dorothy May by
name."

III. — MISTRESS ALICE SOUTHWORTH.

When Mistress Southworth read this letter in the dim, vast chamber of her new home in " Duks Place, near Heneage House," she uttered a little cry, and with one of the impulsive movements of her girlhood flung it into the fire blazing at her feet. Then she covered her face and sobbed for a few moments wildly, passionately ; and at last she rose, and, slowly pacing the long, vaulted chamber, took counsel with her own heart, until at last, coming back to the fireplace, she stood there, a pretty picture, with the ruddy light striking up upon her fair young face, disheveled golden curls, and whitest throat and arms, left bare by the fashion of the rich " padusoy " robe which fell trailing upon the oaken floor.

As fair a picture, and but little older than that of the girl who, half in jest and half in wrath, had pelted her lover with roses in the quaint walled garden of the manor-house six months before, and yet —

The crisp cinder of the burned letter had fallen out from the fire, and lay upon one of the painted tiles of the wide hearth. Smiling bitterly, Alice Southworth stirred it with the toe of her satin shoe ; it crumbled beneath the touch, and caught by one of the draughts eddying through the room, flew in a cloud of black flakes up the chimney and was gone.

" So best — so best ! Smoke and ashes, and the last trace blown to the four winds ! So let it be."

And thus unconsciously echoing the words in which William Bradford had sealed his betrothal, Alice Southworth closed, as she thought forever, the sweetest chapter in her book of life, and turned to the new duties and new ties she had voluntarily if rashly assumed.

IV. — PILGRIMS.

" And you will sail with these others in the Mayflower, Master Bradford ? " said Elder Carpenter, glancing keenly at the young man, who sat looking gloomily from the latticed window of the little Dutch ale-house where they had met for noontide refreshment.

" Yes, I have so resolved," replied he, moodily.

" And your wife and the little one ? "

" They will remain behind — I think."

" Does the dame consent to be so deserted ? "

" We have not yet spoken of it. She can remain with her mother, and come to me afterward," said the younger man, hesitatingly; and Elder Carpenter again glanced keenly into his perturbed face.

" It is a grievous burden to my spirit," said he, after a pause, " that I am denied this means of testifying to my faith. Were it only mine own infirmities and inconvenience that stood in the road I would count it naught, though I perished by the way; but I must not burden you younger men with the charge of one who can at best serve but little purpose in the life you enter upon, and would most likely become a serious charge and trial. Nor can I bear to abide here longer, or to lay my bones in foreign soil. My night approaches, and I will get me to mine own land and sleep where my fathers sleep."

" You will return into England ? " asked Bradford, in some surprise.

" Yes. This ship has brought me letters from my daughter, Mistress Southworth. She has met with heavy affliction in the loss of her good husband ; and she prays me very earnestly to return to her, I and my daughters Mary and Priscilla still unwedded, and abide beneath her roof to the end of my days."

" Master Edward Southworth dead ! " echoed Bradford, blankly.

" The Lord has willed it so," replied the elder, reverently.

" And Alice a widow ! "

" The widowed mother of two little children. Truly she needs a father's counsel and assistance," mused the old man, and, lost in reverie, he did not perceive that with his last words William Bradford had left the room.

Deep in that evening's twilight, as Dorothy sat hushing her child to sleep with the murmured cadence of a hymn, some one entered the room and laid two hands upon her shoulders from behind.

" Is it you, William ? " asked the young mother, softly.

" Yes, wife. I shall sail with the first party of

adventurers in the Mayflower. Will you go with me?"

"Why, this is something more than sudden!" exclaimed Dorothy, trying to turn her face toward her husband, who resisted the attempt, and only repeated: —

"Will you go with me, wife?"

"Where you go I will go, you know full well," was the meek response. "But why have you not told me your will before, that I might have made preparation?"

"I did not know it myself; and I thought that if I went, you and the child would abide a while with our good mother here. But if you will go, Dorothy, it will be a singular favor to me."

And now the wife would not be restrained, but, rising hastily, confronted her husband with looks of undisguised amazement.

"A singular favor to you!" repeated she. "Why, what words are these from you to me, William! Am I not your own true and loving wife, no less bound to obey your lightest wish than anxious to lay down my life, if so I might pleasure you? Why, had you waited until our friends were embarking at Delft Haven and then said to me, Up and follow them! do you think I would have faltered? And had you tried to go without me, William, I would have thrown myself at your feet and wept and prayed and importuned until you gave consent to my accompanying you. Dear husband, what have I done amiss that you should have entertained this cruel thought of leaving me?"

She was weeping now, and clinging about his neck, so that she could not see the ashen face and haggard eyes he bowed above her, as, gently removing those clinging arms, he said : —

"Naught amiss, naught amiss, Dorothy! You have ever been, as you promised to be, a true, faithful, and most loving wife. Mine is all the blame, mine should be the punishment."

"What blame? what punishment? What do your words mean, dear William? And what makes you look so wan and distraught? Have you bad news from England? — they told me that a ship was arrived with letters" —

"Peace, woman, peace! The wife should not too curiously pry into her husband's will, but accept it unquestioned, for is he not her head and law?"

And, with a laugh of bitterest self-contempt, William Bradford left the room and the house.

The next day, when Dorothy Bradford went abroad to consult her gossips about the needful preparation for the voyage and the new life before her, she heard the news of Edward Southworth's death, and clasping her hands of a sudden above her heart, cried out as if in sharpest pain.

"Dear child, what is it? — what ails you?" exclaimed her friend, running to her.

"Nothing, nothing! A sudden pang — I know not what — as if one's heart broke; but hearts do not break in sober truth, do they?"

" No, not so suddenly as that, nor yet without a cause, and we all know you have none, Mistress Dorothy," said the other, sharply eying the pallid face and trembling form of the young woman.

" Not when I am leaving my mother and my little child, and may never see either again ? " asked Dorothy, bursting into tears, and making her escape.

And that day she began to die.

V. — DOROTHY BRADFORD'S JOURNAL.

In the month of August, 1620, the Leyden Pilgrims sailed in the Speedwell from Delft Haven for England, and some weeks later, transshipped into the Mayflower, sailed from Southampton for — God alone knew where.

Let him who would know what human courage and human fortitude, combined with a high faith and confidence almost more than human, are capable of, let him read the record of that voyage, as told in Bradford's own simple and earnest record, so self-forgetful and so unconscious of its own importance that the only fault of the history is that it omits all notice of the historian, except in the vaguest allusion.

Had not other papers remained, — some precious letters, and a few leaves of a private diary in the faint and timid manuscript of a woman, — this story had never been written, or had been based upon mere imaginings, instead of saddest and most undoubted fact.

Let us here transcribe one of these fragmentary leaves literally, except for the modernizing of some obsolete phrases, and the supplying of some words illegible from time and wear.

It is Dorothy Bradford who writes : —

"At last, praise be to God ! we lie within sight of land, but what a land ! Stern rocks, with cruel waves forever dashing upon them, black forests sheltering who knows what fearful creatures, and still more fearful salvages ; snow, ice, desolation at every hand ; no housen, no Christian people, no sign of the work of man ; I had almost said, no sign of the work of God. Such is our new home ; and yet we have no choice but to accept it, for the captain says and swears that he can carry us no farther, and, unless we determine where we will establish ourselves without more delay, he will put us ashore at the nearest point.

"William, with Master Carver, Myles Standish, and some others, has gone ashore in one of the ship's boats, to discover, if they may, what sort of place lies over against us at this present. I trust they will not elect to settle just here, for surely no place can be worse, if as bad. And yet I know not why I should care. All the earth hereabout will be too sternly frozen to give me room. I wonder how they would go about to dig a grave ! — pity to give them so much pains, when this cold, bitter sea washing past my cabin window would bury me in a moment — a little moment !

"Ah, God forgive me ! what wild and wicked thoughts are these! Away ! away ! Get thee behind me, Sathanas ! Last night I dreamed that my mother came to me with my baby dead in her arms, — my baby, my one

child. Ah, child! you never loved another better than
me, and yet I left you — for him. When I woke
startled from my dream, he stirred in his sleep, and murmured : 'Alice! Sweetest, dearest!'

" That was all, for I laid my hand upon his lips, and
he kissed it, and so slept again. Ah, did he know it was
my hand he kissed, or did he still dream? They do not
dream when they are dead, I think. I hope not, surely,
for I would not be haunted with that dead baby, nor yet
with his father, whispering in his sleep: ' Alice! Sweetest, dearest!'

" *Dec. 7.* — Well, they did not pitch upon that spot
where we lay when I last wrote, and now we are moved
farther into a great bay or gulf, and lie again at anchor,
while the men, with Master Bradford among them, are
away exploring anew. They found before some bas-
kets with corn in them, and some signs of rude cabins,
where it is supposed the salvages or Indyins lived,
though now they are gone. But it is weary work noting these things down, and in sooth I have small heart
for even thinking of them. Last night I dreamed again
of my baby, and he wore wings and stretched his little
arms to me. I would I knew if he be indeed in heaven.
I wonder if I could win there if I took my life in mine
own hand, and so went begging entrance. William
speaks no more of Alice, either waking or sleeping, and
in good sooth he speaks but little to me in any fashion.
One might think he was afraid of me, he shrinks so from
my presence, and yet I never reproached him, oh, never
never! How could I, when my whole heart has wasted
itself in vain love and longing toward him? Yes, I
think that is why I must die; my life has wasted itself
like a little brook I once saw at home that came leaping

down from the hillside, and falling upon a sandy plain
was swallowed up, and perished, in spite of all its strug-
gles. Poor brook! Poor Dorothy! I wonder will he
be sorry when I am dead. Ah, how the cold, bitter sea
runs past these windows! I will up to the deck, and
climb over in the chains as I did yesterday, and look
down at the water. Perchance — God forgive me, God
forgive me the awful thought, and yet " —

That is the last, the very last, of the worn and
faded manuscript. Join it to what follows.

In the journal of William Bradford, after a long
and minute account of the perils and adventures of
the exploring party who finally selected the site of
the present town of Plymouth, Massachusetts, as
their point of debarkation, occurs the brief statement that, upon their return to the ship, it was discovered that Dorothy Bradford had fallen overboard
and was drowned.

Only that.

VI. — WILLIAM BRADFORD AND ALICE SOUTH-WORTH.

Almost two years later, Mistress Southworth, fatherless as well as husbandless, received a letter
of which but one torn fragment remains. Let us
add it to our story : —

God he knows, I never wished her death, or failed
in the dismal effort to feign a love I never felt. How ill
I succeeded you shall see, for I send you certain writings
in the fashion of a diary, discovered in one of her coffers

some time after her most untimely end. No eyes but mine have seen them.

And now, Mistress Southworth, — nay, I will say, as I have said many a fair time before now, sweet Alice, — I ask you once again, as I asked you long since (and I think you will remember, as I do, the fair, well-ordered garden, with its bourgeon of bloom and its rich scents of fruit and flowers, and the humming of the bees about the ripened plums), I ask you once again the question that I asked you then and there, and once again I beg you for such answer as truthful woman should give to honest wooer, — will you have me to your husband? And yet, Alice, as I write, the scales fall from mine eyes, and I see as I have not before that I am asking far more of you now than I asked then. I have been the husband of another woman; my worldly estate is mean and impoverished, notwithstanding the title of Governor which my brothers and co-workers here have bestowed upon me since the death of the noble Carver; and the life which I ask you to share is one of labor and self-forgetfulness.

But yet, Alice, I dare to ask you, for within my own heart I carry an assurance of such undying love and respect toward you that it meseems to outvalue all other things, and if it were possible that you could find in your own breast a similar assurance, I think, Mistress, that not your garden, whose bloom and scent lie so fairly in my memory, were a sweeter abode than these rugged rocks and melancholy forests, so we two might be to-gether.

In conclusion, I must say that although I have discoursed at large upon this matter to you, and although much pains and many qualms of doubt have gone to the composition of this letter, I find by reviewing it that I have said nothing of what is in my heart, and have worded my petitions so coldly and so awkwardly that I hardly dare hope you will approve them ; but yet, Alice, I remember me of a time long since when I thought — yet let that pass, and believe that, whether you say me yea or nay, I shall ever be, while life endures,

Your faithful friend and humble servitor,

WILLIAM BRADFORD.

Stitched to this fragment of a letter is another, a mere scrap, written in the cramped, delicate, and almost illegible hand of a woman, and superscribed

To the Worshipful Governor of the Plymouth Colony in Massachusetts Bay, these :

FAIR SIR, — You do remember my father's garden with its roses and its wall-fruit so well that I marvel you should have forgotten the last words ever spoken to you in that garden by me, or rather, the marvel is that I should remember them myself; and yet I do.   I told you then, Master Bradford, — nay, pardon me, I would have writ, Right Worshipful Governor Bradford, — I told you then that it should be a long day and a very long day before you should see Alice Carpenter following you to London and offering herself to you for wife ; and now you ask me to come, not to London, but across seas to the strange New World where you abide, and all with the selfsame purpose.   Truly, sir, I marvel at your hardihood, and again I marvel more at my own sudden lowliness of heart which does not resent as I would have it this arrogance of yours.   Wait until I summon Pride, and ask her counsel.   "Give him the old answer," quoth she, and so, sir, you have my reply.   Yet softly, here speaks another voice ; methinks it is that of Common-Sense. "How fared it with yourself after you gave him that scoffing answer five years ago?" And again : "Mind you, the long day that you promised him has passed, and it is not Alice Carpenter who goes to seek him, but Alice Southworth."

So sit I, listening to my counselors, uncertain which to credit as the true one ; and so, unable to determine the bent of my own mind, I close these lines, and remain, fair sir, your good wisher and old friend,

ALICE CARPENTER SOUTHWORTH.

Post Scriptum. — I omitted to mention in the body of my letter that I am resolved upon emigration, and have taken passage in the ship Anne, bound from Southampton to your colony, for myself, my two children, and my sister Mary, whom you will perhaps remember, and perhaps also may elect to the place in your affections once held by my unworthy self. At all rates, however, we shall have the time and opportunity for considering face to face these matters, so largely and yet so uncertainly spoken of in our letters.

VII. — THE END.

No tradition, no memento, tells us how the governor of Plymouth Colony received this letter of his former love, — this proof that time and distance and sorrow had cured her neither of her audacious coquetry nor her affection for himself ; but this much we do know, that when the Anne arrived in Plymouth harbor, in the last days of July, 1623, it brought among her passengers Mistress Alice Southworth, although neither her boys nor her sister Mary came for another while. But Mary did not marry William Bradford, for, many years after, she died "a godly old maid who never married."

Three weeks after the arrival of the Anne, Alice Southworth and William Bradford became man and wife, and here is the double note of the event made in the governor's private journal by his own hand and hers : —

"This day Alice Carpenter hath answered the question I asked of her six years agone among the roses of her father's garden in Somersetshire, and she hath answered yea, as she should have answered then."

And below, this note : —

"This day, the 15th of August, shall hereafter be known as the long day ; for it is the one promised by that same Alice Carpenter as the day whereon she would wed with William Bradford, whom God forever bless and hold in his holy keeping."

What more do we know? Only that they lived to a ripe old age, and departed, he some years the first, leaving sons and daughters to inherit their name, and perchance their qualities.

NAZARETH PITCHER.

UPON the coast of Massachusetts, a little south
of the headland where Thomas Morton set up the
Maypole of Merry Mount, and that neighboring
height whence Sir Christopher Gardiner watched
the Boston catchpoles coming to arrest him, a
curious little bay makes in, called Floater's Cove.
Ask whom you please, within twenty miles of its
waters, how or when or why Floater's Cove received its name, and you will probably be informed
that the how and the when are questions without
reply, but that the why is " because of the floaters
there."

Pursuing the inquiry, you will further learn that,
owing to some peculiarity in the trend of the shore
and the course of the tides, whatever bread may
be cast upon the waters within fifty miles of this
point is sure, sooner or later, to make its appearance in Floater's Cove, there to be either thrown as
a waif upon its shores, or to wearily wear itself to
fragments by ceaselessly beating upon the rocky
point that guards its entrance.

Holding fast to this clue, you will, if you care to
pursue the inquiry, be led to search the county
records in the neighboring shire town, and will
find that the tract of land granted to Gabriel

Pitcher, yeoman, in 1685, is bounded upon its eastern limit by the waters of Flotsam Bay. More puzzled than you were before, because a new idea begins to stir in your mind, you will close the book, thank the dignified clerk for his courtesy, and go away, not satisfied, but as nearly so as you are ever likely to be, for you will have possessed yourself of all the exact facts to be gained upon the subject. Compassionating your evident desire for information, some one of the half dozen dwellers beside Floater's Cove will direct you to the "old Pitcher place," and, making your way there through fragrant summer lanes, you may be privileged as was I to sit in the woodbine-covered porch of the old, old house, and listen with dreamy faith to the story of an ancient dame, who fills the pauses of her legend with the whirr of such a spinning-wheel as the wife of the first Gabriel Pitcher may have used beneath this very roof; for, as the spinner assures you with triumphant appeal to the solid log-built walls and massive masonry of the chimneys, this is the house built by the first Gabriel upon his newly acquired property.

About half-way between that day and this, the master of the Pitcher house and farm was a Gabriel, who, in addition to his hereditary possessions, had acquired property in a wife and an only child, a daughter, upon whom he had bestowed the name of Nazareth, and whom he educated in the fear of God and the love of duty, as interpreted by the strait rule of Puritan tradition.

It may be that Gabriel enforced this rule a little more strictly than was quite consistent with the comfort of his household, by way of making amends for the fact that he had himself departed from it in marrying a Quaker, who, loving and submissive wife though she had proved, quietly retained and exercised the privilege of separate faith stipulated for in her marriage covenant. With equal exactness did she observe the counter stipulation that her children were to be educated in their father's creed, and Nazareth had assuredly been so educated. But besides the Puritan and the Quaker, the girl possessed a third parent called Nature, and upon her bestowed all unconsciously an adoring faith and tenderness quite foreign to the placid love and duty never denied to father or mother.

Those whom we love, we love to meet without spectators, and Nazareth's reward and indulgence, after the labor of the day, was to wander by herself through the woods and fields, or along the shore, indulging in the dreams and reveries that her father would have called sinful and her mother idle. The third parent, however, approved and encouraged them; and to her only did Nazareth reveal them, not in words, but in snatches of song, in faint lingering smiles, in long, wistful gazing across the quiet waters, in half-unconscious tears and causeless sighs, in the tender touch of her lips upon some unplucked flower, in the fondling care bestowed upon some wounded bird or stranded fish.

"If Nature put not forth her power
About the opening of the flower,
Who is it that could live an hour?"

It was in the dreamy twilight of an autumnal day that Nazareth, somewhat sad and solitary, though why she could not have told, sat upon the beach at the head of Floater's Cove, and amused herself by shaping figures in the mist wreaths creeping in from seaward. Of a sudden one of these shadowy forms grew real, and from an iceberg or a man-of-war fell to the proportions of a little boat, manned and commanded by a gallant young fellow, who presently leaped ashore, and holding his boat by the painter as a landsman might his horse, took off his cap and said : —

"Excuse me, madam, but can you tell me who lives in the farmhouse beyond the hill ?"

"My father, Gabriel Pitcher," said Nazareth, with the blood tingling at her fingers' ends.

"And do you think he would give a night's lodging to a belated traveler?" pursued the stranger, with a frank smile; and as the girl slightly hesitated at answering a question in her father's name, he continued, with a little hauteur : —

"My name is Richard Armstrong, and I am passenger upon the ship Anne Lovering, lying just now in the harbor above here. Finding the time hang somewhat heavy upon my hands, I took a boat this morning and set out for a cruise along the shore. I ran farther than I intended before the wind, and now that I have it ahead, and the fog coming in like a race-horse, I hardly dare venture a night voyage in unknown waters. So, fair Mistress Pitcher, if your father will, as I said, give me shelter, and you will show me the way to his house, I shall owe you both my hearty thanks and such further acknowledgment as you will consent to receive."

"Come with me, sir, and I will bring you to my father, who will answer for himself," said Nazareth, not without a certain quiet pride upon her own part, and then she stood silently observant while Richard Armstrong made fast his little skiff to the boulder upon which she had been sitting, arranged his disordered dress, and finally turned to her, saying with a smile : —

"Your pardon again, mistress, for having kept you waiting, but I am ready at last."

So they went silently up the rocky path, and over the hill, and through the meadow skirting the wood, until, through the shining and odorous orchard, they came upon the house, and Gabriel Pitcher just coming from the barn with pails of frothing milk.

To him the stranger announced his errand in the same frank and assured manner he had already told it to the girl; and, hardly waiting for the end, the farmer gave him welcome in the hearty and homely fashion of the times when words meant deeds, not sound.

In the morning the guest departed, but with an invitation and a promise to repeat his visit before the Anne Lovering should again set sail for England, whence she had come. The promise was kept so well that the Anne Lovering discharged her cargo, and received another, and at last set sail for her appointed port, while Richard Armstrong lingered in the quaint old seaport town which at first he had pronounced so dull, and where now he seemed well content to spend his life. To such questions as were put to him, he answered carelessly that he had no especial business anywhere, that he was traveling to see the world, and that his stay or his departure at any given time were equally uncertain.

So Nazareth no longer wandered alone upon the shore, or through the withering fields and woods; no longer gazed with nameless yearning across the waters, or spent her tenderness upon flowers or birds or fishes. The sun had risen upon her day, and his glory filled her life with joy and beauty.

All this did not come about unquestioned. The mother, through many wise and cautious observations, convinced herself of the probity and moral worth of her daughter's lover, and the father made inquiry of the merchants to whom Armstrong gave his reference as to his worldly standing and repute. The answers to these questions were satisfactory beyond the farmer's expectations ; and, in the confidence of their own bedroom, he informed his wife that Nazareth had done better for herself than ever he had expected to see her.

So the wooing prospered, and at Thanksgiving

time there was a quiet wedding at the old farmhouse, and Nazareth Pitcher became Nazareth Armstrong, while her father, with pride and ambition, and her mother with loving trust, looked on with no thought of misgiving.

It had been settled that the new-married couple were to spend the winter at the farmhouse, and in the spring to take passage for England, the bridegroom's home. But when spring came these plans were changed. Armstrong, who had in the course of the winter made several journeys to the city, for the purpose, as he said, of receiving remittances and news from home, brought back upon one occasion a very grave face and a business-looking letter announcing that his immediate presence in London was absolutely necessary to the safe conduct of his affairs. This letter he showed to Nazareth ; and when she had read it, and looked confidingly into his face, he kissed her and said : —

" You see, sweetheart, that I must go at once."

" Yes, we must go," said Nazareth, placidly.

" Not we, but I," explained the husband, with a look of pain and something more upon his face. " I cannot take you in your present state of health, and in this stormy season of the year. You must wait, and I will come again for you so soon as you can travel."

The poor child turned as white as the snow dashing against the window, and sank suddenly into a chair. It was the first cloud between her and that glorious sun that had risen upon her life, and the shadow fell with an ominous chill upon her heart. She said little, however, and her parents less, in opposition to her husband's plan ; and a week later he left them, with more than one tender charge to Nazareth's parents to keep her safely until his return, and to Nazareth herself so many loving and passionate farewells that the mother at last came between them, saying, gently : —

" Richard, thee will make her sick. Go, and return as quickly as thy business permits. Thou dost not leave thy wife with strangers, but with her own people."

A prophetic sentence, and one that may have risen to the memories of all that little group more than once in the days that were to follow.

A letter sent back by the pilot announced that Armstrong had sailed, and another, two months later, that he had arrived at Liverpool, but after this nothing. Nazareth wrote by every opportunity, and waited with the terrible patience of woman for replies, but none came. The long, hot summer days found her still watching and waiting, a little less confidently now, but still with a patience only to end with life. Her favorite haunt was Floater's Cove ; and here she would sit for hours, curiously watching the waves breaking at her feet, and now and again depositing some waif of town, or vessel, or far-off wreck. Once her mother, softly following, stood watching her long and silently until she could bear it no longer, and, coming forward, drew the bright head to a pillow upon her bosom, saying : —

" Does thee think to find news of him among the floaters, child ? "

" It will come in God's own time, mother," said the girl, turning her white face a little closer to that tender heart ; and so they sat for hours, with never another word between them.

At last Nazareth could go no longer to the shore, and when the golden autumn came, and brought the anniversary of the day she first met Richard Armstrong, her desperate calm gave way at last ; and shutting herself up in her own chamber, her marriage chamber, she gave way to such a terrible passion of grief as in the end nearly destroyed her life, for before morning she was desperately ill, and when she recovered it was with the loss of the great hope and joy that had hitherto sustained her.

The anniversary of her wedding came and passed, and the broken-hearted mother left her daughter's bedside and came to her husband, where he sat alone, gloomily gazing into the embers of a decaying fire.

" We shall lose her, Gabriel ; she is going fast. Our only child is dying, and none can save," moaned she.

" She shall not die ! How dare you say that none can save ? Is this your faith in God, or in your own child ? " sternly demanded the old Puritan, and, rising up, he went straight to Nazareth's bedside and confronted her, not with the tender petitions of love, but the stern and requiring exhortations of his uncompromising belief, demanding that she should rouse herself from the lethargy of soul and body into which she had fallen, should prove herself worthy of her ancestry and of the holy faith in which she had been bred; that she should remember those who had cared and prayed and toiled for her through all her infancy and youth, and make some effort now to repay their exertions by the exertion on her own part necessary to keep life within her wasting body.

To this keen and wintry argument Nazareth listened with wide-open eyes, and cheeks that flushed and paled with emotion. Evidently the shock of such an appeal, following the tender and tearful lamentations of her mother, had at least recalled the dying girl's attention to matters around her which had seemed entirely forgotten or set aside. When Gabriel Pitcher ceased, his daughter humbly said : —

" Thank you, father. I will try."

And try she did to such effect that in a few days she was creeping about the house, the wreck and shadow of herself to be sure, but still alive, and with the weapons of youth and a strong constitution to aid her in the terrible fight she had yet to make against despair.

The winter passed, and the spring came on with more than its usual proportion of furious storms and deadly winds. Floater's Bay was crowded with relics of wrecks and trophies torn from vessels not wholly subdued by the attack of wind and wave. Nazareth, now restored to bodily health, but sadly changed from the bright and hopeful girl whom Richard Armstrong had found waiting for him upon the shore, had resumed her daily walks, and almost every sunset found her seated quietly upon her favorite rock, watching the wild waves at her feet as earnestly as if some day they were sure to bring her back the peace and joy and hope that she so long had lost.

One night her father interposed as she was leaving the house, saying : —

"There will be an awful storm to-night, Nazareth ; I would not go down to the shore. Wait until morning."

"Very well, father," replied she, and waited ; but all the night long her mother heard her softly pacing her chamber, moaning and sobbing, and only pausing while she leaned from the casement out into the black and howling storm. Suddenly she came to her father's door and called to him : "Father ! father ! There is a vessel driving upon White Reef ! They are firing guns. I can see their lights. Oh, father, father, can nothing be done ? "

She was like one mad in the fierce excitement of her hope, and before her father left the house he led her back to her chamber and turned the key upon her, saying to his wife : —

"Go to her, Rachel, and do not leave her for one moment, if you care for her. She fancies that man is aboard the wreck, and she may be down on the beach before you know it, unless you watch."

"Surely I will watch over her, Gabriel," replied the mother, somewhat reproachfully; but when, after helping her husband to gather together the articles likely to be needed upon his expedition, the good woman went to look after her charge, it was too late. The casement swung loose in the furious wind, and the chamber was empty. Like one distracted, the poor mother rushed out into the night, calling and searching, equally in vain, for the sweeping blast bore away her voice, and the darkness and rain blinded her eyesight. She knew not whither her husband had gone, or what point Nazareth would be likely to attempt to reach, so that finally she could only return to the house, and, casting herself upon her knees, pour out her soul in silent prayer, not only for her own beloved ones, but those others who might at that moment be perishing even in sight of rescue. Morning broke and found her still so occupied; but as soon as the light had grown sufficient to enable her to distinguish objects with certainty, she prepared to leave the house, and, in spite of the unabated storm, to seek her child wherever she might have wandered. Upon the threshold she met her husband, and in few words told him their common misfortune and her proposed errand.

"Stay you at home, Rachel. I will seek the child and bring her to you," said he, briefly, and Rachel did not think of disputing his command.

Drawing his hat lower upon his brow, and fastening his coat more securely about him, Gabriel

Pitcher turned his face again toward the sea, and for an hour wandered along the shore among the groups of men looking out to White Reef, where still hung a few timbers and fragments of the wreck. Not one body had come ashore, and no attempt at rescue had been possible from the very moment she had struck.

But none of the watchers had seen Gabriel Pitcher's daughter, and, although several had offered to aid his search, no one disguised his belief that it was useless.

" She 's gone over the cliff in the darkness, and unless she comes ashore in Floater's Cove, never will be heard from again," muttered the fishermen among themselves; but Gabriel, without listening to them, was already on his way to Floater's Cove, unsearched as yet, because it lay in quite another direction from the beach opposite White Reef, where the doomed ship had struck.

Floater's Cove was reached at last, but the driving mist and wrack so obscured the view that the father at first believed his search as vain here as in other quarters. In despair he called aloud : —

" Nazareth ! Nazareth, my child ! "

" Here am I, father," answered a feeble voice, and from beneath the shelter of a cave-like rock appeared the young woman, pale, drenched, and exhausted, carrying an infant in her arms.

" I thought you would look for me, father," said she, " and as I was afraid I could not come over the hill alone, I waited for you."

"What have you there, Nazareth?" asked the father, much surprised, as he wrapped her in the great shawl that Rachel had pressed upon him at the last moment.

"It is a little child, father. It came drifting into the bay, lashed to a spar, and I went through the water and rescued it. I always thought the bay would bring something to comfort me for the loss of its other gift."

She murmured the last words to herself, but her father heard them, and, folding the shawl more carefully about them both, half led, half carried his child and her new-found treasure up the hill and over the well-known field-path home.

"Care for the baby first, mother," said Nazareth, laying the infant in her mother's arms; and, without pausing to question her, Rachel did as she was asked. Not for hours, however, were her exertions rewarded, and more than once she was on the point of abandoning the attempt as useless, when the look of imploring anguish in Nazareth's eyes moved her to renewed efforts, repaid at last by a faint sign of life. In another hour the little creature lay sleeping in the arms of its adopted mother, safe and well.

From this moment Nazareth came back to life.

So far as could be ascertained, the child whom she had rescued was the only survivor of the wrecked ship, which had been so entirely broken up that no clue to its name, size, or history could be obtained; and, unfortunately, a wreck upon White

Reef was not so rare or terrible an event in those days as to call for any extraordinary research or comment. So Nazareth, without opposition either upon the part of her own friends or those of the little girl whom she now considered her own, adopted her into her heart as well as her home, gave her the name of Coral, and grew once more like herself in loving, attending, and petting her little nursling.

And Coral proved herself worthy of the love and care so lavishly bestowed, developing not only such wealth of beauty and grace that even Gabriel Pitcher confessed her " the prettiest thing God ever made," but a sweet and docile disposition, a loving heart, and unusually quick mental capacities.

" Take care, Nazareth," said her mother at last, " lest thy pretty Coral prove a snare to thy feet and a pitfall in thy path. Thee loves her too well, daughter."

The warning rang ominously in Nazareth's ears for many a day; but still she clung to and served her pretty darling, as only a heart so loving and so wounded as hers can cling to what is left after the best is taken.

Again the summer was waning, and the second anniversary of Richard Armstrong's advent had nearly arrived, when one day, as Nazareth sat upon her rocky seat at Floater's Cove and watched the little Coral playing with some bright seaweed and pebbles upon the shore, a hasty footstep caused her to look quickly up. just to catch the glimpse of a dark. handsome face. the next moment buried in Coral's golden hair.

Gabriel Pitcher stood behind, and laid his hand upon his daughter's head. saying brokenly : —

"Nazareth. my child. be strong. The Lord has appointed you another trial."

Without reply Nazareth rose, and. approaching Coral, knelt and put her arms about the child's waist.

The dark face of the stranger confronted her.

"She is mine. The Lord gave her to me," said Nazareth.

"She is mine. I am the mother who bore her," replied the stranger, fiercely ; and little Coral, clinging convulsively to Nazareth, stamped her foot and cried : —

"No, no, naughty lady ! You are not my mother. I will have no mother but this. Her name is Nazareth, and mine is Coral, and that is grandfather."

"Hush, foolish darling !" said the stranger, frowning and smiling at once. "You are no Coral, but my own little Mabel. and you shall go with me to such a beautiful home that you will soon forget all this, and even your new mother and grandsire."

She laughed as she spoke. but in the next moment laid her hand upon her heart with such a look of deadly anguish that Nazareth, forgetting herself and even little Coral. sprang forward to help her, but the stranger warned her off.

"Thanks, mistress ; it is past now. It is only a

pain that comes when I am over-tired or agitated. Just now, it is seeing my little darling there, for whose healthy and merry looks I thank you kindly."

At the word Nazareth fled again to her nursling, and, laying her arms closely about her, cried in bitterness of heart: —

"No, no, no, she cannot be yours, for God sent her to comfort me when I was ready to die. She is mine — my very own!"

At this the father interposed with stern decision. "Daughter," said he, "you may not keep from the woman what is indeed her own, or say that God gave you what was only lent for a purpose. Hear her story, and submit, as a Christian should, to the rod freshly laid upon your shoulders."

So the stranger, obedient to Nazareth's imploring eyes, told how she had been married three years before to a man who could not acknowledge her on account of his family's opposition, and had left her not knowing that she was likely to become a mother. After the child was born she had sought him all over her own country, and others where she could hear that he had been seen. At last she traced him to an American city, and finally heard that he had spent a winter in or near a fishing hamlet upon the New England coast. So, taking her child, she came to find and reclaim him, and it was the vessel in which she was passenger that had gone to pieces upon White Reef the night that little Coral came to comfort Nazareth.

When the storm grew furious the sailors lashed

the mother and child to separate spars, intending
that each should be the charge of two stout swimmers; but no human strength was able to combat
for a moment the fury of the waves upon that
dreadful night, and no sooner did swimmers and
burden touch the water than they were hurled
asunder, and the unhappy mother knew no more
until she found herself on board a British packet
homeward bound, and was told that she had been
picked up some hours previously by a fishing craft,
which, not to delay her own voyage, had put her
aboard the British brig, where she could receive
proper care and ultimately reach a central port.
That her child should have been saved seemed impossible to hope, and at any rate the captain of the
brig absolutely refused to put back for the purpose
of landing his involuntary passenger. So soon, however, as she reached England, she had dispatched
a special messenger to make inquiries in the neigh-
borhood of the wreck for any news of child or
father that could be obtained, and through him
had at last received intelligence not only that
her child was safe, but that her adopted mother
was Gabriel Pitcher's daughter and Richard Armstrong's wife.

"And your husband!" gasped Nazareth, as the
stranger paused, and again laid her hand upon her
side.

"Richard Armstrong is my husband, and that
child is his and mine, born in lawful wedlock,"
said the woman, with sturdy determination.

Then Nazareth fell prone upon the sand, and hid her face from even the light of day.

"Both, both!" moaned she. "Take both, and leave me desolate!"

"Not desolate, for you have God and your father and mother. More than father or mother, you have an unspotted life and a clear conscience," said Gabriel Pitcher, raising his child, and folding her to his breast with unwonted emotion.

Then, without a look at the stranger, he took Nazareth in his arms, and bore her homeward, as he had done the night when she carried her new-found comfort in her arms.

The child, dimly conscious of the change in her destiny, half-followed, half-lingered, weeping bitterly. Gabriel had reached the top of the hill, and paused to rest, when the patter of little feet resounded along the hard field-path, and Coral, flushed and breathless, caught him by the skirt.

"Away, child! Go to your mother!" cried the old Puritan, sternly, and Nazareth moaned upon his breast; but Coral, unheeding all else, cried piteously : —

"She is sick, the woman is. Perhaps she is dead. I cannot go to her. I am afraid!"

"What is that to me? I must care for my own," muttered Nazareth's father between his teeth, and would have held his onward course; but she, who till now had seemed insensible, raised her head, and said feebly : —

"Set me down, father, and go to her. It is the

duty of a Christian man; and she has done no harm, poor woman, to you or yours."

" But you, Nazareth! How can I leave you?"

" Coral will stay with me, or help me to go to my mother. Will you help me, little Coral?" asked Nazareth, smiling wanly, and the child answered joyfully: —

" That will I, mother dear, for you know I am your own little comfort. You call me so very often, and I do not forget anything you say."

" Come then, little comfort, and let me lean upon you for a last sweet moment," said poor Nazareth, taking the child in her arms, and bending over her until Coral's golden hair shone full of diamonds.

Gabriel Pitcher looked at them a moment, then strode away, his face dark, and his heart swelling more with wrath than pity; and had Richard Armstrong stood that moment in his path he had surely found the stern old Puritan a worthy descendant of those who went out to fight, — the Bible in one hand, and the sword in the other.

Beside the rock where Armstrong had made fast his skiff upon the night of his first visit, and where Nazareth had sat and waited for him through the two weary years since past, lay the stranger woman who had come to claim Nazareth's husband and Nazareth's child as all her own, dead, Gabriel at first thought, for her dark face was livid, her teeth set, her eyes glassy, and her form rigid.

" I will call the neighbors to attend her. Why should I bring her beneath the roof she has made

desolate?" asked Gabriel Pitcher of himself, looking down at the prostrate form, with a sense of all
the wrong his only child had borne seething in his
heart; but there came the memory of Nazareth's
plaintive voice, " It is the duty of a Christian man;"
and because he was a Christian he stooped and lifted
her, and carried her, not tenderly but carefully, up
the hill and along the field-path to his home, whither
Nazareth had already made her way, leaning upon
little Coral, and counting as a precious boon every
moment in which the child was yet spared to her.

" Here is Richard Armstrong's wife, Rachel.   If
you can find it in your heart to serve her, do so.
I am going for a doctor," said Gabriel, bringing in
the stranger and laying her upon a couch in the
wide, old-fashioned sitting-room.   And Nazareth's
mother, pale and cold and very gentle, ministered
to the woman who had stolen all that Nazareth held
dear, even to her good name and maidenly repute,
as if she had been her own child.

The doctor came, and after a while restored the
sufferer to consciousness; but in private he warned
Mistress Pitcher that her guest was the victim of a
fatal disease, that her days were numbered, and that
their continuance depended upon the care that was
taken to keep the patient from any fatigue, exposure,
or emotion.

" You must nurse her as you did Nazareth, when
you saved her life a year ago," said the good old man,
unwitting what a stab he was inflicting upon the
mother's heart.

When he was gone, Rachel went away into her own room, and there sought help and strength where such women are sure to find it; and when she came forth it was with a holy light upon her face that all who saw her felt and understood.

Then for days and weeks Rachel and Nazareth bent themselves to this new burden and bore it, not patiently alone, but lovingly and caressingly, and as if it had been a precious and coveted gift; so that before she died the stranger, who had come with bitterness in her heart and the law in her hand to wrest from Nazareth what she had been deceived to think her own, humbly asked forgiveness of her innocent rival for the harshness she had shown, and died blessing her and hers, and leaving her child to them as a precious legacy and remembrance.

So they buried her, bravely putting upon her gravestone —

"THE WIFE OF RICHARD ARMSTRONG."

And little Coral once more was Nazareth's child.

Two years more passed silently and swiftly on. Nazareth, still in the early blossom of her life, had settled into the quiet and completed aspect of a woman whose morning dreams are past, and who has accepted the appointed task of her day. Some threads of silver shone among her wealth of soft, brown hair; her sweet eyes no longer wandered expectant over sea and earth and sky, but looked out upon the world straight and steadfast, content with what lay day by day before them; her voice, clear and soft as it had always been, gained a pathetic tone, the echo of a far-off sorrow ; but besides these, and a certain shrinking from the presence of strangers, Nazareth's life showed no outward sign of the storm that had swept over it. She had resumed her maiden name, and, although more than once besought to change it, quietly expressed her resolution to live out her days in her father's house, content with the duties she there found.

It was thus with her, when one day Coral came home followed by a gentleman, at sight of whose handsome face Gabriel Pitcher rose wrathfully, while Rachel moved hurriedly toward her child as if to protect her. Nazareth alone had power to speak.

" Have you come for your child, Richard ? " asked she, in a sudden agony of fear.

" I have come for you, Nazareth," replied Richard Armstrong, slowly, and with his eyes upon the ground. " Can you forgive me, and consent to marry me, and be my child's mother in very truth ? "

No one spoke, but Gabriel Pitcher's stern features softened, and his wife looked eagerly into her child's face. They had never confessed it to each other, but the stain upon their name was eating deep into both their hearts.

Nazareth looked slowly from one to the other, reading their wishes in their eyes. Then she stooped thoughtfully to kiss the child's upturned face, and finally she looked at Richard Armstrong, who never dared to raise his eyes to hers.

"Come with me, Richard," she said at last; and the two passed out of the house, and over the well-known path, until they stood beside the great rock at the head of Floater's Bay.

Then Nazareth spoke : —

"It is nothing new to me that you should come to-day to ask this question," she said. "I knew that you loved me still, and I knew that you could never forget the cruel wrong you had done me; I knew, too, that your brave, frank heart would at last overcome the shame that at first kept you away. So I expected you, and my mind is quite resolved. Here, where we first met, we will say good-by forever."

He had not expected this, and threw himself on his knees beside her, passionately clasping her hand.

"No, no, Nazareth!" cried he. "I cannot take this as your answer. I cannot believe you will so defeat my hope. Nazareth, I never loved woman but you, and I only left you in the hope that the law might release me from her, and suffer me to make you wholly my own. When I found this release impossible, I dared not return to you, even had you remained forever in ignorance of my deception. I had learned so to venerate the purity and holiness of your life that I could not sully it by my approach. Then, when I knew she had told you all, I dared not come for very shame, even though I then was free to offer what to-day I beg, I implore you to accept. At last I have gathered

courage, and now, oh, Nazareth, you will not deny
me at the last! For the child's sake, for the sake
of your parents, of your own good name! Oh,
Nazareth, will nothing move you?"

She looked him steadfastly in the face, then drew
her hand away, and pointed to the waters rolling
in with their mysterious treasure.

"All the crises of my life," said she, "have come
in presence of these waves. They brought me you,
they brought me Coral, they brought me the news
that what I mourned as lost had never been really
mine; and now at the last they bring me you to-
day. Richard, when they bring me again my youth
and strength, and the glory and freshness of my
life, — when they bring me my maidenhood and the
hope and pride of a young girl's heart, — on that
day I will become your wife. Till then, good-by;
and if, indeed, you sorrow for what you have done,
and will be happier in thinking you have made
some amends, leave me the love and companionship of your child. Let me keep little Coral for
my own; I whom no other child shall ever call
mother."

Her steady voice failed a little as she said this,
and she turned away her face, while Armstrong
sadly made reply: —

"She is yours, dear Nazareth, as long as you will
keep her; and if ever while we live your heart
should turn through her to her father" —

"I have answered you, Richard, for once and for
always," said Nazareth's soft voice, calm and steady

now as it had ever been. And without a word of reply Richard Armstrong slowly went his way. turn ing at the brow of the cliff to take one long, last look at the patient figure seated beside the sea, her eyes fixed upon the dim horizon, her brow calm, serene. and patient beneath the crown of thorns that yet should turn to a wreath of immortal bloom. Then he went his way, and upon earth they met no more.

WITCH HAZEL.

"Chickens and curses come home to roost."

Two men stood upon the brow of Burying Hill overlooking the town and harbor of Plymouth, in the Old Colony. Below them lay the sparkling white beach inclosing the town with one long protecting arm, the green headland called Saquish, and the Gurnet with its lighthouse; beyond all these the ocean, clear, brilliant, and blue, stretched to the horizon, and met a summer sky blue, clear, and brilliant as itself.

The two men who, standing upon the steep summit, overlooked this fair scene were, as the first glance suggested, father and son, Captain Thomas Randall and his boy Philip, as he liked to call the stalwart young man, whose six feet of stature, broad shoulders, and assured bearing imparted a mingled pathos and drollery to the appellation. But Philip was an only son, an only child in fact, and had never yet left his home in the old town, or shaken off the luxurious dependence in which his father still liked to hold him. He had shot, fished, trained and driven his own horses, played cavalier to the merry-making lasses of Plymouth and neighbor towns; had strolled in and out of his father's country-house, and taken two or three voyages to

the West Indies and the ports of the Southern
States in his father's trading vessels ; but, after all
this, Philip Randall's life was yet to begin.

Between father and son lay a new-made grave,
its slate headstone, just set up, proclaiming it the
resting - place of Gregory Randall, aged eighty-
seven ; while under the name and dates appeared
the following verse, gratuitously added by the lap-
idary, who desired to add his mite of respect to
the venerable deceased : —

> " Stop heare, my friend, and cast an eye :
> As you are now soe once was I ;
> As I am now soe you must bee ;
> Prepare for deth and follow mee."

It was to see this headstone properly set that
father and son had mounted the Burying Hill,
and upon it the elder now sadly gazed, while he
said : —

" Yes, Philip, he was a good father and a good
man, and I doubt not has entered into rest and
peace. Mr. Priest seems also to have done his
work well, and we need tarry here no longer. And
yet, Philip, perhaps this may be as good a place as
any to open a matter which lieth somewhat heavily
at my heart."

" And what is that, father ? " asked Philip, his
frank and blithe young face assuming a shade of
concern deeper than the mortuary spot and theme,
or even the death of his aged relative, had brought
upon it.

" My son, it is not matter for alarm or sorrow,

but rather for much rejoicing, and — and — but it behooves us to walk softly in the matter, for there will be opposition and heart-burning; but a man must cleave unto his rights, Philip, — even Elder Faunce and the parson would grant that, would they not?"

"Of course, father; but what rights of ours are periled just now? Have the Frenchmen meddled with your fishing station in the Penobscot again, or" —

"Nay, nay, boy. Wait, and I will satisfy you, as indeed I appointed with myself to do when we came up hither. Philip, you know that yesterday I spent in looking over your grandfather's private papers and such matters."

"Yes, sir," carelessly replied the young man, as the elder, strangely embarrassed, seemed to pause for encouragement.

"Well, lad, I found a very curious document among those papers, — a document which I never knew to exist; and I can hardly suppose my father knew of it, or rather of its value, although the indorsement upon the back seemeth in his handwriting; though why he should have written 'Just so much wasted parchment' across an instrument enriching himself and his children forever, it passeth me to see."

"But what is this instrument, sir?" asked Philip, half laughing; for the elder, becoming absorbed in reverie, stood staring down at his father's grave, with an expression curiously compounded of respect, grief, and reproach upon his handsome features. Recalled by his son's voice, he looked up, stared a moment at him in turn, and then slowly said : —

"It is a deed of entail, Philip, confirming to your great-grandfather, John Randall, and his heirs male, in regular succession, the full ownership, control, and possession of a large tract of land, accurately described and bounded, lying chiefly in this town of Plymouth, but extending into the town of Carver, and embracing not only much valuable land in the outskirts, but a large portion of that in the very centre of the town ; in fact, my boy, including almost all the territory north of the Forefathers' Rock until we reach the Cold Spring."

"But, father, very much of this land is already occupied and built upon," objected Philip. "Why, it would take in those houses upon what they intend to call North Street."

"It will take in all of North Street, Philip," replied Captain Randall, complacently, and meeting his son's look of perplexity and dismay with one of triumphant satisfaction. "It takes in all of North Street, Philip, and you, my boy, will be the richest man in Plymouth Colony ; yes, or in the whole Massachusetts Bay, for that matter."

"But, father, the people who have built upon and improved these lands, supposing them to be their own " —

"They either become our tenants, Philip, or

they make satisfaction for the trespass they have committed, by purchasing their lands at our price."

Philip Randall frowned, and dug his heel thoughtfully into the spongy turf of the hillside where they still stood.

"Entail!" exclaimed he, at length. "Why, who ever heard of an entailed estate here in New England? We have no such institution."

"We live under English rule, and we govern ourselves by English law, do we not?" replied his father, dryly. "What is legal in the parent country cannot be illegal in the colony."

"Perhaps not, father. I have never thought upon such matters, and yet there seems an injustice" —

"Stop there, Philip Randall, and do not accuse your father of injustice in the same breath that you make acknowledgment of ignorance, concerning this matter. Because I have, perhaps, erred in over indulgence toward my only child, do not suppose that I intend to pretermit altogether the respect and deference which is my due from him."

"Surely not, sir; and I pray you to hold me excused if I have failed in either," replied Philip, a little haughtily, while the frown reflected from the face of the father to that of the son brought out a certain harsh, stern, and determined likeness, boding ill for any serious difference that might arise between the two.

But why — except at the instigation of some

demon of perversity, just then whispering at his
ear, — why should Philip Randall have chosen this
time, of all others, to convey to his father certain
tidings sure to meet with determined opposition?
Why prefer just now a request to which the elder
would scarcely have listened patiently in his most
indulgent mood? And yet, just then it was, as the
two in a somewhat sullen silence descended the path
and turned into the Main Street and homeward,
that Philip said : —

" Perhaps, sir, as we are on family matters, it
is a convenient time to inform you that I am thinking of marriage."

" Indeed, son Philip? If it be not intrusive, may
I ask whom you have selected as my daughter-in-
law ? "

" The name of the young lady is Bethiah Hazel,"
replied Philip, half sullenly, half defiantly.

His father paused and faced him, the level rays
of the rising moon falling full upon his face of
stern astonishment.

" Bethiah Hazel ! " slowly repeated he. " What,
the daughter of yonder old webster, who should
have been hung or burned for a witch long enough
ago ?"

" Goody Hazel weaves for a living, and she is
old. As for the witchcraft, I did not suppose we
believed in such matters here," replied Philip,
shrugging his shoulders. " It is fifty years since
those poor wretches were hanged at Salem, and the
world has gone on since then."

"Not so fast as to release children from their duty to their parents, young man," replied his father, sternly. "And once for all, I forbid you to think or speak of this matter further. When you marry it will not be after this fashion, I can promise you."

"I am two-and-twenty, sir," returned Philip, briefly.

"Two-and-twenty fools in one, then!" roared his father. "Do you mean to defy me, sir?"

"Nothing of the kind, father, but only to bring to mind that I am a man grown, and able to judge for myself as to a man's dearest and most personal matters."

"Very fine, — very fine indeed, Mr. Philip Randall; and I suppose you are also prepared to earn your own living, and that of your lady-wife, and of her lady-mother; unless, indeed, that worthy dame is to support you and yours by her praiseworthy arts!"

"I don't doubt I can find means to support myself, and whomever else I may choose to take under my charge," replied the younger man, doggedly.

"And how, pray?" sneered his father, pausing, with his hand upon the gate of the handsome house they had now reached. "Do you remember, sirrah, that everything you have ever used, or possessed, or enjoyed — the very coat upon your back, the very victual that supports you — are all of my bounty; that of yourself you are nothing, and less than nothing, — a beggar, a dependent, a mere hanger-on upon the fruits of my enterprise and industry " —

" You forget, sir, that our estates are entailed," interrupted Philip, with a sneer. His father's face grew livid with rage.

" The entail can be set aside, sir, and it shall be ! I will claim this property to which you presume to tell me I have no right, and then I will take measures either to secure your obedience, or to turn you and your witch's brat of a wife upon the world, with a father's curse for your only inheritance."

" A witch's brat ! " echoed Philip Randall, with an expression which even his father's taunt of dependence and threat of beggary had not called to his face.

" Yes, a witch's base-born brat ! " repeated Captain Randall. " Once for all, sir, I forbid you to visit or speak to her again. I forbid you ; do you understand ? "

" I understand, sir."

" And you will obey ? "

" Most assuredly I will not obey."

" You will not ? "

" I will not obey you in this, so help me God ! "

The two men stood for a moment in the moonlight, looking full into each other's eyes, — those eyes so wonderfully like in their stern, dark determination ; and then, with no gesture of leave-taking, the younger turned and went his way.

" He has abandoned his father's roof forever,"

said the old man, with even then a pang of anguish wringing the heart so filled with anger and disappointment.

Turning into the house, he went directly to a room upon the second floor, devoted to his private use, and called, for want of a fitter name, his study. Here, as the clock was on the stroke of midnight, he was found by his wife, a fair-haired, timid, and delicate woman, who loved her husband but feared him more, while she adored her son with no shadow of fear or doubt.

"Philip has not come in, captain," said she, in a hesitating way, for she had seen them at the gate.

"Well, what of that?" harshly demanded her lord.

"It is late, almost twelve o'clock."

"I know it. Why are not you in bed?"

"I waited for Philip," stammered the wife.

"Well, then, wait no longer. Get you to bed."

"Captain, what does it all mean? Where is the boy? What have you done with him?" And fair-haired and timid though she was, the captain's wife spoke with the courage of a bereaved mother who sees an opening to fight against the bereaver. Captain Randall looked up in some surprise. Very rarely had his wife dared to question him thus, — never, perhaps, with such a look and such a voice.

"What ails you, woman?" asked he, sternly. "Get you to bed, I say; or, stop, you asked about your son Philip. He has gone to marry Bethiah Hazel, and I have bestowed my curse upon him for a marriage-portion."

"My boy!" screamed poor Mrs. Randall, vanquished by this one cruel blow, and in the next moment fell upon the floor in a dead faint. Her husband raised her in his arms, carried her to her chamber, summoned Mehetabel Fry, the servant-maid, and went back to his study so soon as returning consciousness and a flood of tears proclaimed the patient out of danger.

"Yes, go along, you hard-hearted old flintstone! It's little enough you care for fainting, or crying, or dying, for that matter, as long as you get your own way." In which words Miss Fry expressed the widespread and popular estimate of her master's character; but yet few of his townsmen disliked, very few opposed him.

Alone in his study, Captain Randall unlocked the tall, old-fashioned secretary brought from his father's house a few days after the funeral, and taking from it certain papers, among them the Deed of Entail, with the indorsement, "Just so much wasted parchment," he sat studying them, referring occasionally to a rude map of Plymouth and its environs, until the gray morning light crept over the sea and in at his unshuttered window. Just then Thomas Randall stumbled upon what he had been all that night unconsciously seeking, — a link between the two terrible injuries he considered himself to have received at the hands of his son and the course he was obstinately bent upon pursuing ; yes, and a means of punishing at once Philip, the girl who had dared to receive his addresses, and the mother who had allowed her to do so.

" Surely, surely," muttered the captain to himself, as he eagerly read the description of the tract conferred upon Gregory Randall by his gracious majesty Charles I., and his heirs male forever. " Surely, 'the Sagamore's Cypress,' I remember that landmark right well, and it stands fairly to the north of Judith Hazel's hut. Yes, yes, that comes well within my privileges, and, by the sword of the Lord and of Gideon, I will claim that which is mine own."

Then the captain blew out the candles, waning and dying into all sorts of coffins and winding-sheets in the growing morning light, and threw himself upon a sofa for an hour or two of unrefreshing sleep.

Almost at the same time Bethiah Hazel, throwing open the door of her mother's cottage for a breath of fresh air after the sultry night, started back with a little shriek of surprise, for a man was seated upon the doorstep, his head leaned upon his folded arms.

At sound of her voice he rose, and, standing before her, showed the haggard face of Philip Randall. The girl stared at him dumbly, for indeed there was that about him to freeze any words of ordinary greeting, while he looked as silently at her, — looked as might a man who, having given

all that he possessed for the jewel which he covets,
examines it yet once again to make sure that it is
worth the purchase.   And this was what he saw :
A tall and slender girl in early youth, her graceful
figure disguised in a russet homespun dress, the
short sleeves of which left bare a pair of exquisite
arms, while the brief skirts exposed feet and ankles
as bare, as white, and as beautiful as the arms ; a
clear, glowing complexion, dark wavy hair, and a
pair of eyes, brown and bright and fascinating as
the brook that wells out from gnarled oak-roots,
and pauses one moment to eddy and dimple in the
shadow before it shoots forth into the light of common day, — a very beautiful picture, framed in the
low doorway of the poor cottage, and lighted by
the rosy and purplish gleams of coming day.   But
yet the man who has given all for his gem asks for
more than a fair outside ; his purchase must be genuine, pure, flawless, or he has indeed showed himself a fool, and lost all, and more than all.   Upon
Philip Randall's pondering of this truth broke the
girl's fresh young voice : —

"Why, Philip, it is you, and not your ghost,
is it not ?   What is the matter ?   What has happened ? "

"Come out here, Beth.   Come down to the
spring.   I have something to tell you."

"Good gracious, Philip ! what is it ? "   But without reply Philip turned into the little path leading
through the meadow to the spring in the grove, and
Beth followed, her bare white feet daintily treading

the dewy grass, and gleaming out from the daisies and buttercups.

Safely out of sight of the house — for, with man's justice, Philip was coming to hate and shun Bethiah's mother, even while resolved to cling to the daughter — he turned, and, taking her hands in his, said : —

"Beth, you know that I love you, and you know, too, that I have never asked you to be my wife."

"I never expected you would. I'm not fit to be your wife, Philip; and though I do believe you love me, and I love you dearly, Philip, I'm an honest girl, and " —

"And will be no less than my wife, if anything," said Philip, gravely.

"That is it, Philip," replied the child of nature, too pure for prudery. "And so we ought not to be together, and you must not come here any more, and " —

"Stop, child !" and Philip smiled, half bitterly. "You are hastening to forestall my speech of parting; but I did not come here to bid good-by; nor need you arm your pride against one even poorer than yourself. Beth, as I stand here, so stand I in the world, — alone, poor, without money, position, or even the knowledge by which to gain a livelihood. My father and I have quarreled, and he has cast me off, or, rather, I have left him, and never, whatever might befall, will I become again dependent upon his charity. I am a beggar, Beth;

he told me so himself, and I tell it again to you; and before that sun reaches the tops of the trees I shall be gone from Plymouth, gone for many a year, gone to seek my fortune, or, rather, to make it, to earn it, to become a man, for I feel that as yet I am none. Beth, will you have me for your husband, beggar as I am?"

The girl turned swiftly, and laid her arms around his neck, her head upon his breast.

"You are still so far above me, dear," whispered she; and Philip, gathering her closer to his heart, felt that all he had given, and more had it been his to give, was not too much to pay for the treasure of pure and unstinted love thus poured out before him.

After a while the lovers, returning to the things of this world, began to discuss plans by which Philip was to gain a livelihood for the two, and also another plan of more immediate urgency. This was no other than a secret marriage, and Beth's removal to the house of some humble friends of Philip's in Boston.

"Truth to tell, Beth," said he, after all other arguments had failed, "I care not to leave you with your mother longer. She has not favored my visits, and — and — in sooth, I cannot be easy unless you are away from her, and with those I know."

The reason was no reason, as they both felt, Philip knowing in his heart that, should he confess that he feared his father's persecution of both

mother and daughter when he should not be there
to defend them, Bethiah would cling all the more
closely to the parent thus threatened, while she
saw beneath Philip's embarrassment a distaste he
had not always concealed for her mother's speech,
manners, and character. A sudden flash of con-
viction showed the girl that here the path divided,
here the choice between parent and husband was
to be made, — that to possess both was now become impossible; and, clinging closer to her lover's
breast, she made her choice, and sealed it with her
tears.

"Oh, Philip! if I 've got to give up mother for
you, it 's no matter how soon I do it."

"Then come with me now — this morning!" exclaimed Philip, eagerly, and yielding to the im-
pulse to turn his back and withdraw Beth from
that place and that companionship at once, and
without fear of detention. But the girl would not
quite consent to this, and her grief at feeling com-
pelled to thwart any plan of Philip's was so apparent as to disarm him of the displeasure he felt
tempted to use as a weapon. So at last it was
agreed that the two should walk that morning to
Kingston, where they might be married by the
magistrate, as was then the custom of the colony,
and returning the next morning they would then
tell the old mother what they had done, before
bidding her farewell.

But although Bethiah consented to this scheme,
it was as she would have consented to lay her hand

upon the block and suffer it to be chopped off, had
Philip bid her; and even when she had left him to
return to the house and collect the little parcel of
finery without which not even she would consent
to be married, the poor child turned back to clasp
her hands and piteously ask : —

" Oh, Philip! is there no other way? Must I
steal away from her so? Is it right, Philip? is it
right?"

" It must be so, Beth. Does not the Bible say
that for this shall man or woman leave father and
mother, and cleave only to the partner thenceforth
to be one flesh and one life with their own? It
is right, Beth; and I wish it, I ask it, for love of
me."

" I will go, Philip. Wait here, and I will return
anon."

So Beth crept into the house, made her little
preparations, and crept out again without disturbing the old mother, not yet awake; a few moments
later the two set forth together upon the road to
Kingston, and upon the road of their mutual life.

The blithe summer day came up from the ocean,
and wheeled its fervid hours across the sky until
they brought noon, — sultry, breathless, and exhausted; and Judith Hazel, standing in her cottage door, searched the familiar landscape once
again for trace of her missing child. The line of
the sandy road, white and dazzling, stretched away
from her little house toward the town a full mile
before it hid itself in the pine-wood, whose bal-

samic odor, drifting toward her upon the light
breeze, mingled with the sweet, sharp note of the
locust to express a summer heat as no other scent
or sound expresses. But Judith did not heed the
heat, did not smell the pines, or listen to the locust. With one hand set upon her hip, and the
other shading her sharp black eyes, she stood there
in the doorway, a picture as striking, if not as
beautiful, as the one framed by that same doorway
six hours before.

"She's gone, — wiled away by that fellow.
Did n't I tell her what it would come to? But
when did a girl in love listen to reason? If ever
I see him or his proud father — Ha! what's
that?"

The muttering ceased; the wandering eyes fixed
themselves steadily upon the point where the road
emerged from the wood, and never wandered
again; for in the little cavalcade just coming into
sight the bereaved mother saw the promise of an
answer to her cry for satisfaction or revenge. The
central figure of this cavalcade was a man sixty
years old, but tall, straight, strong as youth, — a
man of iron jaw and unflinching eyes, a haughty
bearing and unyielding mien, — a man in whom
all men trusted, because he never yet had swerved
from his word or his will, whether for good or
evil.

"Captain Randall, and two constables at his
back!" whispered the old woman breathlessly;
and then, folding her arms across her breast, she

leaned lightly against the doorpost, and stood waiting for her guests.

The tramp of their horses' feet came up the little
hill, along the sandy track, and paused at her door.
The keen black eyes of the old woman fixed themselves upon the leader's face, but no word or gesture acknowledged his presence. The sheriff and
his assistant leaped from their horses and fastened
them, but Captain Randall rode close to the door
without dismounting. Still looking steadily into
his face, Judith read, as if it had been printed
there, the humiliation and agony through which
the man's soul had passed during the night just
gone. Hard and pitiless and cruel she found it;
and yet beneath, above, pervading this expression,
there lay another, and recognizing it, she grimly
smiled.

"Do you come looking for your son, Captain
Randall?" asked, she, mockingly, at last; and the
sudden spasm crossing the white face of the man
before her told how truly her chance shaft had
sped.

"What have you to do with my son?" demanded he, fiercely, and speaking in a thick, unnatural voice. "I have come here to-day to give
you a warning."

"Ay? And you shall get one in return, I
promise you. I was coming down to see you before night."

"Warning to quit these premises," pursued
Captain Randall, not noticing the intimation.

"'Quit these premises!'" echoed Bathsheba, unmoved. "And why should I quit the house where I was born and bred, and where I mean to die? Why should I quit it, except for my grave, Captain Thomas Randall?"

"Because it is mine, — my property; do you understand? And although my father and grandfather allowed you and others to occupy their land, they never intended to bestow it upon you. The line of my property extends to the Sagamore Cypress in this direction, and that is some rods beyond anything you have ever claimed. The land is mine, and I no longer choose that you should occupy it; do you understand? The house you have chosen to put upon it becomes mine also; but, on condition that you and yours should leave this town and this part of the country, I will give you whatever two honest men will say that it is worth; and you may come to my office to-morrow and receive the money. If ever you come within my reach again, however, I will throw you into jail for rent and damages; and there you may live and die, unless your master helps you out."

During this harangue Judith, hardly changing her position, had gathered herself together, as it were, slightly raised her head, slightly opened her eyes, and set her thin lips closer, while every muscle in her sinewy frame seemed to grow tense and ready for action. As before she had looked not unlike a somnolent serpent, so now she resembled the same serpent, — venomous, startled, coiled for a spring, and sure to carry death in that spring. As Captain Randall paused, and moved his hand heavily across his forehead, she said, in a suppressed voice : —

" You really mean to turn me out of this house, and off this land, where I and mine have lived for fifty years or more ? You really think to drive me from this town, and throw the price of my stolen home at my feet that it may carry me out of your sight ? Is that your meaning, Captain Randall ? "

" Yes. You will leave this house within a week, or I will burn it over your head."

" I will not go."

" You will not ! I tell you, witch, that you shall go, even though you bring your master, the devil, and a legion of his imps to defend you ! You shall go if I drag you from the place with my own hands. Yes, you and that light o' love, your daughter, too."

" My daughter ! And if she be a light o' love to-day, who yesterday was as honest a girl as ever stepped, whose fault is it, Thomas Randall, — whose but your son's ? Yes, his, and none but his ; and of him and you I ask back my girl ; and you shall give her to me, or I will have the town about your ears. What have you done with her ? Where is she ? Where is Philip Randall ? "

" He is gone, and you and she have wiled him away : you with your devilish spells, and she with her wanton smiles ; but I will have my revenge, I will have justice. So sure as God is in heaven, you shall be burned for a witch, and she set in the stocks and lashed out of the town as a lewd and wanton woman ; your house shall be scattered to the four winds, and your name pass into a byword of infamy. You have robbed me of my son, and you shall pay me even to the uttermost farthing, even to the last gasp of your wretched breath and the last drop of your evil blood. You have defied me, and I will not spare you ; so surely as God liveth, you shall die the death appointed for such as you ! "

He raised his hand above his head, as if appealing to Heaven for a witness to his words, while his face flushed a deep red, then returned to its former ghastly pallor, and his eyes fixed themselves upon the face of the woman with a stare of deadly animosity, strangely underlaid with a look of awful terror and distress.

Meeting that wild and terrible look, Judith Hazel stepped one step forward, and, holding his eyes with her own, glittering and snake-like now, she slowly said : —

" And so surely as God liveth — yes, and so surely as the devil liveth, and hath power — I will not die until you are dead before me ; I will not leave my home until you have left yours for the graveyard ; I will not leave this town until you have left this earth; I will not be burned as a witch until you have died like a dog, wanting priest and leech and shelter. You have threatened me, Thomas Randall, and I curse you ; I curse you with the black and deadly curse of the widow and the fatherless, and the poor and the oppressed; I curse you body and soul, — and lo, the curse descends!"

She extended her arm, the long, bony finger quivering like a serpent's tongue, and pointed full in the face of him she had cursed; and as she did so the look of terror and distress grew and grew, and overflowed the look of rage and menace, while the deep crimson flush mounted again across the livid white of the set face, and reached the brain; then, with one wild, gasping cry, and a futile grasp at the fallen rein, Thomas Randall swayed heavily sideways in his saddle, and but for the attendants would have dropped to the ground at Judith Hazel's very feet.

"He is dead. I cursed him, and the curse has fallen!" said she, quietly, and going into her house, shut and barred the door. The two men, more afraid of her than of their dead or dying master, mounted in hot haste and galloped down the hill: a few moments, and even the sound of their horses' feet died upon the sultry air. And there he lay alone, his head upon the witch's doorstone, his majestic figure trailed in the dust she had trodden; there he lay, dying like a dog, as she had said, uncomforted, untended, unsheltered, unforgiven.

Half an hour later the men returned with others, and with a conveyance; but Thomas Randall was dead before they came, and it was only his discolored and fearsome corpse that they carried back

to the terrified and weeping woman who waited
for it, and too late lavished upon it the tenderness
and care for lack of which he had died.

"He was always good to me, — always good to
me ; and Philip has gone too," moaned she, over
and over again ; for, weak in all else, this poor,
pale woman was very strong in loving, and mourned
herself into her grave not many months after her
stern and absolute lord.

The next morning a stout horse paced merrily to
the door of Judith Hazel's hovel, and from his back
sprang Philip Randall and Bethiah his wife.

These were days before telegraph, post-office, or
active communication of one town with another ; so
that no rumor of yesterday's tragedy had wandered
from Plymouth to Kingston, and the young people
had come to make their confession, and to bid farewell to the old mother, if not gayly, at least cheerfully, for the light of the new day, risen upon their
lives, was strong enough and rosy enough to hide,
or at least to overlay, all ugly things of yesterday ;
and Philip, with Beth at his side, could forgive her
mother for the part she had unconsciously played
in his quarrel with his father, — could even forgive
her, almost, for being Bethiah's mother, and had
already explained to his attentive wife how generous
he intended to be toward her after he had earned
the fortune they neither of them doubted was awaiting him.

The door was fastened ; and after Bethiah had
gone round to the brook door at the back, and found

that fast also, Philip knocked long and loudly, and then the two stood waiting, the young man's feet upon the spot where yesterday his father's gray head had lain. Perhaps it was the subtle communication between animate and inanimate nature, perhaps what we now call telepathy, that suggested his next words : —

"Beth, my darling, what if I should leave you here for an hour or so, and go down into the village just to bid my father good-by? He cannot be so hard upon me now that I have gone from his house forever, and may never set eyes on him again ; he must treat me as a man at least, and not as an ungrateful beggar, as he did in our last interview. And then, my mother — I must see my mother again, Beth ; for now that I have you, I love my mother better, because of your common womanhood. Shall I go, Bethiah ? "

"Yes, dear; I would gladly have you," replied the wife, eagerly. "I cannot bear to think that through poor me you should have quarreled with " —

But just then her words were awfully cut short by a wild shriek from within the closed house, — a shriek of mad terror, long, shrill, wavering, piercing the quiet summer morning like the curse falling upon Eden. Beth stopped, turned white and still, and clung to Philip's arm in silent horror ; nor was he undaunted.

"What was it ? " muttered he, at length ; and the two stood looking at each other, as if each would

make sure that his own fancy had not played him a
horrible trick.

" It was real — it was in the house," whispered
Beth, her lips white, and her voice trembling as if
in an ague fit. " Oh, Philip ! what could it be ? "

" It was in the house, and we must enter," replied Philip, recovering himself, and gently putting
aside the little clinging hands upon his arm. " Is
there an open window, a cellar door, any way better than to break down the door ? " continued he,
half aloud, as he glanced about for the means of
entrance.

" The window at the end — the window of my
room — was hardly ever fastened," murmured Beth,
still shaking with terror, but leading the way around
the house.

Philip followed, and presently, raising the little
window, guarded only by its maidenly white curtain, he climbed in at it, and stood one moment irresolute, looking about the simple room, but yesterday a shrine of mystery and love to him.

" Open the door and let me in, Philip, first of
all," whispered Beth at the open window. " If
there's anything dreadful, I want to be near you
when you see it."

Without reply Philip obeyed ; and setting the
door wide open, let the sunshine and Beth into the
grim old house. Then, hand in hand, they searched,
cautiously, shrinkingly, yet resolutely, through
every room, every corner, always expecting to
stumble upon some ghastly sight, to meet some

horrible answer to the question the mind of each was asking. The three rooms below, the cellar, the bedroom above, had all been searched; and then they climbed into the little garret, unused except for lumber, and unlighted except by a single pane of glass at one end. Clinging to each other's hand, and standing close beside the door, the two peered through the darkness, at first with renewed apprehension, then with freer breath.

" No one is here, Beth " — began Philip; and just then a low, unnatural laugh almost over their heads made both start back and look up. There, crouched upon a beam, to which she was busily knotting a rope, sat Judith Hazel, her scant gray hair streaming down her back, her eyes glaring with the fearful fires of madness, her white lips muttering incessantly, with now and then that hideous laugh, so void of mirth, so full of menace.

" What does she say, Philip ? "

"Hark ! my father's name ! "

" Yes, I cursed him, and he was cursed, and fell down dead at my feet, — handsome Thomas Randall. When I was maid in his mother's house I told him how I would go to destruction for a kiss of his proud lips, and he bade me go there if I would, but not for that. Handsome Tom Randall! Oh, how I loved him, and how I hated him! and I cursed him, and he died; laid there in the hot, sweltering sun at my doorstep, and not a hand to brush away the flies from his dead face, — the beast of the field might have kissed his lips then, — and

I sat looking at him until they took him away, and never cared to kiss him then. I cursed him, and he died, and I shall die ; and then he will love me, and I shall have my kiss at last, — yes, at last, and at last, — all things come round at last, and why not that " —

She had the rope knotted now, and the noose about her neck ; and rising suddenly to her feet, with another such shriek as that which had first alarmed them, she flung herself from the beam just as Philip Randall and his wife sprang forward to receive her. Before they could do so, however, the noose drew up about her neck, and the shock, although not fatal, reduced the wretched creature to insensibility. In this condition they removed her to a room below stairs, and while Philip watched beside her Bethiah hastened for assistance. This was not to be found short of the town ; and there the daughter and wife heard news that threw yet an added horror over the scene she had just left ; and yet, with the courage of true love, it was she, and no other, who told Philip Randall the terrible story of his father's death, and upon her faithful bosom he shed the strong and bitter tears of a man's wounded heart.

" He died without forgiving me, without my telling him how well I loved him in spite of all," moaned he.

" But God knows, and your father knows too now," whispered Bethiah, and tenderly kissed the bowed head upon her breast.

Witch Hazel, as she was ever after called, did not die, nor did she ever recover her reason, but spent the rest of her melancholy days in the house she had sworn never to leave, in company with a keeper liberally paid by Philip Randall, and carefully overlooked by his wife, who, amidst all her new duties, seldom failed of a daily visit to the lonely cottage where she had been born and bred.

When at last the unhappy creature died, they buried her upon a little knoll behind the cabin, and for many a year the country folk declared that her ghost was to be met on almost any stormy night wandering between the ruins of her former home and the Sagamore's Cypress, wringing its hands, and moaning always : " I cursed him, and he died ; he fell dead at my feet ! "

But the shadow of this great mystery, shame, and sorrow was lifted at last from the lives of Philip and Bethiah Randall ; and as the years rolled on, and children clustered about their knees, and men spoke well of him, and the matrons made honorable place for her among them, the old story passed into the dim and almost forgotten memories of the past, and the happy present filled all the scene.

The entail was never revived, nor did Philip Randall or his heirs ever claim the great estate that by disuse had lapsed from their possession into the hands of others, until the Revolution came and all matters of private interest were merged in the great public events that left the new country to begin its new and nobler life.

THE FREIGHT OF THE SCHOONER DOLPHIN.

Meeting had gone in. Parson Holbrook was in his seat in the high, ugly pulpit, with the sounding-board overhead; the singers, in the singing seats in the gallery, had taken their pitch from Uncle Jethuron's tuning-fork, and were fuguing "And on the wings of mighty winds came flying all abroad;" the first families of Pilgrim Village were seated in their square pews, each furnished according to the taste or the means of its owners; and the little boys, perched upon the high wooden seats, with no footstools near enough for their little dangling feet to reach, had begun their two hours' fidget, — when the door, just closed by black Pompey, the sexton, opened slowly, and Major Cathcart walked up the broad aisle in his usual dignified and deliberate manner. Every head was turned to gaze upon him, every face wore an expression of astonishment and disapproval; the singers, finishing their hymn with hasty quavers of discomfiture, leaned over the front of the gallery and gazed down upon him, and even Parson Holbrook bent his powdered head sidewise to look sternly at the great square pew where his wealthiest parishioner was uncomfortably seating himself with an attempt at unconscious dignity.

A moment of silence fell upon the place, — that awful, pregnant silence which speaks as no words can, — and then Martin Merivale, the man whom Pilgrim Village always chose as its representative in colonial assemblies, and who led public opinion as he willed in the town where his honorable, steadfast life had thus far passed, rose in his place, deliberately did on his heavy cloak, took his hat in his hand, cast one meaning glance across the aisle into the questioning eyes of Major Cathcart, his old associate and neighbor, and then walked slowly down the aisle. He had not reached the door before Dr. Holcom rose to follow his example, and then Squire Vale, and then the Oldfields, father and son, and finally every man in the congregation who counted himself a person of the least consequence, or able to set an example, until, when black Pompey at last closed the door, and with a joyous grin sat down beside it, the church, so lately filled with the pith and sinew of the stanch old colony town, was empty, save of women, children, and Major Reginald Cathcart, whose ashen-gray face had never moved after the first from its stern straightforward gaze, or his dark eyes blanched, or his heavy eyebrows unbent from the frown of defiant endurance which with some men is the only sign of agony.

And agony it could not fail to be ; for this man, to-day so openly and deliberately thrust from their midst by his fellow-townsmen, counted himself only three days earlier their autocrat, claiming by birth, wealth, and haughty self-assertion the place yielded to him in virtue of these qualities, as that of Martin Merivale was thrust upon him in recognition of his own personal character.

But why this terrible insult? Why this stern intimation that the men of Pilgrim Village considered the presence of one so lately their magnate so great a pollution that they preferred even to lose the privilege of public worship to suffering him to join them in it?

It was 1774, and the Governor of Massachusetts, in right of his commission from King George of England, had sent to demand the payment of a tax levied upon the colony for the support of the foreign soldiers, sent over with the avowed purpose of holding the mutinous province in subjection. Pilgrim Village took this demand from "the man George" into consideration, argued upon it, prayed over it, and finally declined to accede to it, but in so mild and temperate a manner that the governor considered the refusal only a formal protest, and proceeded to enforce his demand by appointing certain collectors of the revenue throughout the colony, and for the town of Pilgrim Village commissioning Major Reginald Cathcart to this odious office.

When the news came down to the old town, its men smiled after the slow and solemn fashion of their kind, and said, "The governor does not know the mind of the people even yet, it seems."

But the next day a rumor pervaded the town, --

a rumor of dismay and incredulity, yet deepening hour by hour to certainty. Yes, Major Cathcart had accepted the commission, and announced his intention of carrying out its instructions. That was on the Saturday, and we have seen the result upon the Sunday.

As the door closed, Parson Holbrook rose and prayed long and earnestly for the welfare of his native land, and the safety of those whose fathers had been led to these shores, even as the children of Israel were led out of Egypt to find' safety and freedom in the land their Lord had promised them, and he closed with a petition for protection against all enemies, both without and within, — the foreign foe and those of their own household who had turned against them, and whose evil counsels might, he prayed, be turned to foolishness and dishonor.

Then came the sermon ; and, laying aside his carefully written discourse upon the Urim and Thummim, Parson Holbrook preached extemporaneously and mightily from the text, " Put not your faith in princes," diverging finally into the story of Judas, and the high crime of domestic or social treachery.

When all was over, and the choir had sung, " See where the hoary sinner stands," black Pompey threw open the doors, and stood aside, as usual, to meet and return the kindly greetings of the congregation ; but as Major Cathcart strode down the aisle, his head erect, but his face white and withered, as if he had just arisen from a bed of torture, even Pompey turned his back and stood staring intently out of the open door while the stricken man passed by. But Major Cathcart looked neither to the right nor the left; and if others besides Pompey had intended to show their disapproval of his presence, they found no opportunity, for the king's collector passed quickly through the little throng outside the door, and down the main street until he reached the grave, handsome, middle-aged house so strongly resembling its master, and quietly opening the front door, passed directly upstairs, and was hastening to the shelter of a room at the back, known as " the major's study," when from the open door of one of the principal bedrooms came a gentle yet eager call: " Reginald, do come in here."

The husband paused reluctantly and, turning his head toward the door, but without showing his face at it, replied, " What is it, Hepzibah? I am going to my study."

" Not first, dear. Please come and see me for a moment. I am all alone."

Without replying, the major obeyed and, passing into the handsome, shadowy room, stood beside the bed, where lay a woman whose fair and delicate face bore the patient, almost angelic look of one who has suffered very long and very cruelly, but whose pains, meekly borne, are consciously drawing to their final close. She was Major Cathcart's wife, and the only being the cold, proud man had ever loved, and she was dying.

He stooped and kissed her tenderly, asking, "How have you been this morning, dear?"

"As well as usual. But you, Reginald? How has it been with you? I knew by your step upon the stair that you were suffering, and your face tells the story. Oh, my darling husband, they have insulted you, as we feared. Is not it so?"

"Yes, Hepzibah, they have insulted me, and so cruelly that I will no longer live among them. I have resolved that we will go to the northern provinces. We have good friends at Halifax, good and loyal to the king whom these anarchists are preparing to defy."

"Even the parson and the doctor, reasonable and law-abiding men as they are, say that the colony should be free," said the invalid, timidly, and stealing her thin hand into her husband's. But he frowned impatiently.

"This is not talk for women or children," said he, coldly. "And you are of those whose conversation should be in heaven. It would better become Parson Holbrook to tell you so, instead of disturbing your mind with matters so unfit for it at any time."

The wife remained meekly silent a moment, and then, softly pressing her husband's finger, said: —

"My love, you will wait until I am gone, will you not, before you leave Pilgrim Village?"

"Gone, Hepzibah! — gone where?"

The wife looked up with tearful eyes, but her reply was prevented by the sudden entrance of a young girl, her cheeks flushed and her eyes bright with anger and excitement.

" Father, John Belknap has been in, and told me of the insult they have offered you," exclaimed she. " It is a shame, a burning shame, and I hope you will show them " —

" Dolly, I am not very strong to-day, dear, and you are speaking loudly and unadvisedly."

It was the mother's gentle voice, and Dolly, who would have joyfully taken the part of Joan of Arc, or even Boadicea, fell upon her knees directly beside her mother's pillow, soothing the invalid, and accusing herself of all manner of evil in forgetting even for a moment the consideration and tenderness owing to her.

Major Cathcart stood looking at the two for a few moments, then quietly left the room, and a little later dispatched a servant with a note requesting the immediate attendance of Dr. Holcom. The worthy physician was one of those who had left the church so pointedly a few hours earlier, and the proud man, thus insulted, by no means forgot or forgave the insult, but the feelings of the husband were stronger than all others at that moment, and Hepzibah's words had startled him with a new and terrible idea.

The doctor came, was closeted for half an hour with the major, made a short call upon his patient, and left the house. A little later Major Cathcart summoned his daughter to his private room, and addressed her, briefly and almost sternly : —

" Dolly, Dr. Holcom does not disguise from me the cruel truth known for some time to him and to your mother. She is dying, surely and swiftly. Did you know it ? "

The girl hid her pale face between her hands. " Mamma has said it, but I hoped " — Her voice died away, and her father's filled the space.

" Hope no longer. He says two or three months are as much as we may look for, and even that brief respite depends upon quiet and her accustomed comforts. She must on no account be removed even from the room where she now lies. But this people about us will not wait two or three months before they carry out in act the treason they already talk, and I, as the avowed friend of the king, and ready and willing to execute his will in this rebellious province, shall very probably fall one of their first victims ; or if not personally, shall surely suffer in property, and be stripped of land and house and even personal belongings. Were your mother able, we should all migrate at once to the still loyal northern provinces ; but as it is, you must go alone, carrying such valuables as we can collect, and remain with your uncle in Halifax until — Perhaps — God's goodness is without limit — perhaps I may bring her with me."

" Must I leave my mother ? " cried Dolly, in dismay. " What matter for our possessions, compared with the comfort of her last hours ! And how can she spare me ? and, oh ! how could I spare her ? "

" Girl, there are perils in time of anarchy and

war of which you know naught, — perils for a
young and comely woman of which I may not
speak. Your mother will be cared for, since it will
be the one duty of my life to care for her, and it
will be removing a weight from my mind to know
that you are safe, and shielded from the possibilities
of evil. Say no more ; it is decided."

Dolly, stout-hearted as she was, dared say no
more, for the girl of a century ago was trained to
obedience as the first duty of her sex, and to silence
and respect for the authority of man as the next ;
nor was Dolly's father a man to soften the stern
and unquestioned rule every head of a household
felt bound to exercise in all particulars. So the
preparations for the young girl's departure went
quietly and silently forward, and the schooner Dolphin, a small coasting craft partly owned by Major
Cathcart, received a cargo so various in its character that neither master, mate, nor the attentive
loungers who inspected the process of loading could
positively determine her destination.

Not until the very last days before the Dolphin's
sailing did any one outside the major's own family
surmise that his daughter was to be a passenger,
and so rapidly, even secretly, was her luggage carried aboard that very few persons saw it at all.
Among the rest was one article singular enough as
part of a young lady's outfit, especially so healthy,
active, and blithe a girl as Dorothea Cathcart : it
was one of those large, square, stuffed easy-chairs
still to be found in old country-houses, sometimes

dishonored in the lumber-loft, sometimes carefully preserved in cover of white dimity or gay old-fashioned chintz in the chamber of the grandmamma. This one was covered in green moreen, and had stood in Mrs. Cathcart's own bedroom, although that dear lady had not been able to occupy it for many a day. A short time after the decision with regard to his daughter, Major Cathcart removed this chair to his own study, and both he and Dolly occupied themselves over it in a very mysterious fashion for many hours, until at last the girl deftly sewed a wrapper of tow-cloth over all, and said to her father, who stood watching the operation : —

" There, father, it will stand in the cabin, and I shall say that it is covered lest any but my dear mother should use it, and I am taking it to her invalid sister in Halifax, whom I am about to visit."

" I doubt not your shrewd wit will suggest many a quip and turn," replied the major, with a grim smile ; " but take care that you do not pass the bounds of truth and discretion."

" I will take heed, father. The barrels are all ready, are they not ? "

" Yes, and shipped. Here is the bill of lading ; " and Major Cathcart took from his pocket-book and handed to his daughter a slip of paper worded thus : —

Shipped by the Grace of GOD, in good order and well conditioned, by Reginald Cathcart, in and upon the good Schooner called the Dolphin, whereof is Master under GOD for this present voyage William Peters, and now riding at anchor in the Harbour of Pilgrim Village, and by GOD's Grace bound for Halifax, to say, Twenty barrells and boxes of sundries on Acct. and Risque of the Shipper, and consigned to Cathcart and Kingsbury, Halifax. Being marked and numbered as in the Margent, and are to be delivered in the like good Order and well Conditioned at the aforesaid Port of Halifax (the Dangers of the Seas only excepted) unto said Cathcart and Kingsbury or to their Assigns, he or they paying Freight for the said Goods, Sixpence per cw., English Curryancy, with Primage and Average accustomed. In witness whereof the Master or Purser of the said Schooner hath affirmed to two Bills of Lading, all of this Tenor and Date, one of which two bills being accomplished, the other to stand void.

And so GOD send the good Schooner to her destined Port in safety. AMEN.

Dated in Pilgrim Village, October the 15th, 1774.

WILLIAM PETERS.[1]

Dolly rapidly ran her eye over the familiar form, for her duty had been to play the occasional part of confidential clerk in her father's business, and she smiled as she returned it to him, saying: —

" 'Barrels and boxes of sundries?' Well, and so they are. China and books and household gear are sundries, no doubt, although I dare say your partners think it is mackerel or " —

" It does not concern the other owners of the schooner, since I ship my freight at my own charge and purely as a private venture," interrupted Major

---

[1] The above is a literal copy of a bill of lading given in Boston shortly before the Revolution.

Cathcart, hastily. " But be careful, Dolly, that you say not a word either here or upon your voyage as to the nature of these same sundries, for William Peters is a fanatic as bitter as the worst, and if he got wind of the matter now, nothing would be more likely than that he should persuade Merivale and the rest to throw off the mask at once, and confiscate my goods to the republic they talk of founding. Even at sea you must be careful, for this man is quite capable, even in the harbor of Halifax, of giving the order to 'bout ship, and bring you and the easy-chair and the barrels of sundries all back to Pilgrim Village. It is a large errand for so young a woman as you, Dolly, and you will need to be wily as the serpent, though innocent as the dove."

" I think I can do it, father," said Dolly, quietly; and as the major looked in his daughter's face, he thought she could.

The morning that the Dolphin was to sail, Captain Peters found that Thomas Wilson, his first mate, had fallen down the steep ladder leading from his house to the shore, sprained an ankle and broken a wrist, and was obviously unfit for a voyage. As he grimly meditated over this reverse, he encountered a flushed and breathless young man, who thus accosted him : —

" Splendid weather, captain. I 've a mind to make a cruise with you up to Halifax."

" Cabin is all engaged and paid for, John Belknap," replied the skipper, gruffly. " That old

Tory Cathcart is sending his daughter up there to bring down troops upon us, or something of that color, I 'll warrant. I wonder the owners don't see through it and refuse; but he 's paid for the cabin and both staterooms, so that madam should not be spied upon, I suppose."

" Oh, never mind; I 'll go as clerk, or purser, or steward, or even as a foremast hand. I can hand, reef, and steer with any man, you know, and hard work, or hard fare either, don't frighten me."

The skipper looked meditatively at the young man, and turned the quid in his cheek, then carelessly asked : —

" Did you know that fool Wilson has tumbled down the cliff steps and disabled himself, at least for this voyage ? "

" Your first mate ? Hullo, skipper ! Is that what you mean ? Will you give me the berth ? "

" Hold hard, lad ! What are you squeezing my old flipper for, and what 's your rage for Halifax just now ? Is the English lass that was here last year up there, or have you quarreled with your uncle, or " —

" Never mind why I want to get to Halifax," replied the young man rapidly, seizing upon this version of his eagerness to ship in the Dolphin. " But saying I do, will you give me Wilson's place ? "

" Why, yes, Belknap, and be glad to get you; for I 've seen you handle a boat round the harbor here and up on the fishing-ground often enough to know that you're worth having aboard, even if you — But look here; there's the gal. She's got to have the after-cabin, and her meals are to be separate, and no one knows all the fine airs she'll put on. Maybe you couldn't stand it, and I don't know as I can. The little she-Tory!"

But John Belknap did not seem in the least disturbed even at this prospect, and no other objections coming up, the bargain was soon concluded, the young man's name set down upon the schooner's books as mate, *vice* Thomas Wilson, discharged, and he at once entered upon his duties. One of the first of them was to receive and place the last articles of Miss Dolly's luggage, including the arm-chair, which he was about to have stowed in the hold, when the young lady herself came off, attended by her father. At sight of the first mate standing beside the open hatchway, reeving a line around the chair, Miss Dolly showed signs of some embarrassment, whether arising from the sudden appearance of her old friend and schoolfellow, or from his employment, no one can say.

"Oh, John — but the chair is for my cabin, if you please; are you helping Captain Peters get ready?" stammered she; and the mate, hardly less disturbed, replied, in much the same style: —

"Certainly, Dolly — of course, Mistress Cathcart; it will be as you direct, surely; and — yes, of course; I am mate of the Dolphin, you know."

"You mate of the Dolphin? Since when, John Belknap?" asked Dolly's father, severely.

" To-day, sir. I was looking for a voyage, and wanting to go upon my own business to Halifax; and as Wilson is disabled, I took the place," replied Belknap, a little more coherently, and meeting as best he might the piercing regard fixed upon him by the major from beneath his shaggy gray eyebrows. At last the veteran slowly spoke : —

" You have a right to your own business, as you say, John Belknap, and I have known you boy and man for an honest, honorable, and true-hearted fellow, until this foul breath of treason swept through the land, tainting you among the rest with its poison. And so knowing you, I give this girl into your charge, to guard her with all respect and modest courtesy to her journey's end, remembering that her lonely and unprotected state should be her best defense from even an idle word or look. Will you accept the charge, and give me your hand upon it, John ? "

" Indeed I will, Major Cathcart, and you may demand account of her when I return as strictly as you will. I shall not be ashamed to give it."

As the young man spoke, he held out his hand. The elder grasped it heartily, and for a moment the two gazed steadily into each other's eyes. Then John turned to resume his duties, asking : —

" Did you say, Mistress Dolly, that you wish this chair in the cabin ? "

" If you please, sir," replied the girl, demurely; and presently the great clumsy structure was wedged in between the table and the transom at the stern of the little schooner, taking up much more than its share of room, and greatly disgusting Captain Peters by its presence the first time he came below. There was little to say, however, this cabin having been secured as far as possible for Dolly's private accommodation, the captain and mate only visiting it for meals, which they took at a different hour from their passenger, and sometimes of an evening, spending the other hours off duty in the house on deck or in their staterooms. The weather was, however, so lovely that Dolly also spent much of her time on deck ; and as the mate of the schooner was, of course, obliged to stand his watch, whether he liked it or not, and the quarter-deck was his appropriate place at such times, it naturally fell out that the young people were a good deal together, and Dolly found the anxious kindness and attention of the mate a pleasant relief from the decided gruffness and half-concealed suspicions of the captain. Whatever arrangement he could devise for her comfort was sure to be made, even at risk of displeasing his superior, and Dolly had often to beg him not to attempt to serve her so openly or so much, lest he should bring trouble upon both their heads. John promised, but the very same day broke the promise, for, having noticed that Dolly, try as she might, failed to arrange a comfortable seat by the combination of a three-legged stool and a shawl, disappeared from the deck, and presently returned, bringing, with the aid of one of the sailors, the great easy-chair, in which he had noticed that Dolly usually sat when in the cabin.

"Boom won't swing over it, sir," grumbled the man, as he set it down near the wheel.

"No more it won't," replied John, a little perplexed. "Well, if she needs to go over, we can turn down the chair, Mistress Dolly. At any rate, you 'll have a comfortable seat."

"My eye! won't the old man growl when he comes on deck and sees that 'ere!" muttered the sailor, slowly returning forward; but Dolly, too pleased with the attention to heed its consequences, seated herself in the chair like a little princess, and thanked her gallant knight so prettily that he altogether forgot the boom, the sail, the captain, and the schooner, until the wind, which had been fitful and gusty all day, and of late had seemed dying out altogether, suddenly revived, gathered itself together, and came swooping down from out the angry sunset as if determined to punish those who had failed to respect its power and guard against its attacks.

"Mr. Belknap, sir, what are you about, to let the schooner go driving ahead with such a breeze as this coming on?" shouted an angry voice; and John, who had been seated on deck at Dolly's feet, suddenly remembered that he was first mate of the Dolphin, and that she was in immediate need of his attention. His first act was to draw Dolly from her seat, and then to throw the chair upon its side, just in time to avoid the great boom, which came flying over, as the captain fiercely cried to the man at the helm: —

" Port your helm, you lubber, — port ! Mr. Belknap, is this your watch on deck, or is n't it ? "

" The flaw struck us before any one could have looked for it, captain, or I should have been ready; but there 's no harm done yet," replied Belknap, in some confusion, and forthwith began to bellow a series of orders so numerous and vociferous as to drown the steady stream of grumbling abuse that the captain distributed upon his mate, his passenger, her father, and the chair, which latter he strode across the deck for the express purpose of kicking.

" Please not injure my chair, sir," remarked Dolly, standing pale and haughty beside it. " To be sure, it cannot kick back again, but still it may not be safe to abuse it."

Captain Peters was an angry man, and more than one cause combined to increase his wrath and render him glad to vent it where he could. He hated Tories in general, and Major Cathcart in especial ; he had not found the major's daughter as genial and familiar as he imagined all young women ought to be ; he had not felt quite satisfied with his mate's deportment toward the young lady or toward himself ; and, to cap all, he had been suddenly aroused from his after-dinner nap by the steward's knocking down and breaking a pile of dishes ; finally, perceiving with the instinct of an old seaman that all was not right with the schooner, he had come up the companionway just in time to meet the squall, and to see that the first mate was in no wise attending to his duties. Remembering all these causes of aggravation, let us condone, so far as possible, the next words and act of the irate skipper, for the words were too profane to repeat, and the act was to seize the poor unwieldy old chair in his sinewy grasp, with the avowed purpose of heaving it overboard.

But the purpose was not effected, for, pushing past him, Dolly seated herself upon the cushion, as upon a throne, and with flashing eyes and trembling lips asserted herself and her rights.

"Captain Peters, if you throw this chair overboard, you will throw me with it. How dare you, sir, to use such language toward me, or to lay hands upon private property intrusted to your care?"

If the captain had been angry before, he was furious now, and roaring profanely, "Dare! I dare lay hands on any old Tory's goods! — ay, and on his brat too, if it comes to that!" he seized the girl's arm, and attempted to drag her from the chair. Dolly did not scream, but her mute resistance was more than the skipper counted upon, and he was grasping for the other arm, when a lithe figure flew with a bound from the top of the house to the deck beside the chair, and a sinewy hand upon the captain's throat hurled him backward with irresistible force.

"What does this mean? What was that man saying or doing, Dolly? I'll fling him overboard, if you say so," panted John Belknap; but before Dolly could reply, the captain, foaming with rage, was upon them, threatening his mate with irons and close confinement on bread and water, and Dolly with nothing less than hanging on the same gallows with her old Tory father. Belknap, however, had already recovered his mental poise, and standing between Dolly on her throne and the captain, quietly said to the latter : —

"See here, Captain Peters ; in the new times that you are so fond of predicting, you say there are to be no masters and no servants, and one man is to be just as good as another, or better, if he can prove himself so. Now why shouldn't we begin these new times here and now ? Say I 've as good a right as you to command this schooner, owned in part by my uncle, and say that I 've as good a chance as you of the men's good-will, what 's to hinder me from trying to take the head of the concern ? I could do it, and you know I could, and five minutes from now could call myself master of the Dolphin, with the power of ordering irons and bread and water to anybody I chose. I could do all this, I say; but I 'm a quiet and law-abiding man, and apt to stick to my word when it 's once passed, and I don't forget that I shipped for mate and not for skipper ; so if this young lady and her property are to have such treatment as she has a right to expect, and such as was engaged and paid for by her father, and if she 's content to have it so, I 'll agree to let by-gones be by-gones, and return to my duty as mate. What do you say ? "

Captain Peters stood for a moment glaring at his

mate with red and angry eyes, then turned away, paced the deck twice up and down, paused, and said, in as nearly his usual tone as he could manage : —

"Mr. Belknap, see everything made snug for a gale ; we shall have one before dark. Mistress Cathcart, I must have the decks cleared, and this chair carried below at once."

"Certainly, Captain Peters," replied Dolly, willing to accept even so rusty an olive-branch as this ; and as she descended the steps of the companion-way, followed by two seamen bearing the chair, John Belknap went forward to attend to his duties ; but as the chair remained for a moment poised at the top of the steps, a sudden flaw caused the Dolphin to lurch so violently that chair, sailors, and all were precipitated down the steps and into the little after-cabin together, all suffering more or less in the descent, — the men from bruises and abrasions, but the poor chair from the loss of a leg and fracture of an arm. The sailors would have raised it up on the three remaining legs, but Dolly suddenly begged them to leave it alone, and without apparent intention, interposed between it and them so as to nearly hide it from view, while courteously turning them out of the cabin, and closing the door behind them.

Soon after, Mistress Dolly herself left the cabin, begged a few nails and a hammer from the steward, and, returning, carefully reclosed the door, and proceeded to use them so vigorously that the sound of her hammer resounded even through the howl-

ing of the swiftly risen wind and the trampling of
the seamen overhead as they obeyed the clear and
rapid orders of the first officer.

The breeze grew to a half gale, then to a gale,
and at last to a storm so furious and resistless that
at the end of the third day the Dolphin lay, mast-
less and rudderless, a mere unmanageable hulk
rolling in the trough of an angry sea. The boats
were got out, manned, and ready to push off, when
John Belknap came down to the cabin for Dolly,
who rose from her knees and met him with a white
but very calm face.

"Come, Dolly, they cannot live a moment beside
the wreck, and I think the captain would be glad
of an excuse " —

"He has found it!" interrupted Dolly, as a
dark object swept past the cabin windows, breaking
for an instant the sullen glare of the green and
foamy waves. Belknap leaped on deck. It was
true. The captain, perhaps unable to control his
men, perhaps driven by the waves, had allowed the
boats to leave the side of the vessel, and already a
dozen oars' lengths divided them.

"We are deserted," said a calm voice beside the
young man, as he stamped and vociferated madly
upon the deck.

"Yes, Dolly; and, Dolly, I would give my life
for yours, if so it might be saved."

"We shall both be saved, John, I am sure of it,
I feel it, — we and the trust that my father has
committed to me."

" What trust, Dolly ? "

" The arm - chair and the barrels and boxes
below."

John stared, and wondered if the poor child were
going mad under this terrible strain ; but the peril
was too pressing for words, and John Belknap was
a man of act rather than speech. Persuading
Dolly to go below, he busied himself in rigging a
rude substitute for a rudder, and then in getting
up a slender spar to serve as jury-mast. With
them, feeble and incompetent as they needs must
be, he gained some control over the schooner, — sufficient at least to keep her before the wind, and
thus avert the immediate danger of swamping.

The night passed, and the next day. Dolly con-
trived to find and prepare food for her guardian,
who never was able to leave the helm, although he
slept grasping the tiller, and became almost too
much exhausted for speech or thought. But help
was at hand, and the storm was past. As the sun
set he threw a clear flood of light across the sub-
siding waters, and in its gleam shone out the top-
sails of a bark plunging along toward them. The
signal raised by the girl, under her lover's direction,
was seen, and an hour later the Fairy Queen lay
alongside the Dolphin. The next morning the
arm-chair, the twenty boxes and barrels, and, last of
all, Dolly herself, were transferred to the British
bark, whose captain had consented to carry the
young lady's property as well as herself to the port
where he as well as she was bound.

Arrived, Dolly was welcomed by her uncle, to whom she at once confided her charge, and received in return no measured praise and commendation.

"Your father says it is your own dowry, lass," remarked the uncle, folding up his brother's letter. "So let us see to what it amounts, and place it in safety."

The china, the books, the stuffs, and the household gear were released from the boxes and barrels, and then the poor old arm-chair was ripped up, and the fine old family plate, brought from England by the major's father, the brocades and silks that had been treasures of Dolly's grandmother, and still waited for occasions grand enough to shape them into robes, a casket of hereditary jewels, and finally the title-deeds of property both in the Old and the New World, were all produced; and Dolly told of the perils the poor chair had passed on board ship, and how it had fallen down the companionway, and the silver coffee-pot had peeped out and nearly betrayed the whole secret, and how she had protected it and cobbled it up, and how she had been glad to be left on board by the retreating crew that she might not abandon the charge her father had confided to her.

"And now, uncle," said she, in conclusion, "I have promised, if you and my father approve, to marry John Belknap; and he never suspected a word of all this."

"In truth, that is the most wonderful part of the story," cried jolly old Ralph Cathcart. "Not one girl in a hundred would have shown your patience and courage, my lass ; but not one in five thousand would have kept a secret so faithfully and long, especially with a sweetheart at her elbow. Well, when the young man comes to-night, tell him of your dowry, and tell him I 'll answer for my brother's consent, as well as my own. He touched upon the matter in his letter."

The next news from Pilgrim Village told Dolly that her mother was at rest, and her father had accepted a brevet commission in the royalist army. Then came an interval of months, and then a hurried scrawl written upon the field of battle, and with it a letter from the chaplain of the regiment, telling Dolly that she was an orphan.

" No one on earth now but you, John," sobbed the poor child in her lover's arms.

" And I will try to be all that earth can give, with a looking on to something better," replied he.

And tradition says he remembered his promise, and that Mistress Belknap was a happy, a prosperous, and a most honored wife.

And the old arm-chair ? It stands beside me, hale and hearty, in spite of Dolly's cobbling.

MISS BETTY'S PICTURES.

WHEN I was a child in the dear old New England seashore town where I was born, my daily walk to school led me past an isolated house known as Miss Betty Thorndyke's, inhabited only by that lady and one old negro servant woman, popularly supposed to be a witch.

Various circumstances combined to invest this house, at least to my childish mind, with an awful yet fascinating interest.

> " Over all there hung a cloud of fear,
>   A sense of mystery the spirit daunted,
>   And said as plain as whisper in the ear, —
>   'The place is haunted!' "

Certainly it had a peculiar aspect. It was a large house, gambrel - roofed, unpainted, and weather-stained to a dull gray color, rendered more gloomy by spots of gray-green lichen creeping like a disease all down the shingled walls. The air all about it seemed filled with a deadly stillness, — no bird sang, nor dog barked, nor cat sunned herself upon the weedy doorsteps. The only life about the place seemed indeed to intensify the desolation, for in the twilight the old negress flitted out, basket in hand, to supply the simple wants of the household, and always Miss Betty "walked." I

don't know what idea of terror that simple word
conveyed to my childish mind, but I think I connected it with some story of "Spirit's Pasture,"
where "old Maglathlin" was said to "walk;"
but at any rate, every window of that gray old
house was closely and constantly shuttered, except
two in the second story, which we all knew were the
windows of Miss Betty's own room, and through
those might generally be seen the figure of a tall,
gaunt woman, always clothed in white floating garments, and always wringing her hands with a mo-
notonous yet convulsive motion. I never passed
the house without hiding myself behind the great
gateposts and pausing as long as I dared, to watch
this figure, and sometimes in summer when the
windows were open, to listen to the dull murmur
of her voice; what it said I could not generally
make out, but once or twice, creeping close beneath
the dusty lilacs that buried the fence, I made out
the words, "Oh dear, dear! Oh dear me! Oh
me!" words simple enough in themselves, and yet
so fraught with an anguish never dying yet ever
new, that I always crept away from beneath the
hedge, after hearing them, with an aching heart
and tearful eyes.

I was not a very happy child, being an orphan,
and not fond of the relatives who had adopted me.
My stirring aunt had no children, and kept no servants, so there did not seem to be anybody of
whom I could ask Miss Betty's story. Once I
mentioned her to Alice, my favorite playmate, but
she said contemptuously : —

" Pho, she's only an old crazy woman, — nobody cares anything for her ; the boys say they'd fire stones at the windows, if it was n't for the old black thing that lives with her : *she*'s a witch, and could kill you any minute, just as easy!"

I flushed, but remained silent, for I felt that Alice was taking but a vulgar and outside view of the subject, and I would not have my childish dreams disturbed, either with regard to her own character, or Miss Betty's history.

That night, however, I sat beside the window of my little bedroom, revolving a daring scheme, and when at last I quietly undressed by moonlight, I had resolved upon its accomplishment. I did not pause as I passed the old house next day, and hardly looked at it ; I felt that I must hoard my strength, and stifle my emotions to support me when the time should come.

The moment that school was dismissed in the afternoon, I hurried away, not heeding the various invitations of my playmates, and, seeking certain well-known nooks of wood and meadow, soon collected a really beautiful bouquet of wild flowers, mingled with some long stems of wood strawberries, whose sweet musky odor mingled deliciously with the more delicate flower perfumes. With this in my hand, I hurried on, nor paused until, with dizzy eyes and chokingly pulsating heart, I stood upon the threshold of Miss Betty's door and, raising the heavy iron knocker, woke the long-sleeping echoes of the awesome house.

Long silence followed my first summons, but mine was one of those timid natures which, once aroused, will dare all and do all, but cannot retreat. I knocked again more loudly, more resolutely ; a few moments, and the door opened, slowly and groanfully ; like the door of a long-closed tomb.

It was the old negress, as I had expected, who stood and glared silently and irresolutely at me. I did not wait for her to speak, but hurried on : —

" Here are some flowers for Miss Betty, — I think she will like them ; may I carry them up ? "

The old woman paused ; peered earnestly into the little pale face before her, and finally, without speaking, took me by the arm, and drew me in, closing and barring the door behind me.

I shivered all over ; would she kill me, and throw me in the well, like little Sir Hugh and the Jew's daughter, which my aunt used to sing ? I did not know, but followed resolutely as she led me through the long and dark entry to a small side staircase ; up this we groped, and paused silently until the hand of the old woman fell upon the latch of a door, which she opened ; then my heart gave a great throb of relief, for it was really Miss Betty's chamber, and there, dressed in her loose white robe, paced Miss Betty up and down, up and down, still wringing her hands, and moaning over and over : —

" Oh dear ! Oh dear ! "

She did not look at us until the old woman hobbled up to her, and laying a hand upon her shoulder said : —

"Bucra pickaninny bring lilly posie to Missy; look, honey-plum, see de pitty posie."

It is impossible to describe the coaxing, pleading tone of the old woman's voice, as she thus addressed the piteous figure before her. Evidently to her, instead of a middle-aged, heart-broken woman, Miss Betty was a suffering child, who must be coaxed and petted that she might forget her little sorrows. The tears rushed to my eyes; I longed, baby that I was, to change places with Miss Betty, and give all to be thus loved and cared for.

Miss Betty paused in her walk, took the flowers, gazed at them eagerly, inhaled their fragrance, and then throwing them down, covered her face, and burst into a wild fit of crying.

I shrunk back frightened, and stood irresolute, while the woman, lifting the slight figure of her mistress, laid her upon the bed, and taking from a drawer some aromatic vinegar, bathed her forehead and temples.

Presently the invalid became more quiet, although she still wept silently, and my eyes wandered from her to the mysterious chamber in which I found myself. It was a large, low room, with an uncarpeted floor, and rich old mahogany furniture; what, however, particularly attracted me were the pictures. These were five in number, evidently portraits, and the idea at once occurred even to my inexperienced mind that they were members of one family.

One was a gentleman, dressed in a flowing robe

of Indian silk, such as I remembered my aunt to have shown one day to a visitor, as belonging to my grandfather. In one hand he held an open letter, with a finger of the other pointing to it, while his dark, serious eyes seemed fixed so intently upon my face that I felt as if I were the person whose attention he had been waiting all these years to attract to that now illegible line. Opposite, hung the picture of a lady whom I at once decided must be his wife. She had a sweet and pensive face, somewhat delicate and languid too, as if she did not feel very strong. She was dressed in a soft, smoke-colored silk dress, with a gauzy scarf about her shoulders ; in her hair, and on her neck and arms, were ornaments of pearl and opal, which I remember thinking well suited to her fragile loveliness, although I did not then know either the names of the gems, or why they suited me so well in the picture.

The next portrait was that of a young man about twenty years old, I should judge from recollection. He looked very much like his father, except that his face wore an eager, impatient expression, as if life held out so many pleasures to him that he could hardly bear to wait long enough to have his picture painted. In one hand he held a wide-brimmed hat and a riding-whip, while the other rested on the head of a great dog, who looked eagerly up in his face.

Next to this young gentleman's portrait hung that of his sister, an exquisitely lovely young girl, about sixteen, but already dressed in her bridal robes. Among her dark curls were twined orange flowers and buds, which drooping down were lost upon the whiteness of her pearly neck and shoulders ; besides the flowers, she wore no ornaments except the lace that flowed as a veil behind her back, and draped with its soft folds the round white arms and little hands lying clasped upon her lap. She was seated in a garden chair, and from the tree above her head hung great festoons of gorgeous flowers, which years after I recognized as passion flowers. The eyes were downcast, but their darkness was visible through the transparent lids, and the black lashes showed upon the pale, clear cheek. About the little rosy mouth played a half smile of bashful pleasure, and the skillful painter had thrown over the whole figure just the air of a pretty consciousness suited to a young girl wearing her bridal dress though not yet a bride.

The last picture hung over the bed, as if Miss Betty did not care to look at it so much as the other, and yet it was very pretty, representing a little child, with merry blue eyes and golden hair, seated upon the grass, the lap of her white frock filled with bright flowers, among which her little fat hands were plunged, while her eyes were raised to a great orange held just beyond her reach by a black woman, who laughed from every one of her white teeth, and from every fold of her gay turban.

It may seem to some persons unnatural that I should notice so many little particulars in these five pictures, and be able to describe them so minutely after these many years, but I was a quiet and observant child, thoughtful beyond my age, and was often storing up food for memory, while those about me thought me engrossed in play, or too young to understand what was going on. Besides, this was not the only interview which I had with Miss Betty's pictures.

I had just concluded this first examination, and was turning to begin again, when the negro woman (whose name I afterwards found to be Judith, or as Miss Betty always called her, Maum Judy), turned round from the bed where her mistress was now sleeping, and coming toward the door seized me by the arm and hurried me out before her, nor did she pause to speak till she had put me out the front door, and was closing it behind me ; opening it a little way just as I thought it shut, she put out a skinny hand, patting me gently on the head, and muttered in her hoarse voice : —

" Good pickaninny, — Maum Judy tank pickaninny, but dontee ever come here again; make poor lilly Missy cry, see de posies dat she use'a pick."

The door closed, and I hurried home, my heart beating proudly with the consciousness of having successfully achieved a perilous enterprise, and come safely out of unknown dangers.

Although longing to see and know more of Miss Betty and her pictures, I did not think of again intruding after Maum Judy's injunction, until one day, about a fortnight after my visit, as I

walked slowly by the house, looking eagerly up in
hopes of seeing Miss Betty, which I had not done
for some days, the door slowly opened, and old
Judy's dark and withered face appeared in the
aperture. She silently beckoned to me, and without hesitation I obeyed the summons. Once inside
the house, with the door locked, the negress
breathed more freely, and patting me again upon
the head, said sadly : —

"Lily missy berry tic — drefful weakly, chile, —
'pec she won't nebber git ober dat ar fright; wants
to see bucra pickaninny dat bring her posies.
Must n't talkee much, she so berry weak."

"No, ma'am," replied I timidly to this caution,
and we again climbed the dark and narrow staircase and, opening the door, Judith admitted me to
the chamber of the pictures, where Miss Betty lay
in bed. She looked paler and weaker than she
had done when I saw her before, but her eyes had
a softer and quieter look, and when she saw me
she smiled a little, which I had never seen her do
before.

"Come here, little girl!" said she, putting out
her thin white hand, and taking mine; "I thank
you very much for bringing me the flowers, — they
have made a great change in my life. What is your
name, dear ?"

"Salome, ma'am," replied I, timidly.

"That is rather a sad name, but you do not look
like a very merry child; perhaps it suits you as a
blither one would not do. Will you stay with me a
little while this morning ?"

"Thank you, ma'am, I should like to very much," said I, mentally resolving to risk the "tardy mark" and the loss of my "nooning" for the sake of seeing a little more of Miss Betty.

"That is right," said she, smiling again. "It is long since I spoke to any one but poor Maum, who has been faithful to me through all, and I should like to talk a little to-day."

"Would you please, then, ma'am, to tell me a little about the pretty pictures here?" asked I quickly, forgetting, in my eagerness, not only my own natural reserve, but the caution impressed upon me by Maum Judy, who had not entered the chamber with me, being probably detained by some domestic duty.

Miss Betty did not answer me for a moment or two, but her eyes, wandering from my face, visited each picture in succession, filling the while with tears, and her hands, slowly folding together, began the old motion, and her pale lips softly whispered:

"Oh dear! Oh dear!"

I was quite still and silent, fearing lest I had been the means of making the poor lady worse in body and mind, but after a little while she looked at me again, wiped her eyes, and said kindly: —

"Yes, Salome, I will tell you about them, for I think about them always, and it will be no worse to speak. That gentleman was my father, that lady my mother, that my only sister, that my brother, and the picture above my head which I cannot see, is myself and Maum Judy, who was then, as now, my kind and faithful nurse.

" I was born in one of the West India islands,
where my father had gone from here some years before. My first memories are of such flowers and
fruits as you see there, and of all the beauties of the
tropics. These pictures were painted by an artist
whom my father brought from one of the great
cities, on the occasion of my sister's marriage. I
remember her, just as she looked then. I remember the gay wedding, and how we all cried when she
went away. After that I remember nothing for
some time, — I was but a little child, — but I know
she was there the dreadful night, she and her baby.
I suppose she had come on a visit, or perhaps to live,
— but she was there. That night, I was in bed,
and was wakened suddenly by my pale, beautiful
mamma, who snatched me up, and held me close to
her breast, while her hot tears rained down on my
head. She ran with me into her room, and crouched
down behind the bed, still sobbing, but warning
me to be quiet. Presently there was a great noise
outside, and a crowd of servants rushed into the
room : they were all field hands, and I did not
know any of them ; the house servants loved us all
and would not join. They soon found us, but when
they seized my mother she did not stir. I do not
know whether she had fainted or was dead ; I hope
she was dead. One man took her, and another
me, and carried us to the great saloon. There
was my father, pale and bloody, tied hand and foot
to a marble statue. He looked weak, but brave as
ever ; if he had been free and had a weapon, he

would have driven them all before him, even then.
My brother lay upon a couch, dreadfully wounded,
and breathing slow and hard; my sister, with her
baby in her arms, stood between two fierce-looking
negroes. I think her wits were gone, for she smiled
as she looked about her, and cooed to little Lota
when she held up her hand.

"The slaves whispered together, and then one —
he did not belong to our plantation, I am sure —
stepped out from among them, and asked my father
something which made him very angry. I do not
know, but I suppose he offered to spare his life
on some disgraceful terms, for my father said very
loud and quickly: —

"No, villain! The only mercy I ask is that I
may see my wife and daughter dead before me."

"The great black made no answer, but, swinging the hatchet which he held round his own head,
buried it in my father's forehead.

"I saw them all die; oh, child, I saw it all! The
little baby lay upon the hearth, her mother beside
her — my brave, noble brother, my mother, — all
murdered — all! They would have seized me, but
Maum Judy snatched me from the man who held
me, and hurried away. I was saved, but I suppose
the terrible shock had shattered my senses, for I
was a child then, and now my hair is turning gray,
but I remember nothing since, till the flowers that
you brought me; my life ended there.

"Maum brought me to this country, she says, and
to some of my mother's friends; finally we came

here. They recovered some of my father's property, among the rest these pictures, and they have been for many years my world, — they and this old house which was my mother's home."

Miss Betty paused, breathless and pale. I was crying so much that I could not speak, but I kissed the white hand which lay outside the bed, — kissed it again and again. Miss Betty did not cry or speak, but I think it would have been better if she had, she was so very white and still. So we sat, motionless and silent in the solemn room, until Maum Judy came softly in to look after her nursling. Stealing up to the bed she bent over, evidently expecting to find Miss Betty asleep ; but as soon as she saw the white face, and dim, languid eyes, she turned to me almost fiercely : —

"Go 'way, bad pickaninny — go right 'way. Did n't me tellee no talkee much, no let lilly Missy talkee? Now here she all gone — clean tuckered out. Go long wid you ! "

Frightened and unhappy, I crept to the door, venturing only to pause and press one more kiss on the beautiful pale hand, which did not move in response; then I opened very softly the door, and stole down the dark stairs to the gloomy hall beneath. It was almost more than my little fingers could accomplish to withdraw those ponderous bolts, but I labored eagerly upon them, for there was something in the air of the old house which hung upon me like a nightmare, and I felt so intense a longing to escape into the fresh, free air, that I believe I should have made my way through the solid door rather than to remain within it. This feeling, however, gradually wore away, and after a few days I used to look up at the old house as longingly as ever, but I never saw either Miss Betty or her pictures again.

A month later, and one Sunday evening, the church bell tolled solemnly and slow. My Aunt listened quietly, and said : —

" That's for poor Miss Betty Thorndyke, — *her* troubles are over at last, thank God. "

THE LOVE OF JOHN MASCARENE.

A STORY OF COLONIAL BOSTON.

THE harvest moon shone full and bright upon Deacon Elnathan Paddock's barn in Roxbury, some three miles from Boston Common, and with her flood of white splendor royally snubbed the red and smoky flare of two or three dozen pitch-pine torches, set here and there to light the interior of the great sweet place, filled to overflowing with the new crop of hay stacked in the mows, and the varied grain piled upon scaffoldings in the fragrant glooms of the roof.

High heaped in the centre of the barn-floor lay a great pile of maize, or Indian corn, still in the husk, and around it some twoscore merry lads and lasses, divided into couples, were seated upon benches, boxes, logs, or trusses of hay, all busy in stripping the golden grain of its covering, chattering like a flight of blackbirds, comparing the growth of the little pile of gleaming ears rising between each couple, jesting, laughing, shouting, or, when a red ear was discovered in some girl's hands, watching with decorous glee as the happy swain seated next her claimed the forfeit of a kiss.

Do not, however, fancy that these young people were rustics, or hoydens, or lacking in the proprie-

ties by which gentlefolk are supposed to be hemmed
about in all ages of the world. These were sons and
daughters of the very best among the townsfolk of
Boston and Roxbury and Newtown, or Cambridge
as it is now called, for Deacon Paddock, besides this
barn and farm, owned a fair brick house on Long
Acre Lane, now Tremont Street, in Boston, and it
was his son, Major Adino Paddock, who planted the
row of elms in front of the Granary Burying-ground,
so shamefully cut down by city step-fathers not long
since. Yes, these young people were both well-nur-
tured and well-moraled, but the fashion of their day
differed from ours; the moon was just the same
that looked down upon you, my dear, on the night
you wot of, but the kiss which John most innocently
bestowed upon Rebecca and she most innocently
accepted was quite another thing from that which
So-and-so wanted to give you and you would not for
all the world have permitted.

Times change, and manners with them, and it
is to be hoped human nature adapts itself to the
change.

I mentioned Rebecca, and so reminded myself
that she is my heroine, and I have a story to tell
about her and John Mascarene, who sat next her,
and, as I hinted, took advantage of her husking
a red ear of corn to kiss the cheek next to him,
watching with satisfaction while it rapidly assumed the same hue as the friendly ear of maize.
But the next moment Emily Parker, sitting opposite, also husked a red ear, and Thomas Phillips

hastened to follow Mascarene's example, so that
under cover of the fresh peals of laughter hailing
this event John could quietly say in Rebecca's
ear : —

"You didn't want me to give you that kiss,
Ray!"

"What makes you think so? A husking kiss
doesn't signify more than a Pope Joan or a forfeit," replied Mistress Rawson, a little coldly, as
she picked two or three ears from the heap, and
slyly peeped to see that none of them were red.

"That's just it," replied Mascarene, discontent-
edly. "You wouldn't let me give you a kiss in
earnest, although in sport you can't help it."

"You know so much, John Mascarene!" exclaimed Ray, flashing a splendid glance upon him
out of great dark eyes now full of mocking light.

"Am I wrong? Ray, do you mean that I am
over-timersome?" And the young fellow bent
eagerly forward, trying to catch once more those
eyes, now glancing in every direction except his.

"Ray Rawson, did you ask my lord to grace our
poor festivities, as I bade you?" demanded lively
Lois Paddock, across the heap of corn.

"Yes, Lois, I gave him your message," replied
Ray, her cheeks again blazing up with the superb
color John Mascarene was wont to watch for, although now he did so with angry eyes and lower-
ing brow.

"And he will come at your bidding, I am well
assured, if not at mine," laughed Lois.

" He is coming. My brother Will and he promised to ride out together," replied Rebecca, briefly.

" Here they are now," muttered Mascarene. " Rebecca, you 'll rue it yet, — my word for it, lass ! "

" Rue what, you simple fellow ? Bidding Sir Thomas Hale to Lois Paddock's husking, pray ? "

" Setting your foot on an honest man's heart, to climb up to a coronet."

" A baronet has no coronet, Johnny. 'T is a bloody hand you mean."

" Ay, the bloody hand may well grasp yours, wet with my life's blood."

" Pooh, John ! if it were midsummer I'd say you were sunsick, and as 't is, perhaps the moon is to blame. Sure 't is something more than nature ails you ! "

" Here they are. Come you with me and greet them, Ray. Adino, come ! " And Lois, assuming a pretty little air of dignity with her office of hostess, went forward, followed by her brother and Rebecca Rawson, to meet the two young men waiting, for a moment, upon the threshold, the glory of the moonlight at their backs, the smoky flare of the torches in their faces.

" Good-evening, Will. You are welcome, Sir Thomas Hale. You do our poor merry-making too much honor," said Lois, with sweet formality.

" When beauty that would embellish a throne chooses scenes rustical for its setting, its humble admirers can do no better than to follow."

And Sir Thomas Hale bent low, sweeping the threshold with the plumes of the hat in his left hand, while with the right he raised Lois's pretty fingers to his lips. From which speech and action it will be seen that this young gentleman was a very fine gallant indeed, and quite superior to poor John Mascarene, who was only skipper of a schooner trading to the West Indies for fruit, and assumed no other manners or language than nature and respectable training had furnished him with. But then, Sir Thomas Hale claimed the Lord Chief Justice of England as his uncle, and had gained his breeding at the court of Charles II., the Merry Monarch, where, just now, Nell Gwynne, the orange-girl, set the mode.

"And fair Mistress Rawson!" exclaimed the courtier, kissing her hand also, in a sort of polite ecstasy. "Ever blooming, ever radiant! Will your majesty deign to allow me a seat at your side and instruct me in this bucolic pastime at which you are so gracefully engaged?"

"With pleasure, Sir Thomas," replied Rebecca, more flattered and pleased than she wished to show, and Mascarene, whose eyes had never left her face since Sir Thomas was announced, sprang from his seat, saying, with what he meant for indifference: "Here is a seat at your disposal, Mistress Rawson. I have had enough of the bucolic pastime."

It was a mistake, and he felt it so, poor lad, but it was not ten minutes ago that he had kissed her, and she had been his sweetheart since they played

together, two happy children, in the green, shady
foot-path known as Rawson's Lane, leading from
Long Acre to Marlborough Street. The names
of these places are changed, and to-day we say
that Bromfield Street, where never blade of grass
or even city tree is seen, connects Tremont and
Washington streets, but human nature has never
changed a whit in all the two centuries lying between that day and this, and although Rebecca
Rawson's flower-garden is now a row of glaring
shops, and although John Mascarene's home in
School Street, hard by, is now a fine City Hall,
and neither maid nor man dwells in either, I
doubt me not that at this moment the pavement
of both Bromfield and School streets is beaten by
the feet of lovers just as madly jealous, and sweet
girls just as foolish and as blind, as those who
were alive on the evening when Rebecca came
home from Lois Paddock's husking, escorted by
Sir Thomas Hale, with careless Will riding on
ahead and poor John Mascarene following just in
sight, and wondering if he would go to-morrow
and volunteer on one of the king's ships, or if he
would marry Dorothy Alden and be happy, in spite
of — And here he had to stop thinking, and set
his teeth hard, for he was but three-and-twenty, and
had a loving heart, albeit as brave a one as ever
faced a foe.

A few days more, and the town's talk was that
Rebecca Rawson was engaged, or, as they called it,
contracted, to Sir Thomas Hale, and her father was

something more than pleased, for being already
secretary of the Massachusetts Bay Colony, he was
naturally discontented with his position, and counted
to be governor; a promotion which Sir Thomas air-
ily assured him could be managed by his uncle, the
chief justice, in less time than it took to speak of
it. Just how, Sir Thomas did not mention, and the
good secretary was too dazzled to inquire.

As for Rebecca, it is hard to say how she felt. A
crumb of her father's ambitious nature worked like
leaven in her sweet girl-nature, and the flowery
speeches and ornate manners of her titled admirer
made a deep impression upon her inexperienced
fancy. She liked the idea of being called My
Lady, and of going to court and vying with duch-
esses and marchionesses, every one of whom, as Sir
Thomas assured her, would wither with envy at
sight of her transcendent beauty and incomparable
toilets.

And then she should help her father to the position he so much craved; and her brothers — oh,
there was no vanishing-point to the glittering vista
opening before her eyes!

John! Well, John was out of sight. He had
sailed a few days before the engagement was announced, and would not be back before the wedding. Ah, well! Those childish follies could not
last! So Ray, alone in her own pretty bedroom,
took an ear of red corn tied up with a blue ribbon
out of a coffer upon her dressing-table, and went
toward the fireplace. But the hearth was cold and

empty, and the chambermaid would wonder at seeing such a matter lying there ; and — after all — poor John — Then with a little sigh, a little smile, a little blush, the ear of red corn, with its true-lover's knot of blue, went back into the coffer, and stayed there for a great many years, — as many as Rebecca lived.

The colonial secretary was a widower, and a very verjuice-tempered sister of the late wife kept the house, and wintrily mothered Rebecca. She was a gentlewoman, however, and a notable house-keeper; and the secretary, with his long purse in hand, had bidden her furnish forth the future Lady Hale with everything that would befit her high estate and the position at court Chief Justice Hale was to procure for the bride of his favorite nephew. Aunt Becky, nothing loath, went about this commission with zeal, and the two or three leading linen-drapers of Boston town, and the India merchants who had already begun to import silks and feathers and goldsmith's work cunningly wrought into fabrics for dresses, and certain French traders who ventured upon buying small amounts of Parisian gauds to sell to such dames as dared purchase and wear them, — all these good traders were roused up and laid under contribution, and each produced his best, and exerted himself to procure better from incoming vessels, until finally Rebecca, tired, bewildered, fascinated, and yet not quite content, saw a dray driven up to the side door of the great wooden house in the bowery lane, and watched while twelve boxes and mails were piled upon it, all filled and crammed with her own clothes and household linen, — the largest and most expensive outfit, as Aunt Becky proudly declared, ever yet bestowed upon a Boston bride.

"And so it should be," replied Secretary Rawson, loftily ; "for no Boston maid hath ever made such a match as our maid hath."

And he was right, poor man, — he was right !

The next morning dawned cold and stormy. An east wind blew in the fog from sea, and moaned and sighed around the gables of the great house, and cried shrilly through the keyholes, and sobbed in the wide chimneys with almost a human voice.

"Let us have a fire upon the hearth, — at least in the hall, Rebecca," suggested the master of the house to his sister. "'T is a shrewd and nipping day for riding, and our friends will be chilled, albeit 't is called July."

So a fire was kindled upon the hall-hearth, and, whether it was the wind, or the long dampness, or the effect of the sudden heat, certain it is that, as Ray stood before the mirror in her own room, and Aunt Rebecca herself was pinning the bridal veil around her head, while one maid held the little satin slippers, and another the fan and handkerchief and nosegay, a great crash sounded through the house, drowning the wailing of the wind and shaking the solid oaken frame.

"Good Heavens ! what is that ? " cried the bride, sinking into a chair, her face as white as her paduasoy gown.

" Don't faint and muss your veil, child ! " cried
Aunt Becky, running out of the room, followed by
both the maids ; and Ray, presently gathering her
strength, followed, and looked over the balusters of
the great square staircase into the hall below, where
men and maids, and some early guests, and the secretary himself, were gathered in dismay about a
confusion on the hearth.

" 'T is the great mirror fallen and shattered ! "
cried Aunt Becky.

" Ay, the shield above slipped down, and tore the
mirror from its holding," added the secretary, in a
somewhat annoyed tone ; for, although as practical
as most men of his generation, he would not have
chosen to break a mirror or throw down his ancestral shield upon his daughter's wedding-day.

" And oh, see here, father ! " cried ten-year-old
Grindall, grubbing in the smoking ruin. " The
shield is broken and burned, and only the head of
the raven in the crest is left ! Caw ! Caw ! "

"Oh, oh ! What an omen ! — what a fearful
portent for a wedding-day ! " shrieked Aunt Becky,
after all as superstitious as a softer woman, and her
speech was echoed by a sobbing wail from above as
the bride sunk fainting upon the staircase.

Of course the secretary reproved everybody, and
Aunt Becky scolded Ray, and Parson Richardson,
who had come all the way from Newbury to marry
the daughter of his old parishioner, clearly proved
to anybody who would listen, that omens and por-
tents were really not infallible, and that he himself

by steadfast faith and prayer had averted all misfortune from his own home, although the mirror
in his own state bedroom had fallen and splintered
into a thousand pieces.

" But you had not your escutcheon burned,
and only a raven's beak left to caw misfortune,"
expostulated Aunt Becky, tearfully ; and the minister replied, with a shrewd twist of his mouth : —

" Nay, dame, — that was I saved by the lowly
estate of my ancestors, who claimed no coat-armor."

So the wedding went on, and the feast was
spread, and bumpers of generous wine, not to mention rummers of mighty punch, brewed of old Jamaica, with a dash of arrack, were drunk to the
health of the bride, and Sir Thomas, growing somewhat glorious himself, favored the company with a
description of his uncle Sir Matthew Hale's mansion in Grosvenor Square, and his country-seat at
Hampstead, and invited his friends then present,
one and all, to visit him at whichever of those
stately homes he might be residing when they
should arrive in England.

But in those days men did not pay much attention to after-supper talk, or invitations, and the
secretary soon led the attention of his guests away.

A few days later the Three Brothers sailed
proudly down the harbor and past the Outer Light,
already planned, and so to sea, bearing not only Sir
Thomas and Lady Hale, with two or three other
passengers, but those twelve solid boxes of plenishing, and a thirteenth which Rebecca had packed for

the voyage, throwing in at the last moment, half shyly, half pettishly, the coffer holding that red ear of corn with its blue ribbon which she had determined to leave behind, and yet could not quite destroy.

" Beshrew the thing, 't is bewitched ! " exclaimed she, with an angry smile, and tossed it among her shoes the very morning they were to sail.

The Three Brothers had a somewhat tempestuous passage, in spite of the summer season, and when on the thirtieth day, at evening, she anchored opposite the new Commercial Docks off Rotherhithe, Ray was so weary with ship-life that she implored her husband to take her ashore at once, and if it were too late to seek her uncle Grindall Pirne's house in the Strand, she vowed she would not complain of the meanest tavern accommodations, so that she had room to move around and a solid floor beneath her feet.

Sir Thomas, whose courtly manners had become somewhat tarnished by the long sea-voyage, considered the petition for a few sullen minutes, and then said : " As well soon as late, so it must be. Get your night-rail and what gear is needed for a night."

" Nay, but I must needs have the mail out of our state-cabin," pleaded Rebecca. " I have naught at hand else wherewith to present myself at Uncle Pirne's in the morning. 'T is but a little box, Thomas."

" Well, well, have thy way, dame. Thou 'rt a

good lass and a comely, Ray. Give me a kiss, and I'll call for a boat, and the mail shall go in it."

My Lady Hale held up her sweet lips to the proffered kiss, and her husband, taking her chin between a thumb and finger, stood looking into her face for a moment with strange, troubled eyes, then, muttering something like an oath, turned hastily away, and was seen no more until he sent down to summon his wife to the boat, which presently landed both passengers and box at the foot of one of the innumerable flights of stairs serving the purposes of wharves and quays to Old London.

"We'll sleep at the Mermaid, sweetheart," said Sir Thomas, as they landed. "'T is not so good as the best, nor is it so bad as the worst, but 't is close at hand from these stairs, and the waterman will carry up the box on his shoulder."

"As you will, dear. Oh, what a huge town this London looks to be!" cried Rebecca, staring about her.

"Ay, 't is a thought bigger than Boston, and a man can find a quiet nook for his meditations now and again, as he cannot in your village yonder."

My Lady made no reply to this enigmatical remark, and presently the couple arrived at the Mermaid, where Rebecca was shown at once to a good-sized and comfortable bedroom, and, with her box and a tub of water, spent a happy hour, coming down to supper so sweet and smiling that Sir Thomas revived some of the forgotten compliments and courtesies, and his wife once more felt content.

The next morning at an early hour Sir Thomas called a coach, and placing My Lady and her box within it, directed the driver to Master Grindall Pirne's house in the Strand, bidding the girl make his compliments to her relatives, and look for him, with two or three of the boxes, in time for both of them to dress for dinner. Lest he should make any error in selecting those mails needed for immediate use, Sir Thomas took the keys of all, even of that ark wherein, securely hidden among some winter clothing, lay a bag containing two hundred golden guineas, a parting present to his daughter from the colonial secretary so soon to become governor.

The lumbering coach, pitching and swaying along the unpaved streets, was almost as bad as the ship, and glad, indeed, was the wayworn traveler when, stepping gingerly down its rickety steps, she found herself standing at her kinsman's door, and bade the serving-man tell his mistress that Lady Hale had arrived.

" I am at hand, fair niece," responded a pleasant voice, and down the broad stairway came a buxom and cheery dame, who affectionately bade the weary girl welcome, ordered the servant to pay the hackney-coachman and bring in the box, and presently led her young kinswoman into a fair chamber overlooking the river, where breakfast still lay, in hopes of her arrival.

For some hours Rebecca was well content, but noon came, and dinner-time, and not till toward night did the boxes arrive, and then it was the whole twelve, instead of two or three, with a message from the captain that nothing more belonging to Lady Hale was on board.

"But where is Sir Thomas?" demanded his lady, who, getting no reply, at last insisted upon herself seeing the drayman, who said his orders came only from the mate of the Three Brothers, and he knew naught of any Sir Thomas, — not he, but would be paid for his job, and that speedily.

Dame Pirne attended to this part of the business, and so soon as it was over sent a messenger to the counting-house, who presently returned with the worshipful master of the house, who looked grave enough at hearing the story, and prepared to go himself at once to the Mermaid tavern and see if news could there be found of the missing man.

"And I will go with you, uncle, for I saw the landlady last night, and she looked hard at us both, and she will know if she has seen my husband since," said Ray; and though both her uncle and aunt demurred, the somewhat spoiled child would not be denied, and it ended in all three taking boat at the Pirnes' private stairs, and landing soon after sunset at the Mermaid.

The landlady was not hard to find, but no sooner did Master Pirne begin to question her than she cried : —

"Marry, but I knew that was no wanton! Poor lass, I pity her, — I do, indeed, — but there's no help for it, since the villain has already a wife and three babes down in Canterbury."

But here Rebecca interrupted her, with an air of wounded dignity.

" Nay, dame, 't is of no villain that we speak, but of Sir Thomas Hale, my husband, who was with us in this house last night. You mistake the person."

" Nay, then, poor lamb, 't is you do mistake the person. The gallant who was with you here last night is but too well known to me and my goodman, for many is the score he has run up in our bar and never paid until we had the bailiffs after him. He is indeed a sort of lackey and hanger-on to Mr. Thomas Hale, nephew of Sir Matthew, the Chief Justice, but his own name is Thomas Rumsey, and five years ago he married, in this very room, Betsey Martin, my man's cousin, who was serving us then as bar-maid, and would have been in your case to-day had we not looked out for her " —

But before the last words were spoken Rebecca's aunt had caught at her tottering form, and now they laid her upon the floor, so cold and white and still that for some time none knew if merciful death had released her, or if she yet must suffer more. Presently, however, she revived a little, and her relatives had her home with as little delay as possible, closing their doors upon the disgrace that threatened their respectable house.

A long illness followed, and in the course of it, needing some more linen for her patient, Dame Pirne caused one of the twelve great boxes to be broken open, and finding in it nothing but stones and shavings, she went on to the other eleven, with a like result.

An inventory in the box Rebecca's persistence had rescued told what a rich plunder Thomas Rumsey had secured, even to the bag of guineas ingeniously noted " C C Spades " in the schedule.

The worthy couple said nothing of this discovery to their niece, but Master Pirne dispatched a sharp fellow to Canterbury with instructions to trace Thomas Rumsey's history in that place, and to discover, if possible, where he might be found ; for, as the worthy merchant argued, although his niece's honor and happiness were hopelessly lost, her guineas and napery might be recovered, and would be a good deal better than nothing.

But Thomas Rumsey was much too practiced a villain to be caught in this simple fashion, and in the end it was concluded that he had escaped over-seas with his plunder the very day of seizing it.

Months passed, and creeping back to life and health, Rebecca Rawson meekly but persistently insisted upon going down to her bachelor brother Edward, rector of an obscure living in Horseman-den, in Kent, where, as she gently said, she could pass her days in such labors of charity and lowli-ness as befitted her condition, besides comforting the loneliness of her brother, who, knowing all her story, urged her to come and work out her salvation in his company and after his stern Calvinistic methods.

And so she went, first tearfully writing a meek refusal of her father's entreaties that she would return to his roof and protection, for, as she said,

"Penitent though I am for the headstrong folly and pride that cast me into my present estate and made me prefer a glozing villain to an honest man, it were too hard a penance for me to come back and stand, as it were, in the pillory of my native town, a warning and a moral to my former play-mates. So rest content, dear and honored father, and let me abide for yet awhile with my brother and his poor people."

The secretary, never to become governor, felt the force of this reasoning, and mournfully waited, going in and out of the old house in Rawson's Lane with a mien sadly shorn of its old confidence, until, when years had passed, his son Will wrote to his "sweet sister Ray," and bade her hasten home at once, for the father was failing day by day, and mourned for his favorite child.

To this appeal the daughter could not say nay, nor would Edward have kept her back, although in losing her, he said, he lost his right hand; and Uncle Pirne, being applied to, soon found a vessel bound for Boston by way of the Barbadoes, a trifling détour in those days, and in due course Rebecca, with only the one box she had brought ashore from the Three Brothers and another that Aunt Pirne insisted upon furnishing, again set sail to cross the Atlantic; but oh, what a different Ray! what a different voyage!

Different, too, in that this voyage was short and prosperous, and in no more than fifteen days from leaving Rotherhithe, the Smiling Susan dropped

anchor off Bridgetown, doomed capital of smiling
Barbadoes, and Rebecca, going ashore with the captain to spend the few days of the Susan's stay
here, was met upon the quay by a grave, bronzed
and comely gentleman who turned pale at the sight
of her, yet extended both eager hands, crying :
" My Lady — nay, Ray, is it you ? "

" Yes, Rebecca Rawson in very deed, and glad,
indeed, to see John Mascarene once more," faltered
the poor girl.

" Ho, Captain Mascarene, and so we 're here together once more ! and I 'll warrant you 've secured
the best of the sugar and coffee, as you did last
time ! " cried Rebecca's companion, jovially ; and
Mascarene responded, with an effort at the same
tone : " Nay, Burton, you 're safe this trip, for I am
after indigo, and have sent my schooner round to
St. Lucia (only he called it Sent Loozee) to ship
a lot I have stored at Soufrière, and I shall only
take sugar enough to make out a cargo, that is, if
you leave me enough to sweeten my coffee on the
home voyage."

" Ho ! ho ! ho ! Your coffee, man ! Say grog
and shame the devil ! " roared Captain Burton.
" When may the Red Ear be at Barbadoes again ? "

But Ray did not hear the reply. The Red Ear !
Why had John Mascarene chosen so grotesque a
name for his schooner ? It used to be the Morning Ray, — and Rebecca smiled faintly and sadly,
remembering how, for old times' sake, she still
cherished that ear of red corn, with its true-lover's
knot of blue.

It was some hours later, when the great tropic moon stood high in heaven, and Rebecca lingered yet a moment upon the veranda before bidding her old friend good-night, that he gently, carefully, and with many misgivings, told the poor stricken girl that to all the rest of her grief was added orphanage. The secretary, never holding up his head again after his terrible disappointment, had died the very day that Mascarene sailed from Boston, and it was sympathy, no less than undying love, that so agitated the honest fellow in meeting her upon the quay.

"It is God's warning that I am unforgiven!" moaned Ray, her sweet faith tinged with Edward's Calvinism.

A week later, the Smiling Susan was ready for sea, and Rebecca bade farewell forever, as she said, to her old playfellow, for she had resolved to tarry only so long as the Susan did at Boston, and to return in her to end her days in Horsemanden with Edward.

But not yet had the Susan left Bridgetown Harbor when a storm broke upon her, the like of which she had never encountered before, nor could now resist, for it was the harbinger of that terrible earthquake which destroyed Port Royal, in Jamaica, and so vexed the neighboring seas that many a stout craft was wrecked that day without ever understanding how it came about. Of these was the Smiling Susan, and as she parted amidships and staggered to her ruin, brave Captain Burton's last act was to lash his pallid charge to a stout spar and launch her overboard to avoid the vortex of the sinking ship.

He soon lost his own hold, but the lashings held; and Mascarene, raging like a madman up and down the beach, saw the spar tossed by the breakers almost at his feet, dragged it ashore with a thousand perils of his life, and bemoaning himself over the dead body of his love, found it still held a sigh; and by such exertions as only heroes and lovers make, he cultivated that sigh into a breath, and the breath into a life, and was at last rewarded by a sweet faint smile and a whispered word.

Well, we have not time to tell all the story, and the rest is so easily imagined, except, perhaps, the one incident of Rebecca's box coming ashore almost unharmed, and her shyly producing from its depths an ear of red corn tied about with a faded blue ribbon. A shabby thing and a worthless, most people would say, yet no gold that ever was counted down, not his cargo of indigo and sugar happily saved from the earthquake, would have bought that ear of corn from John Mascarene.

They did not go back to Boston, nor yet to England, nor does tradition tell where they set up their home, but they were married, and sailed away from Barbadoes some weeks later; nor although Captain Mascarene often made that port in later days, did he ever bring his wife with him, or say where she abode. Let us trust, however, let us believe, that the latter days were better than the first with her, even as clear shining after rain is purer and fairer than the cloudless day can be.

THE LAST OF THE PROUD PULSIFERS.

FAR back in the old colonial days of Boston there stood, upon what was then its most aristocratic street, a large four-square family mansion, substantially built of the small dark bricks imported from Holland, relieved and enriched by freestone copings and ornaments.

This house belonged to a family prominent enough in their day, although now forgotten, — a family whom all men respected, and some loved, and who had gained by their leading characteristic the title, almost universal among both those who feared and those who loved them, of the Proud Pulsifers. However this title may have been deserved, or however it may have been gained by his ancestors, it belonged to Major Plantagenet Pulsifer, as his stern dark eyes and gray hair and stately figure did, by the right of birth, necessity, and the eternal fitness of things. It was a common saying among the common people that Major Pulsifer trod the earth as if it were not worthy of such honor, and certain it is that he found its ordinary level too low to serve as his dwelling-place; and when the street whereon his building-lots lay was graded and lowered, he refused to have a single shovelful of earth removed from his own premises.

so that after the work of street-making was accomplished the Pulsifer estate remained high and dry above the leveling flood, like Ararat above the waters ; and upon this pinnacle of pride did Major Plantagenet Pulsifer build his house, laboriously gaining access to it by four long flights of sandstone steps reaching from the pavement to the front door.

To this elevated position Major Pulsifer one day brought home a bride, daughter of a family as old and well-nigh as proud as his own; and yet despite birth, marriage, and elevated position, Death, that terrible democrat and leveler, found out the poor lady while yet in her earliest bloom, and summoned her away from husband, house, and her little daughter Margaret, not yet old enough to know her loss.

Major Pulsifer did not marry again, and he and the little girl remained alone with four servants in the aristocratic seclusion of the great house at the top of its four flights of steps. The child grew to girlhood, to womanhood, and upon her twentieth birthday her father, Major Pulsifer, announced to her : —

" I have settled an alliance for you, Margaret; you are to become the wife of my friend Morgan's son."

" John Morgan ? " asked Miss Pulsifer coldly ; but her father saw the sudden light which kindled in her eyes, the swift blush that rose to her cheek at the name, and he smiled almost like other men, as he said : —

"Yes. You have seen the young gentleman. He is not disagreeable to you, I trust."

"He is not disagreeable to me, sir," replied Miss Pulsifer, and there the conversation ended. That evening the Morgans, father and son, climbed the four flights of sandstone steps, and in the grim old library, with its oak wainscoting, and its shelves filled with books, each one of which was a sentinel set to defend the domain of the past from the encroachments of the future, the marriage contract was agreed upon, the formal consent of the parents given, and finally the two young people were left to express their own opinions upon this matter, so thoroughly their own, and yet in which they had been allowed, hitherto, so little voice. John Morgan was, as befitted his sex, the first to speak, and he found nothing better to say than —

"Margaret!"

And Margaret said nothing, but suffered her hand to lie in that which had clasped it so tenderly, and laid her head upon the breast to which it was so closely drawn, and in very truth behaved not like a daughter of the Proud Pulsifer at all, but like the veriest village-maid who ever confessed herself both loving and beloved.

There is a picture painted by one of Copley's predecessors, and already in his stately style, representing Margaret Pulsifer in the early days of her betrothal; it shows her tall and slender, and queenly of figure, wearing her brocade and point-lace and smouldering rubies as if they were as much part of herself as the form they clothe ; it shows her with the dark hair and hazel eyes of her race, with a clear brunette complexion, and proud sweet lips on which a smile of triumphant love seems forever dawning, — a smile so subtle and so full of an inner joy knowing not its own revelation, that no observer has looked long upon that pictured face without turning from it to its proud possessor, and asking in some form, " What made her so happy ? What is her story ? "

The rubies were John Morgan's betrothal gift, and from the necklace depends a single gem, heart-shaped, and of surprising size and beauty, whose shifting fire has been so cunningly caught and imprisoned by the artist that one seems to see it flicker and change with every breath of the proud bosom that bears it ; and he turns again to the morsel of yellow paper in his hand, remnant of the letter in which well-nigh two hundred years ago John Morgan wrote, in the crabbed Saxon script, of his day : —

" And this ruby hearte I send you, trew love, that bye it you may see how firm of constancie is the hearte that I long agoe gave you, and as the ruby is bright and warm of color, so burns my love within that other hearte, and as the stone is cold and sad of itself, so is that other hearte cold and sad wanting warmth from you, and as I humbly pray you, mistresse, to hange the jewel about your neck, and warm its coldness with the warmth of your own bosom, so would I, did I dare, beseech of

you to grant my lowly and despairing love some
hope of return, some warmth of life, some promise
of shelter within the sanctuary of that same gentle
bosom."

It was the fashion of the day to thus profess
despair and lowliness of mind, but the promise that
the wily lover asks was his already, as who can
doubt that reads the eyes and lips of that fair
lady's pictured face and marks the glow in the
dusky core of the ruby heart.

The picture was but just finished, so says the
story, and the splendid preparations for the bridal were but just begun, when Death once more
mounted the stately steps, ringing his scythe against
each one as he advanced, and grimly holding above
the solid sandstone the shifting sands of his glass,
in which so few grains yet remained for him whom
Death had come to seek.

" Major Plantagenet Pulsifer ! " rang out the
summons.

" Here ! " replied the soldier, too proud to dis-
obey, even had the power of disobedience been his,
and forth from the mansion upon its scornful em-
inence was borne the body of its master ; and of
all the Proud Pulsifers only that weeping girl remained, heiress and sole representative of her line.

All thoughts of marriage and merrymaking were
laid aside at once, and a short time after the funeral
John Morgan, in the interests of his betrothed,
took passage for Virginia to settle there some matters connected with the estates Major Pulsifer had

possessed in that country before coming to the Massachusetts colony.

A voyage to Virginia was in that day something more of an affair than the tour of Europe is to-day, and when Margaret Pulsifer bade her lover good-by, it was with the feeling that she was risking all that life had left to her, and her farewells partook of the solemnity of a renunciation. The lover, man-like, laughed at her fears, and failed to comprehend the vital importance to her of what to him was but an event in the ordinary course, and rather a pleasing excitement than a danger.

" I know not what it is that you dread so much, sweetheart," said he in their final interview. " Certes it is not the time, for it will be but a few months at most ; and not my health, for I am a stout fellow, not to be upset by changes of climate or the discomfort of travel. Nor do you fear that I should forget you, my Margaret ; surely not that ? "

" I should be loth to offer myself such slight, even if I could so insult you as to suppose you false," replied proud Miss Pulsifer, with a faint light breaking through the tears in her hazel eyes, — a light which John Morgan was well pleased to see, and kissing the heavy eyes, laughed a little as he said : —

" Nay, Margaret, I should be afraid to play thee false were I so inclined, for thy father's daughter would slay me with a look."

But Margaret at this looked pained, and remained silent, and John Morgan, still in his light way, filliped at the ruby heart at her throat, and said : —

"And moreover, lady mine, do not I leave my heart always with you, and its visible emblem always before your eyes? Look at the ruby day by day, Margaret, and remember all that I wrote when I gave it you."

"I will remember, John, and you, too, remember," sighed Margaret; and then came the parting, which left one so lonely, so sad, so objectless in the seclusion of her mourning home, while the other, thrown at once into the excitement of a new life, new scenes, new companions, his attention and his resources constantly called into action, soon felt the pain of separation become intermittent, and very tolerable to be borne, even in its most serious attacks.

Eight months from the day when John Morgan sailed out of Boston for the Virginia colony, he set foot again in his native city, and hastened at once to the house upon the hill, where Margaret Pulsifer, her heavy mourning a little lightened, lest it should too much dampen the joy of her lover's return, and her own face as bright as if mourning, loss, and sorrow were words stricken once and for all out of the language, waited for him.

But spite of the brightness and the joy, John Morgan saw at the first glance that all was not well with his betrothed. Her slender figure had become fragile, her rich color came and went with hectic brilliancy and haste, her eyes were over-bright, her thin hand parched and hot, and an ominous low cough disturbed her speech.

"Why, Margaret! why, darling! you are not well: you are ill, and I never heard of it!" exclaimed the lover, holding both the fevered hands, and looking anxiously into the delighted eyes that devoured his face.

"Oh, no, John, not ill, never fear! A little ailing just now, perhaps, and not quite so strong as when we used to ride our ten miles before breakfast; but now you have come, I shall be well anon. I have fretted too much after you, though shame on me for confessing it."

But John Morgan remembered the beautiful young mother, object of his boyish admiration, who had faded and died in her earliest bloom in spite of all that love and wealth and the Pulsifer will and pride could do to keep her. So busy was he with these thoughts that when, some time later, Miss Pulsifer asked playfully: —

"And where is the little cousin you promised me?" he started and stared aghast, then struck his hands together in comic despair, exclaiming: —

"What, Ruby? What will she say to me when she knows that I altogether forgot her; for when the ship touched the wharf I bounded off, meaning but to speak to you, and look upon your sweet face, and then be back before she missed me. And here I have been with you these two hours, and might have stayed two more, but for your reminder."

" Is her name Ruby ? " asked Miss Pulsifer with a smile. " Do you know, John, that you never told it in your letter ? You only said, ' The child of your mother's cousin, Pynsent, is left an orphan and penniless, and what will you do for her ? ' "

" And you replied like your own noble self, my Margaret, ' Bring her to me, and I will be her mother, and her fortune ; ' I showed her that letter, Margaret."

" Showed it to her ! She is old enough to understand such matters, then ? "

" Old enough? why, she is a woman grown, — eighteen years old, at least," replied John, laughing at the great eyes Margaret fixed upon him, and laughing a little nervously, too.

" A woman grown ! Why do not you call her Mistress Pynsent, then ? " asked Margaret, a little haughtily.

" What, when she is your cousin, and so soon to be mine as well ? " replied John, tenderly, and the proud head sank to the resting-place he offered, and the warm blood flowed again into the dusky cheek, but now so pale.

"There, then ! Go and fetch my cousin, and see that you take the blame of your neglect upon your own shoulders, truant ! " said Margaret at last ; and when her lover was gone, she rang the bell, and bade Judith, her grim-visaged old housekeeper, prepare a separate apartment for the guest, whom, fancying her a child, she had intended to take into her own bedroom.

"For she is a young lady, Judith, and not a baby, as I fancied," continued the mistress, absently, — "a woman grown, and her name is Ruby."

"Ruby? That was a great name among the Pynsents always," replied the old servant, and Miss Pulsifer, vaguely echoing the name, "Ruby!" put up her fingers, as was her habit twenty times an hour, to feel the ruby heart hanging at her neck, — that heart which was to typify the constancy, the warmth, the truth of her lover's heart.

An exclamation, almost a scream, arrested Judith on the threshold and brought her to the side of her mistress as she stood, tottering and pale, one hand grasping at her throat, her wild eyes searching the floor in every direction.

"It is gone, Judith! Oh, Judith, find it, find it!"

"What is gone, dear mistress? What shall I find?" asked the old woman, half believing that her nursling had suddenly gone mad.

"My heart, my ruby heart! It is gone, and I can find it nowhere! Oh, what will he think, when he bade me keep it so safely!"

"Nay, it is no fault of yours, dearie. Sure you did keep it like the apple of your eye. Sit you there and rest, while I look for it; it will not be far away, for I saw it the moment before Master Morgan came up the steps. We will have it anon, — just a little patience, Mistress Meg; we will have it, we will have it."

And murmuring her phrases of encouragement over and over, the old woman, upon her hands and knees, began groping beneath the chairs and tables, turning up the edges of the heavy Turkey carpet which covered the middle of the room, peering into the dark corners, poking away the ashes in the wide fireplace, searching, in fact, in every place likely and unlikely of which she could think, and in one as vainly as in another. The ruby heart was lost, and Margaret, who had alternately aided in the search and returned exhausted to her chair, was repeating for the thousandth time, " It is gone, it is gone forever ; and what will he think of me ? " when a carriage drove to the door, and old Judith, who was just then shaking the folds of the moreen curtains, already thoroughly searched three times, glanced through the window, and exclaimed : —

" Here is your cousin, Mistress Margaret, and your eyes red, and your dress in disorder ! "

" Take her to her own room at once, Judith, and leave some one to wait upon her ; then come back to me, and make me ready to receive her," ordered Miss Pulsifer, struggling back to the needs of daily life, chief among which she had been bred to consider the preservation of her own dignity. But when Judith returned to her mistress, she found her prostrate upon her bed, and gasping under an attack of the pain at her heart which so often of late tormented her. The best alleviation for this was perfect rest and darkness, and thus it chanced that neither John Morgan nor his charge, Ruby Pyusent, saw Miss Pulsifer again until, in the early twilight, she glided ghost-like into the great drawing-room, where he sat sad and silent beside the fire, while restless Ruby flitted about the room, glancing at everything, asking questions, making exclamations, standing on tiptoe to look at herself in the concave and convex mirrors hung upon opposite piers, spinning round and round in a dizzy dance, trying the notes of the neglected harpsichord, behaving herself, in fact, like the very spirit of youth and mirth and gay unrest.

As Miss Pulsifer entered the room, John Morgan sprang to his feet, and hastening to meet her, detained her a few moments near the door to hear his whispers of sympathy and trouble at her illness, and joy at once more seeing her; for indeed he had been very sad and lonely in the last hour.

This over, he led her toward an arm-chair by the fire, and smiling at the fairy who stood watching them, he said : —

" And this, dear Margaret, is your cousin Ruby, as she allows me to call her. She has like me been waiting most impatiently for your appearance and better health."

" You are welcome, cousin," said Miss Pulsifer, with more, perhaps, of stately courtesy than hearty cordiality in her tone; but it was an age of ceremony, and this was one of the Proud Pulsifers, remember. However, she held out her hand as she spoke, and drawing the girl toward her, kissed her

upon the forehead, then stood looking smilingly
down upon her, for this little Ruby was in the *mi-
gnonne* style, with floating golden curls, childish
blue eyes, skin of rose and pearl, and the tiniest
stature, as pretty and as charming altogether as
can be imagined ; and so her stately cousin seemed
to think, for as she looked down upon the little
thing, her eyes grew softer and the smile upon her
lips sweeter, until Ruby suddenly raised her face
for another kiss, exclaiming : —

" I 'm so glad I came, dear cousin Margaret ! "

Miss Pulsifer stooped to meet the lips so confidingly raised to hers, but as she did so a sudden
and startling change swept over her own face, and
she paused as if stiffened to stone in that bending
attitude, her eyes fixed in absolute horror upon the
white throat of the girl before her. And well
might she pause, for hung about that slender throat
by a fine gold chain was a ruby heart, her own ruby
heart, as she knew the moment her eyes fell upon
it, — the ruby heart which her lover had so mean-
ingly given to her as a pledge of his own heart, and
which she had worn that morning, and lost when
he departed ; even as she fixed her swimming eyes
upon the token, the flickering fire shot up in brilliant flame, lighting the inmost centre of the jewel
with a vivid glow, like the eye of a merry demon
exulting over her dismay. For one wild moment
heaven and earth seemed mingling in the mad confusion of Margaret Pulsifer's brain, but in the next
the pride of her proud race rose up like armor and

shield and staff; and standing upright, she said some words of courtesy, dropped the hand of the young girl, and returned to her chair unaided. As she did so, John Morgan, with a lover's privilege, drew a stool to the side of the easy-chair and seated himself close beside her, with a whispered phrase which should have called the blush to her cheek and smile to her lip, but Margaret, neither blushing nor smiling, answered the love-whisper with a few calm words of little meaning, and led the talk to other matters.

Presently, when once more quite sure of her own strength, she spoke the words that pride had silenced in their first wild outburst, and which now came almost carelessly from her lips : —

" That is a pretty jewel at your throat, cousin. I suppose you chose it for its name."

" Yes, it is a ruby, to be sure, and I am Ruby," replied the girl, laughing and dimpling, and withal casting so conscious and so mischievous a glance toward John Morgan, that Margaret felt a cold, sick faintness creeping over her, and feared that she should swoon before their eyes ; a rushing as of many waters filled her ears, but through it came her lover's laughing voice : —

" Ask her where she got it, Meg, and see if she dare tell you."

With a mighty effort Miss Pulsifer opened her swimming eyes and fixed them upon the face of the girl, still set in that look of merry defiance, still turned toward John Morgan. Commanding a voice which seemed to herself to sound from some far-off icy depth, she spoke : —

"It was a true-love token, I suppose, and young maids are not so fond of confessing such."

"Why, yes, cousin, I have already told Master Morgan that this was a token from a dear friend unknown to him, and I take it ill that he should insist upon talking on it, especially before another."

"I only insisted because, as I said this morning, it is so like a jewel that I wot of. You know the one I mean, Margaret."

"It is very like one that I have sometimes worn," replied Miss Pulsifer, coldly.

"That was my meaning. You do not wear it to-night," and John Morgan looked almost reproach-fully at the stately white neck of his betrothed.

"No, I have lost it, I believe," replied she, care-lessly.

"Lost it! Oh, Margaret, lost my ruby heart!"

"Lost it or had it stolen, which I think more likely; but had I known I was to be thus shrewdly called to account for your gift, Master Morgan, I had never taken it."

"Margaret!" whispered the lover; but Margaret met his pleading eyes with a look so full of proud contempt that his own fell in angry confusion. Turning to Ruby, who, during the half-whispered conversation between the lovers had been frolicking with the cat upon the rug, he asked almost sternly :

"Will you let me take that ruby heart, Miss Pynsent?"

"Marry, no, not when you ask in that tone, my master. Do you mean to play highwayman and rob me outright?"

"No, but here is some strange coil, and it is you only who can explain it. Miss Pulsifer has lost a jewel so like to that upon your neck that " —

"It is of no consequence, none at all," interposed Miss Pulsifer, very coldly. "I certainly have lost a ruby heart, but my cousin has already declared that this upon her neck was a love-gift from some one unknown to us, and I would not insult her by asking proof or explanations of her word. Let the matter rest, it is of no consequence."

"Surely not of consequence to any one if not so to you, madam," replied John Morgan, now seriously offended, but still staring impatiently at Ruby, who suddenly grew grave and much confused, glanced from one to the other, while her trembling fingers fumbled at the clasp of the little chain. Undoing it at last, she slipped off the heart, and holding it toward Miss Pulsifer, softly said: —

"Take it, cousin, if it is yours, I never knew that."

"Mine, girl! How should it be, if your tale is true?" asked Miss Pulsifer, coldly, and never extending her hand for the jewel, although her hungry eyes devoured it greedily.

"I did not know — I was wrong — I thought that Master Morgan was jesting when he asked where I got it; he knows, if he would but speak," stammered Ruby, helplessly.

"*I* know! What in Heaven's name does this

mean? What snare is laid here to catch me trip-
ping?"

And John Morgan, springing to his feet, glared
from one to the other of the young women in angry
bewilderment. Miss Pulsifer met his look with
one of superb disdain.

"Big words and loud tones are but a coward's
refuge," said she, icily. "Ruby Pynsent, if you
choose to explain this matter, do it now, and
briefly. If you do not choose, or if you do not
dare, it shall rest forever, and we shall wish Master
Morgan good-night — and good-by."

"He — he gave it to me this morning," sobbed
Ruby, crouched in a heap upon the rug, her golden
hair tossed across the blue brocade of her dress as
she hid her face upon her knees, while the mocking
firelight played over her lissome figure and the
ivory of her arms and the golden curls, and centred
at last in one blinding spark deepset in the heart
of the ruby lying upon the floor beside her.

Miss Pulsifer rose to her stately height, and
pointing down at the lovely picture, turned her
eyes upon John Morgan's bewildered face.

"Have you never a word or a kiss to comfort
her?" asked she, "or are you already false to her
too?"

Then, while he stood reeling beneath the contempt she had hurled at him from lip and eye, and
every line of her majestic figure, she drew her dress
aside and swept past him and out of the room with
never another word or look. As she neared the

door, John Morgan sprang after her, stopped abruptly, and striding back seized up the weeping child, and standing her before him, both her hands in his, looked with stern imploring into her face.

"Ruby! What is this all? Have you gone mad, or have I? How could you say that I gave you this accursed bauble? Why, it was my betrothal gift to Margaret, and she thinks I stole it to give again to you."

"And so you did! At least, I knew not whence you had it; but this I do know, that when you came again to the ship, and found me crying because that you had gone and left me, forgetting me so soon, when we had been such friends, and seeing me crying, you felt sorry, and perhaps — perhaps, my tears they told you" —

"But the heart, Ruby, the heart!"

"Why, when you saw me crying, you came to me and put your arms about me and — and — kissed me twice,— nay, why will you make me tell it over? and then you slipped the ruby heart into my bosom and ran away out of the cabin, and I, thinking you gave it in loving jest, and would not that I should speak of it, hung it about my neck, and when after we were here you asked me where I got it, I thought again that it was jest, and I told you a story, thinking to make you laugh; and when you asked me before my cousin I did not want to say out that you gave it to me, and I did not know what you meant" —

"I see it now, I see it all!" exclaimed John

Morgan, dropping the hands he held, and gloomily staring into the fire. "When I came here this morning I embraced Margaret, as I had a right to do, and the ruby heart fell off and lodged in my clothes; and when I went back to the ship and embraced you, as I had no right to do, it fell out into your bosom, and I, stung by remorse to think that even by one kiss I had been faithless to my love, rushed away before I could see what had befallen, and you understood it all wrong, and — all is over between Margaret and me."

"No; why do you say that? I will go and tell her how it was!"

"What! tell her that I took you in my arms and kissed you within the hour after rejoining her!" exclaimed John Morgan, bitterly. "Good sooth, I fancy that tale would not mend matters much with a woman like Margaret Pulsifer. Nay, Ruby, the kiss was a sweet one, and I say not that it was so much amiss to have given it, but it is like to cost me dear enough, — dear enough."

And with the jewel in his pocket John Morgan left the house right sadly, yet trusting more than he would own to Margaret's love, his own honest purpose, and the cooler judgment of the morrow.

But on the morrow Miss Pulsifer was too ill to see any one, and poor little Ruby went creeping about the house with a weight of vague remorse at her heart, and a fluttering of guilty terror whenever upon the stairs or in the passages she encountered Judith with her stern eyes and cold white face.

Judith, knowing a little and guessing more of
the ill-fortune that had befallen her mistress' love-
affair, visited all that ill-fortune in her own mind
upon the golden head of Ruby, whom, with woman's
justice to woman, she chose to consider as the
temptress who had seduced John Morgan into
unfaithfulness to his liege lady, and perhaps
induced him to steal the ruby heart whose loss was
the beginning of all this sorrow and disturbance.

Early in the morning and several times through
the day Morgan mounted the sandstone steps, at
first confidently demanding admittance, afterward
sadly asking news of his betrothed, who was, as
Judith curtly informed him, when at last he insisted
upon her being summoned to answer his inquiries,
"too sick to see strangers."

"But I am no stranger, good Judith," pleaded
the lover, trying to slip a gold piece into her hand.

"Better, perhaps, if you had been, Master
Morgan. Thank you, sir, I have no occasion for
your money," replied the old nurse, and as he still
stood upon the threshold she quietly shut the door
in his face, and went back to the darkened chamber
where Margaret Pulsifer lay between life and death,
the terrible physical pain at her heart deadening
the still sharper mental pain that had preceded it.

"Will she get over it, think you, sir?" asked
Judith, eagerly following the grave physician to the
stairhead, and looking up in his face with the dumb
beseeching of an animal who believes in the limit-
less power of his master, man.

" She may, — indeed, nurse, I think it pretty certain that she will get over this attack, but the next ! "

Then sadly shaking his head, the old man who had seen Margaret's mother die, and who had closed her father's eyes, dashed a sparkling drop from his sleeve, and went slowly down the stairs.

A week later, as Judith watched the thin, sad face and listless figure of her mistress, who had now for two days sat up for a while, and always chose to sit in a chair drawn close to the front window of her room, she said : —

" Master Morgan has been here twice to-day asking for your health, Miss Margaret."

" Has he? When he comes again I will see him, Judith," replied Miss Pulsifer, gently, and the jealous eyes of the old servant marked well the color which came and went, and the fluttering pulsation which almost choked the sick girl's breath. She saw, and scowled bitterly even while she said with forced serenity : —

" So you shall, if you will, Miss Margaret ; but Doctor Eustis says that we must be more than careful about excitement of any sort."

" When Master Morgan calls, show him into the dressing-room, and I will see him there," replied Miss Pulsifer ; and Judith had been too long a servant in that house to remonstrate further. She revenged herself, however, by muttering in John Morgan's ear, as she led him up the stairs an hour later : —

"The doctor says it is over-excitement that made her sick, and more of it will kill her. So have a care, young man."

"I will be careful, Judith," replied the lover, meekly; and indeed his white face and weary eyes showed that sorrow, and it may be a fiercer tormentor, had been busy with him since last the old nurse saw him.

"What a coil this love-making brings," thought she, eying him keenly, yet not so angrily; and opening the door into the little dressing-room, she motioned him to enter, and softly closed it behind him. Mindful of her caution, the lover advanced with a smile upon his face, and as little emotion in his manner as he could contrive, toward the wan figure in the great easy-chair beside the fire, and obeyed without remonstrance the feeble gesture which bade him seat himself at a little distance, without even touching the hand that made the gesture.

"I am very sad at seeing you so ill, Margaret," said he, choking down the torrent of passionate sorrow and love and terror that rose to his lips.

"Thank you, John, and I do not doubt it," replied Miss Pulsifer, gently, and then after a little pause went on : —

"I sent for you as soon as I could be allowed to see you, John, to say how sorry I am for speaking so that night. It was a bitter insult to your honor, John, my fancy that you had played me false; I should have trusted you more, and honored you better. If ever you came to loving another woman, you would tell it to me before ever you did to her, I am sure of it. So now, if you like to tell me how all this matter came about, and why that poor child fancied you had given my ruby heart to her, — tell me ; and if you do not wish to, why say so, and either way I am content, and believe without another word that you have done naught, said naught, thought naught unbecoming a man of honor, and mine own promised husband."

But in hearing those noble and gentle words John Morgan lost all control of his own emotion, and throwing himself upon his knees, hid his face upon her lap, as he sobbed out : —

"Oh, Margaret, Margaret, slay me with your scorn, despise me, hate me if you will, but do not speak to me like that, for I am not worthy of such trust."

"Not worthy of my trust!" echoed Margaret, pressing her hand upon her tumultuous heart, and sighing wearily. "Oh, John, if I had died before I heard you say that!"

"Hear me, Margaret, then judge me, and I swear to abide by your judgment, be it what it may." And rising from his knees and standing with an arm upon her chair, but out of sight of those steady, truth-compelling eyes, John Morgan told the story through, not hiding that during the long voyage he had been tempted by Ruby's innocent fondness and childish unreserve to treat her in a familiar, almost caressing manner, which might perhaps have led her to believe that he meant more than he ever did, and to allow her thoughts to rest upon him in a way he had never intended.

"I did but think of her as a child until that morning when I found her crying, and reproaching me that I had forgotten her in seeing you," stammered the lover, feeling all the humiliation of his confession, yet glad that it was made, and only anxious now to hear Margaret's reply.

"And so she loves you, and you went well-nigh to loving her, and the ruby heart that pledged you to me dropped away from me and gave itself to her, and you carried it to her, although you knew it not?"

"Oh, Margaret, noble Margaret, priceless Margaret, you do not mean, you do not believe, that I loved her, or could love any woman but you!" and John Morgan, half-crazed with grief and terror and remorseful love, threw himself again upon his knees, and seizing her hands, bathed them with tears and kisses. Margaret looked down upon him, serene and still, as saints may look at men still struggling with the sin and sorrow they have left behind. At last she said : —

"Dear John, let us say no more, now, — perhaps ever. If I had been as I was once, I think it might be that I could not forgive that you, having had my promise and my kisses, should have forgotten them even for a moment ; but, dearest, I stand to-day where I can see that pride is but mortal, and love is immortal. While I live, John, you are mine own betrothed, and none shall come between us; no, not until I am laid in my grave shall any other have a right to say, 'I took him from you,' — after that — John, John, help!"

So crying, in her anguish, she rose stiffly upon her feet, her whole frame rigid and shaken, one hand clenched upon her heart, and one pressed to her lips, through which gushed a stream of bright blood.

Morgan, horror-stricken, clasped her in his arms and carried her into the next room, at whose door stood Judith, white with terror and rage.

"Go, go! you have killed her! Leave her now to me!" cried she, pushing him from the room, and bolting the door upon him.

But Margaret was not dead, nor did she die for weeks, although she and all about her knew that each moment might be her last. White and still and smiling, she lay upon her death-bed, cautious lest by a breath, a word too much, she should snap the attenuated thread still linking her with life and love. Hour by hour, day and night and day and night again, John Morgan watched beside her, hardly leaving her for an instant, grudging every act of ministration offered by another, absorbing every look, every word, every sigh that escaped her.

"He will die too," whispered Ruby to Judith, with whom she had made her peace, and gained permission to spend much of her time in the sick-room.

"Very like he may, and why should he not?

When she is gone, what has he to live for?" asked the old nurse; and Ruby, whose bright eyes were always in these days heavy with tears, stole a look at the bed, saw John Morgan's white face set so steadily, so yearningly, so full of passionate and despairing love toward that other face scarce whiter, but more transparent, and so showing yet more plainly the eternal love lighting it from within, until whispering to her own heart, "They do not need you; they do not even know that you are here," she stole away to cry herself sick in the dark vastness of her own bedroom.

At last there came a day when the pale lips of the dying girl silently shaped " Good-by! " and with their last consciousness pressed a faint kiss upon the trembling lips that feared to press them too closely in return lest that last breath, cold as the air from the door of a newly-opened tomb, should be rudely shaken and cease an instant sooner. It ceased, the dark eyes closed with the love light not yet faded out of them, a faint sigh fluttered past the lover's cheek, and all was over ; over for both of them, as old Judith thought at first, for John Morgan, utterly exhausted and overborne, fell forward from his knees to his face as that last sigh stole past his cheek, and lay with his head upon her hand, to all appearance lifeless as herself.

But Judith knew no love save for her nursling, and so soon as she found that the young man had only swooned, she ordered him carried away, and sternly turning to Ruby, said : —

" And go you after, and nurse him. There are two of you, and here are two of us."

The dead body of Margaret Pulsifer lay in state for a week, as was the regal fashion of her race, and the third day, as she had ordained, her last will was opened and read in the presence of her enshrouded form. This will, carefully drawn by the family solicitor, was somewhat lengthy, and was expressed in all the formal phraseology of such documents, excepting a few clauses inserted at the end, and in the faint and uncertain characters of a woman's dying hand. These we will transcribe : —

" And it is my request that my betrothed husband, John Morgan, be at my funeral, all over mourning, and follow next after me.

" And to my cousin, Ruby Pynsent, I leave, besides the estates which are in some sort hers of right, my kind love and best wishes ; and if this same John Morgan and Ruby Pynsent do find it in their hearts to marry when I shall have been a full year in my grave, they have my consent and my approval and my prayers both now and then.

" And all my jewels and clothes I leave to Ruby Pynsent, excepting the necklace of rubies and the heart belonging to it, which will be about my neck when I die, and these I desire shall be buried with me.

" And if there is any creature in this world who fancies himself or herself in need of my forgiveness, I do now, in the presence of the God to whom I haste, most fully, freely, and solemnly forgive them.

" And so, good-by, world."

The body of the instrument bequeathed nearly the whole of the great Pulsifer property to Ruby Pynsent, with careful provision for all the old servants and dependents of the house, and in especial a handsome annuity to Judith, who enjoyed it for barely two years.

To John Morgan was bequeathed the portrait already described, and the furniture of Margaret's bed-chamber, with the request that he would himself use it " so long as he shall live a bachelor."

So Margaret, last of the Proud Pulsifers, was borne to the grave, and John Morgan, "all over mourning," followed next after her who thus clung to her right in him, even while bestowing him and all her riches upon another woman ; but from the grave he turned away to wander to and fro through the earth for another year, and when it was over he came home, and — we all knew that he would do it, did we not ? — married Ruby Pynsent, who had patiently waited, sure, with the wisdom of even the weakest woman, that he would come at last.

Yes, they married, and Margaret's bedroom furniture was with remorseful care stowed away in a little locked chamber at the top of the house, where moth and rust and mould and rats soon made an end of nearly all except a few of the love-letters in her ebony writing-desk, one of which love-letters is already quoted. The portrait was better used, for it hung in the state drawing-room, the room where Miss Pulsifer's last will was read in

presence of her dead body, and Ruby never entered the place without glancing first at the picture
and then at the centre of the room; and though
the hearth might be heaped with logs and the sunshine stream in at the great south window, that
room had always a chill for her, and perhaps for
her husband also.

But there! Margaret Pulsifer forgave them, and
blessed them, even after she knew herself dying to
leave them alive and together; and if she could do
it, why should not we?

THE FIRST AND THE LAST.

It was the last December of the eighteenth century. All night a fierce northeast snowstorm had been hissing and drifting through the frozen air, pelting angrily at the shuttered and curtained windows of the rich, and shrieking with scornful laughter as he forced his way through the ill-fitting casements and loose doors of the unfortunates who could not keep him out, clutching at them with icy fingers as they cowered over their poor fires, and spreading over the garret-beds in which they sought to hide from him a premature shroud of pitiless white snow.

But with morning the storm ceased, and a little before noon the sun, peering from behind his clouds, seemed to wink with astonishment at seeing how much had been done in his absence.

Not only the sun, but Mr. Phineas Coffin, guardian of the " town's poor," in a town of the Old Colony, was astir, and, standing at the door of the " poor- 'us," bent a contemplative eye upon the progress made by two stout youths who were clearing the snow from the sidewalks and paths upon his premises, and soon perceived that a trial of skill and speed was going on between his own pioneer and a lad similarly engaged on behalf of the next estate. About half way between the rapidly approaching competitors stood a rough-hewn block of stone, marking the boundaries of the two fields of labor.

To first reach this, the winning-post, was evidently the emulous desire of each. As they approached near and nearer, the snow flew from their shovels with a force and velocity which would certainly have reminded Mr. Coffin of a steam snow-plough, had he ever seen or heard of such a thing, which he most assuredly never had.

Each boy performed prodigies of skill and valor. The " poor-'us " lad evidently gained, and his patron did not conceal a wide smile of satisfaction ; the rival looked up, saw it, was stung with generous rage, threw himself with fury upon his shovel, and in three enormous plunges laid bare his own side of the post, before " poor-'us " had come within a foot of it.

Then, clapping his numb fingers upon his thighs, the successful champion uttered a melodious crow, which so disgusted the spectator that he was about to retire within doors, when his eyes fell upon a thinly-clad, timid-looking woman, who was advancing along the newly-opened path, casting deprecating glances at the two boys, who from peaceful rivalry were now proceeding to open warfare, carried on with the ammunition so plentifully spread before them.

Nor was the alarm of the poor woman groundless ; for, as she advanced into the battlefield, she found herself saluted upon the breast with an immense snowball, which, being of loose construction, adhered persistently to the folds of her red broadcloth cloak, forming a conspicuous and remarkable ornament to that garment.

" Come, stop that, you young limbs, or I 'll " — shouted the chivalric Phineas, hastily gathering, as he spoke, material for a formidable missile, which, being completed before the sentence, was used by him as a ready means of rounding his period, being at once more forcible and easier to come at than the words which most men would have chosen.

Besides, Nathaniel, the poor-house lad, turning round at sound of his master's voice, presented so fair a mark, with his gaping mouth, that, half involuntarily, the snowball left Mr. Coffin's hand, and the next instant formed the contents of Nathaniel's open mouth, leaving, however, a liberal surplusage to ornament his cheeks, chin, and nose.   The recipient of this bulletin choked, spluttered, and pawed at his face after the manner of a cat who has tried to eat a wasp.

His rival did not seek to conceal the expression of his triumph and derision, the consequence of which was, that, as soon as " poor-us " could see, he fell upon his antagonist, and both immediately disappeared from view in the bosom of an enormous drift.

" Come right along, ma'am," called Mr. Coffin to the horror-stricken woman, who stood contemplating the spot where a convulsive floundering and

heaving beneath the snow showed that the frozen
element had not yet extinguished the fire of passion
in the breasts of the buried heroes, — "come right
along, and don't be scaart of them young uns.
They're dreffful rude, I know; but then, boys will
be boys."

The woman returned no answer to this time-hon-
ored defense of youthful enormities, but, hurrying
on, reached the door, saying : —

"How's your health this morning, Mr. Coffin ? "

"Waal, ma'am, I'm pooty middlin' well, thank
ye," replied Phineas, slowly, and with an evident
effort at recollection ; then suddenly added, with
more vivacity : —

"Why, it's Widder Janes, — ain't it ? Declare
to goodness I did n't know ye, with yer hood over
yer face. Walk in, Mis' Janes, and see my woman, — won't ye ? "

"Waal, I dunno as I can stop," replied the widow,
beginning, nevertheless, to shake the snow from her
scanty skirts, and to stamp her numb feet, which
were protected from the biting cold by a pair of old
yarn socks, drawn over the shoes.

"I was wantin' to see ye, a minit," continued she ;
"but Mis' Coffin allers keeps cleaned up so slick, I
don't hardly darst come in."

"Oh, waal," replied Phineas, with a chuckle of
satisfaction at the compliment to his wife. "Ye
look nice enough for anybody's folks. Come right
in, this way."

"I dunno how 'tis," continued the visitor, as she

followed her host through the long entry, "that
Mis' Coffin can allers be so forehanded with her
work, an' do sich a master sight on 't, too.   She
don't never seem to be in the suds, Monday nor no
time."

Mr. Coffin had reached the door of the "keeping-
room" as the widow concluded her last remark ;
but pausing, with his thumb upon the latch, he
turned, and, looking over his shoulder, whispered,
with an emphatic nod : —

"Fact is, Mis' Janes, there ain't sich a great
many women jest like Mis' Coffin."

"There ain't no two ways about that," murmured
Mrs. Janes, assentingly, as the door was thrown
open.

"Walk right in.   Here, Marthy, the Widder
Janes has called to see you this morning."

A quiet, middle-aged woman turned round from
the table, where she was fitting patches to a pair
of pauper trousers.   Her face was sweet, her voice
low, and, though she was of middle age, every one
agreed that "Mis' Coffin was a real pooty woman,
an' a harnsome woman, too."

"How does thee do, Keziah Janes ?   I am glad
to see thee.   Take a seat by the fire, and warm thee
after thy cold walk."

"I can't stop a minit ; but it 's as cheap settin'
as stannin', I do suppose," replied the widow, with
a nervous little laugh, as she seated herself in the
proffered chair upon the clean red hearth, and
opened her business by saying : —

" I was wautin' to speak with you, Mr. Coffin,
about poor Mr. Widdriuton."

" Widdrinton, — who 's he ? " inquired Phineas.

" Waal," commenced the widow, settling herself
in her chair, and assuming the air of one who has
a story to narrate, " you know I have my thirds
in the house my poor husband left. It wa'n't
sold, as it had ought to ben, — for Samooel (that 's
his brother) never 's ben easy that I should have
the rooms I have ; but they 're what was set off for
me, an' so he can't help himself ; on'y he 's allers
a-thornin' when he gits a chance.

" But that ain't nyther here nor there. What I
was a-comin' to was this. Ruther better 'n a year
ago, a man come to me and wanted to know ef I
used all my rooms. I told him I had n't no use for
the garrit, 'cept to dry my yarbs in (for I think
yarbs are drefful good in case o' sickness, Mis' Coffin, don't you ?). An' then he said he wanted a
place to sleep in, an' his breakfast an' supper, an'
wanted to know if I would take him so.

" Waal, I thought about it a spell, an' I concluded I was too old to mind the speech o' people,
and I had n't no other objection, so I said he might
come, — an' he did, that very day.

" Waal, at fust he had some kind o' work to do
writin', an' he seemed to git along very comf'table,
— at least, fur 's I know, for I was out tailorin'
all day mostly, same as I be now ; but last fall the
writin' seemed to giu out all to oncet, an' he begun
to kerry off his furnitoor an' books to sell, an'

finally he paid up all he was owin' of me, an' told
me he did n't want no more meals, but would find
himself.

"Waal, I told him, that, seein' things wuz as
they wuz with him, I should n't take no rent for the
garrit, an' I could dry my yarbs there jest as well
as ef he wa'n't there; an' he looked kind o' red,
and held his head up a minit, an' then he thanked
me, an' said, 'God bless you!' an' said he'd pay
me, ef he got any more work.

"Waal, he did n't git no more; an' after the
furnitoor an' the books, his cloze begun to go.

"Then I begun to be afeard he did n't have
nothin' to eat, an' oncet in a while I'd kerry him
up a mess o' vittles; but it allers seemed drefful
hard for him to take 'em, an' fin'ly he told me
not to do so no more, an' said suthin' to himself
about devourin' widders. So I did n't darst to go
up agin, he looked so kind o' furce an' sharp, till,
last night, I reck'n'd the snow would sift in through
the old ruff, an' I went up to offer him a comf'table
for his bed. I knocked; but he did n't make no
answer, so I pushed the door open an' went in. It
was a good while sence I'd seen the inside o' the
room, for when he heerd me comin' up, he'd open
the door a crack an' peek out while he spoke to
me; so when I got inside the room and looked
about, I was all took aback, an' gawped round like
a fool, an' no wunder nyther; for of all the good
furnitoor and things he'd brought, there wa'n't
the fust thing to be seen, save and 'cept a kind o'

framc covered with cloth stannin' aginst the wall, an' an old straw-bed on the floor, with him on it, an' a mis'able old comf'table kivered over him."

"And this bitter weather, too! Oh, Keziah, what did thee do?" asked Mrs. Coffin, in a tearful voice.

"Why, I went up to the bedside (ef you may call it so), an' said, sez I, 'Why, Lor' sakes, Mr. Wid-drinton,' — an' then I hild up, for I ketched a sight of his face, an' I thought he wuz gone for sartin. He wuz as cold an' as white as that 'ere snow, an' it wa'n't till I 'd felt of his heart an' foun' that it beat a little that I thought of sich a thing as his comin' to. But as soon as I found he 'd got a breath o' life in him, I did n't waste much time till I 'd got him wropped up in a hot blanket with a jug o' water to his feet, an' some hot tea inside on him. Then he come to a little, an' said he had n't eat nor drank for two days and nights."

"O Keziah!" sobbed Mrs. Coffin; while her husband, plunging his hands deep into his breeches pockets, and elevating his eyebrows till they were lost in his shaggy hair, exclaimed : —

"Good Je-hoshaphat!" which was the nearest approach to an oath in which he ever indulged.

"An' so," pursued the widow, after enjoying for a moment the consternation of her audience, — "an' so I thought I had better come an' see ef he could n't be took in here ; not that I would n't do for him, an' be glad to, fur as I could, but he ain't in a state to be left alone, an' you know my trade takes me away consid'able from home, — an' which, if I don't foller it, why, when I git a little older, I shall have to come here myself, an' be a burden on your hands an' the town's."

"We would take good care of thee, if thee did come, Keziah," said Mrs. Coffin, in whom the habitual equanimity of the " Friend " had conquered the emotion of the woman. " Though I do not deny that it is pleasanter and better for thee to support thyself, as thee always has done."

"I don't doubt you would be good to me, Mis' Coffin, an' thank ye, ma'am, kindly for a-sayin' of it; but you know innerpendunce is sweet to all on us."

"Surely, surely, Keziah ; and now, Phineas, I suppose thee will see at once about this poor man, won't thee ?"

"Yes, Marthy, yes. I 'll go right off and see one of the selectmen ; and I reckon by the time you git a bed ready for him we shall be along."

Phineas accordingly bustled out of the room ; and Mrs. Janes, after lingering a few moments, took her leave and returned to her charge, inwardly congratulating herself on having so new and interesting a piece of intelligence with which to lighten her next day's " tailoring."

Mrs. Coffin, left alone, stood for a moment considering, and then, opening a door, called gently : —

"Faith !"

"Yes, mother," replied a voice whose soft tones

seemed the echo of her own. A moment after, a slender, dark-eyed girl, about twenty years of age, entered the room, and said cheerfully : —

" What is it, mother ? "

" I have somewhat to tell thee, Faith."

And the Quakeress repeated, in calm, unemphatic language, the story narrated by Mrs. Janes.

" The poor man will soon be here, Faith," continued she, " and I wanted to ask what thee thinks should be done with him. Thee knows there is no room that can have a fire in it, except the one where Polly and Susan sleep, and they are both too sick to be moved into the cold " —

" He shall have my room, mother," said Faith, without hesitation.

" Thy room, child ? "

" Yes, mother ; and I will sleep here on the couch. I should like it very much indeed ; for you know I never have been able to be quite the orderly and regular girl you have tried to make me."

" Thee is a good girl," said the mother, quietly.

" Not half so good a girl as I ought to be, with so good a mother," replied Faith, throwing her arms about her mother's neck and kissing her fondly.

The elder woman returned the caress with an involuntary warmth, which, pure and natural though it might be, was yet at variance with the strict rule of her sect, that taught her to avoid everything like compliment or caress, as savoring of the manners of the " world's people."

So, after one kiss, she gently repelled the girl, saying : —

" Nay, Faith, but it sufficeth.   Go, then, if thee will, and make ready thy chamber for this sick man, while I prepare him some broth."

An hour later, a pung or box-sleigh drew up at the poor-house door, and from it was lifted a long, gaunt figure, carefully enveloped in blankets and cloaks.   As he was taken from the sleigh, he feebly murmured a few words, to which Phineas Coffin replied kindly : —

" Don't be scaart, — it's all safe, and Nathaniel will fetch it right in after us."

" What! this 'ere ? " queried the youth called Nathaniel, while he lifted from the sleigh, some-what contemptuously, a long flat something, care-fully enveloped in a cotton case.

" Yes.   Fetch it along this way," replied Phineas ; and Nathaniel followed the chair, in which the sick man was carried, into the pretty little maiden cham-ber that Faith had so quietly relinquished to one who, as she thought, needed it more than herself.

Mother and daughter stood ready to receive their new charge, and see him comfortable in the warm, soft bed which they had prepared for him.

" Thee will soon get rested now, friend, and go to sleep, — won't thee ? " said Mrs. Coffin, in her gentle voice, as she turned down the sheet a little more evenly.

" Where is it ? " panted the exhausted sufferer, trying to look beyond his kind nurse into the room.

" What does thee mean, friend ? "

" It is this thing, mother," said Faith, bringing it forward, and leaning it against the wall at the foot of the bed. " He brought it with him," continued she, in a low voice ; " and father says, he did n't seem to care half so much about his own comfort as to have *that* safe."

" It is my — property, — all I have — left. I won't be — parted from it. You — sha'n't take it — away," gasped the sick man, in an excited tone.

" Thee shall not be parted from it, friend," said Mrs. Coffin, soothingly. " Surely we would not deprive thee of what is thine own, and what thee seems to value so much. Now if thee will try to go to sleep, I will stay with thee the while, and when thee wakes thee shall have some broth to strengthen thy poor body."

" Let — let *her* stay. Go away, — the rest of you," whispered the feeble voice, while the weary eyes rested upon Faith's grave, sweet face.

" Thee means my daughter ? Faith, does thee wish to stay ? or had thee rather I should ? "

" I will stay, mother, if he wishes it."

" Very well, daughter. When thee is weary, come down, and I, or one of the women, will take thy place."

Mrs. Coffin left the room, and Faith, her sewing in her hand, was about seating herself by the fire, when the voice of the stranger summoned her to the bedside.

Turning, she found his hollow and gleaming eyes

fixed sternly upon her, while a long, lean finger was pointed alternately at her and the frame leaning against the wall.

" Girl ! "

" Can I do something for you ? " asked Faith, kindly.

" Don't you look at it — or let any one — else, while I 'm — asleep."

" I certainly will not."

" Promise ! "

" I do promise."

" Swear ! "

" Nay, friend, that would be wrong," replied the girl, unconsciously adopting the phraseology of the Quakers, while expressing a sentiment learned from them ; for though Faith had been brought up outwardly in the creed of her father, she had, without being aware of it, adopted many of the tenets to which her mother held.

" I will promise you very solemnly, however," continued she, " that I will neither look at yonder thing nor allow any one else to do so ; and you will be wrong to doubt my word."

" I don't. What is your name ? "

" Faith."

" A good omen. Mine is — Ichabod."

" Ichabod Widdrinton ? "

" Ichabod. Call me so, — all of you."

" Very well, if it is your name, we will. Now you must go to sleep."

" Sit there, — where I can see you."

Faith complied with this request, although uncertain whether it was not prompted by a distrust of her promise. The stranger soon slept, and his young nurse then made a more attentive survey of his features than she had yet done. He seemed not over forty years of age, and would, in health, have been considered a handsome man, — although the fine silky hair, thin beard, sensitive nostril, and delicate mouth could never have expressed much of strength or resolution.

The traces of disease and starvation were painfully apparent; but it seemed to the thoughtful Faith that behind these she could perceive in the sorrowful, downward curve of the lips, in the lines of the hollow, throbbing temples, in the gloomy light of the dark eyes, symptoms of a long corroding care, which, though secretly, had done its work of devastation more surely and more ruthlessly than the more apparent foes.

" How he must have suffered! " murmured she. It seemed as if the tone of gentle pity had penetrated the light slumber, and reached the heart of the sick man, — for, opening his eyes, he looked at the girl with a wan smile, whose sadness held both an assent and a benison.

From that moment, until the welcome end of his broken life, Ichabod would patiently endure no tendance but Faith's; and she, with the calm and silent self-abnegation of her order (for Florence Nightingale is but a type, and there are those all about us who lack but her opportunities), devoted herself to him.

Her mother sometimes remonstrated, and begged her to yield her place in the sick-chamber to her or to one of the pauper women; but Faith, whose grave sweetness concealed more determination than a stranger would have guessed, simply answered: —

"Dear mother, what is a little fatigue to one as well as I am, compared with the pleasure of making this poor stranger's death-bed happy and quiet? — which it certainly would not be, if he was crossed in his fancy for seeing me about him." And the conscientious mind of the mother was forced to yield assent to this simple logic.

A few weeks thus passed, and then the sick man became a dying man. The pauper inmates of the house were all willing and anxious to watch beside him through the long nights, but Ichabod received their attentions very ungraciously; nor was it till Faith told him, in her kind, decided way, that she could not stay with him at night, that he consented to allow the others to do so.

At last there came the evening when the physician said to Mrs. Coffin, as he entered the room where she sat with her husband: —

"He won't last till morning, — 't is impossible."

"Then thee had better watch beside him, Phineas. It is not fitting that Faith should do so."

"Certain. I'll go right up and send her down," replied Phineas, readily.

But when the arrangements for the night were made known to Ichabod, he caught hold of Faith's

dress, as she stood at his bedside bidding him good-
night, and gasped out, —

" No, no ! — you ! — I must have — you ! I shall
die — die to-night!   And — and I want to tell —
to tell you something.   Stay, — stay, Faith ! — it 's
the last — last time, and I — I shall never trouble
any one — any more."

"Let me stay, mother ; father, do ! " pleaded
Faith, looking from one to the other.   " I should be
very unhappy, always, if I was obliged to deny him
this last request.   I shall not be afraid, mother ;
and Betty can sleep in the chair by the fire, if you
wish it, so as to be at hand, if " —

" Well, child, if thee feels a call to do so, and it
will make thee unhappy to be denied, I will hold
my peace.   But thee must certainly have Betty
here, and promise to send her to call me, if Ichabod
should be worse, — won't thee ? "

Faith gave the required promise, and in a short
time the chamber was prepared for night.   The old
woman (whose skill in the last awful rites which
man pays to man caused her always to be selected
for such occasions) slept soundly beside the glowing fire, the dying man dozed uneasily, and Faith,
shading the light from his eyes, opened the large-
print Bible which her mother, careful both for the
well-being of her daughter's immortal soul and tem-
poral eyesight, had recommended for her night's
perusal.

The hours passed slowly on, unmarked by change,
until as Faith counted three solemn strokes from

the old clock in the passage, the sick man suddenly awoke.

Coming at once to offer him the draught for which he always asked on awakening, Faith was struck with a change in the face of her patient. The eyes were at once calmer and brighter, the look of uneasy pain had disappeared, and the thin lips wore almost a smile.

"Dear Faith," said he, in a gentle voice, which yet was stronger and more unbroken than any she had heard from him before, "how good you have been to me! I am dying; but do not call any one yet. I want to talk to you a little, first. Put another pillow under my head, and raise me, — so. Now light your other candle, urge the fire to a brighter blaze, and then uncover — it."

The girl, very pale and quiet, stirred the fire till its ruddy glow brightened every nook of the little whitewashed chamber, and made the old crone beside it wince and mutter in her sleep. Having shielded her from its fierce light, she then, with trembling fingers, opened a little penknife which lay upon the table, and cut the twine with which the cover was sewed at the back. The last stitch severed, the cloth fell with a solemn rustle at her feet, and disclosed — a picture.

Faith examined it with much attention and some curiosity. It was the full-length figure of a man, dressed in rich robes of office, his powdered hair put back from his forehead, his left hand resting on the pommel of his sword, his right clasping a roll of parchment. The expression of the face was grave, majestic, and noble; and yet between those handsome features and the attenuated features of the dying pauper Faith soon perceived one of those resemblances, strong, yet indefinable, which are so apparent to some persons, so undiscoverable by others.

" A noble gentleman, Faith, — was he not ? " said Ichabod, at length. " And they say his picture does not do him justice. He was an English gentleman of property and station, — the heir of a good fortune and honorable name ; but he left all to come here and help found this new country, — this glorious land of freedom and conscience, — where every man has perfect liberty — to starve in his own fashion.

" He came, and was a great man among them. He built the finest house in the village of Boston, and then came hither, where they made him governor and named a bay after him.

" He went home for a visit to England, and there he had this picture painted by the court-painter of those days, and brought it back with him, as a present to his wife.

" He was father of many children, mostly girls, and finally died in a very dignified and respectable manner, full of years and honors, as they say in story-books.

" His handsome property, being divided so often, made but rather small portions for the children, and several of the daughters died unmarried.

" Then the family began to decay, and each succeeding head found it a harder struggle to keep up the old hospitalities and the traditional style of living. They died out, too. The lateral branches of the family-tree never flourished, and one after another came to an end, till about forty years ago the remnant of the family blood and the family name was centred in two cousins, a young man and a girl. They met at the funeral of the girl's mother, and found in a short conversation that they were the sole living representatives of the old name.

" They married, gloomily helping on the Fate who pursued them by uniting their two threads of life in one, that thus she might sever it more easily. I was their only child, and they named me Ichabod, which means, as perhaps you know, the glory has departed.

" It is a sad proof of how deeply the bitterness of life had entered their souls that, even in the supreme moment when they clasped their first-born in their arms, the name which rose from heart to lip, and which they bestowed upon him, was in itself a cry of anguish and despair.

" The husband soon died. Man breaks, woman bends, beneath the crushing weight of such a life. My mother lived, a dark and silent woman, till five years ago. Then she died, too, and I inherited my ancestor's portrait and the curse of the Withringtons.

" I tried to work, to earn my bread, as men all about me were doing. But no, — the fate was upon me, the curse pursued me. Everything failed which I attempted. I sunk lower and lower, until the name and the picture, which had been my pride, became a shame and a reproach to me. I abandoned the one and concealed the other, re-solved to reveal neither until the moment arrived when death should wipe out the squalor of life, conquer fate, and expiate the curse.

"Quick, Faith, quick! The hour has come. Take the knife you just held, — cut the canvas from its frame, — cut it in fragments, — lay it on the blazing fire. We will perish together, — the First and — the Last."

"Nay, Ichabod, give it to me," said Faith, shrink-ing from the proposed holocaust. "I will always keep it, and value it."

"Would you see me fall dead at your feet, while attempting to do for myself what you refuse to do for me?" asked the dying man, with feverish ardor, and half rising, as if to leave his bed.

"No, no, — I will do it, since it must be so," exclaimed Faith, eagerly. "Lie down again and watch me."

Ichabod sunk back upon his pillows, and gazed with eyes of fitful light, as the girl, opening the keen knife, cut slowly and laboriously round the margin of the stout canvas, which shrieked beneath the blade, as if the spirit of the effigy which it bore were resisting the fearful doom which threat-ened it.

At last the picture was entirely released, and

Faith silently held it up before the eyes of the dying man, upon whose face had come a dull, leaden blankness, and whose eyes were painful to watch as they struggled to pierce the film which was gathering over them.

"Burn," he hoarsely murmured.

With a sigh, Faith cut the picture into strips, and laid them gently, reverently, upon the coals heaped in the large fireplace.

The greedy flames leaped up to grasp their prey, and Faith turned sick and faint as she watched them fasten upon that noble face, which seemed to contract and shrivel in its anguish as they seized upon it.

She gazed a moment, painfully fascinated, then turned toward the bed, — but as her eyes fell upon Ichabod's face, she started back, and, rousing the old woman from her slumber, sent to summon her mother.

Mrs. Coffin came immediately, — but when she entered the chamber, the last fragment of the canvas was shriveling in the flames, the last sigh of the dying man was parting from his white lips.

They had perished together, — the First — and the Last.

.

NOTE. — It may add to the interest of this story to know that it is literally true. The great-grandson of one of our early New England governors died in a poorhouse, with the portrait of his ancestor as his only possession.

WRECKED AND RESCUED.

IT was a dark night of December, 1790, and the clock in the study of Rev. Isaac Hepworth, the clergyman of a New England seacoast town, had already struck the hour of twelve, when that divine finished and laid within his desk the sermon on which he had been too busily engaged to note the lapse of time.

Late as was the hour, the Rev. Isaac did not immediately retire to sleep, choosing rather to rest his weary brain and relax his constrained muscles by an idle half hour beside the cheerful fire. So, throwing on another log, he wheeled round his study chair, settled himself comfortably therein, and placed his slippered feet upon the fender.

"A-h! This is comfort!" murmured the Rev. Isaac Hepworth, neatly folding the skirts of his dressing-gown across his knees.

Some fifteen minutes of intense quiet passed, and the clergyman, succumbing to the united temptations of fire, chair, and weariness, was dropping into a luxurious doze when he was suddenly and thoroughly aroused by a low tap upon his study window.

Springing to his feet a little nervously, Mr. Hepworth drew aside the curtain and peered out.

A man's face, dimly visible in the darkness, was pressed close to the glass, and met the clergyman's astonished gaze with a reassuring nod.

"Oh, Jarvis, is it you? Wait, and I'll let you in."

Jarvis nodded again, and, falling back into the gloom, went round to the door, which Mr. Hepworth had opened very quietly, that he might not disturb his sleeping household.

"Well, Jarvis, what's the matter?" asked he, anxiously, when the two were shut into the snug little study.

"Why, something very queer's the matter, sir, and I'm right glad I found you up, for, according to my reckoning, the fewer that's let into it the better; and as soon as I see the lights in these winders, I said to myself, 'There, there won't be no need for Mis' Hodson's knowing nothing about it.'"

"About what, Jarvis?" asked Mr. Hepworth, mildly, as his sexton paused to enjoy the satisfaction of a vulgar man who possesses a secret which he intends and yet grudges to impart.

"Well, sir, it wa'n't more than half an hour ago, and I was snug in bed sleeping as sound as any babe, when my wife she nudges me, and says she: —

"'John,' says she, 'there's some one a-knocking at our door.'

"'Pho! go to sleep, woman, and don't be disturbing me with your silly dreams,' says I; for I did n't like to be woke up, sir; and I was just a going off agin, when sure enough I heard a kind of softly knock on my front door, sounding just as if some one wanted to wake us up, and yet hated to make a noise.

" Well, I jumped up and h'isted the window.

" ' Who's there ? ' says I.

" ' A friend,' says a man's voice, though I could n't see no one 'cause of the dark.

" ' Hain't you got no name?' asks I, kind of sharp, for it 's a main cold night, sir, and I wa'n't overly comfortable.

" ' That 's of no consequence. I want to speak with you, if you 're the sexton of Mr. Hepworth's church, and you shall be paid handsomely for the trouble of dressing and coming down,' says the voice.

" Well, sir, I considered that it wa'n't noways Christianly not to hear what a feller-creter had to say, ef he wanted to say it bad enough to come out sech a night; and so says I : —

" ' Hold on, and I 'll come down soon 's I 've put on my trousers.'

" So I shet the winder, and though my wife she wa'n't noways willing, and took on consid'able for fear 't was a plan to rob and murder, or else a ghost, I bade her hold her tongue, and down I went, and jest stopping in the entry to say over a prayer and a verse, I ondid the door and held up my candle to the face of the man that stood outside.

"He was young and noways frightful to look upon, and he says right off : —

" 'That 's right, my friend,' and he put this 'ere piece of money in my hand [showing a golden guinea] ; and says he: —

" 'Now, I want you to come right along to the church, and open the door for me and my companion to go in, and then you must summon the clergyman to perform a marriage ceremony.'

" 'Why, sir,' says I, ' ef so be 's you want to be married, why can't you go to the tavern and wait till morning ; or ef suckumstances is sech as you can't wait, go to the minister's own house and be married in his study. Folks here don't never go to the meeting-house sech times, and more 'n all, it 's as cold and colder there than 't is outer doors.'

" Upon that, sir, the man he got kind of impatient, and says he : —

" 'Friend, it ain't advice I want of you but sarvice.' And with that he put inter my hand this other piece of money."

And the sexton complacently displayed a second guinea.

" Well, sir, upon that I considered, as I did n't know anything onlawful in a man's being married in a meeting-house at twelve o'clock at night, ef so be as he was a mind to, and the minister was a mind to marry him, so says I : —

" 'Well, Mister, you wait outside till I get my lantern, and I 'll show you the way to the meeting-house and let you in, and then I 'll go and tell the minister about it, and ef so be as he's a mind to come, why he will; and ef he ain't a mind to, why he won't.'

"'Has he a wife?' says the man next.

"'No, he hain't,' says I.

"'Have you a wife, then, goodman?' says he.

"'Yes, I have,' says I. 'And a good wife, too. It's she that was the Widder Jones, and darter to old Samwel Rubbles of this town.'

"I was a-going on, when the man he broke right in.

"'Can you persuade her to rise and accompany us to the church?' says he.

"'Lord, sirs,' says I, right out (for which I hope I'll be forgiven), 'what upon earth ken you want o' her?'

"'My companion, the young lady that is to be my wife, should have the support of a woman's presence at such a time; and besides that, it is necessary to have two witnesses to the marriage,' says the man.

"'Wa'al, I don't know jest what to say,' says I, kind o' considering, and, sir, that man he slips this other piece o' money inter my hand." And from his dexter pocket the venal sexton extracted a third guinea, and added it, with a humorous air of innocent astonishment, to the two already in his right hand.

"And then you went and called your wife?" suggested Mr. Hepworth, dryly.

"Why, yes, sir. I considered that it *was* hard

for a young woman to go and be married in a meeting-house at twelve o'clock at night and no womenfolks about; and I consaited that Marthy like enough would take a notion to go, and be kind of riley ef I did n't give her the chance; and more 'n all, I heerd her jest then call my name mighty softly over the balusters. So says I, ' Wa'al, I 'll go see,' says I ; and I shet to the door and went upstairs, and there was Marthy dressing herself faster 'n ever I see her before, and all fer hurrying me off to get you."

"And were the strangers all this time out in the biting cold ? " asked Mr. Hepworth, reprovingly.

" Why, yes, sir. I thought 't was safest so, for we never know what shape Satan may come in to destroy us, and I felt more kind o' easy to keep 'em outside. Marthy, when she got dressed, she went down and asked 'em in, but it wa'n't no wish of mine, nor she did n't stop to ask my leave. Women-folks is dreadful kind o' headstrong sometimes, sir, though I s'pose you hain't never had no call to find it out," said the sexton, sighing.

" And these strangers, where are they now ? " asked the clergyman, who, already cloaked and hatted, stood with the door in his hand waiting for his companion to precede him.

" In the meeting-house," said Mr. Jarvis, taking the hint, and passing out. " They would n't come in, noways ; but when I went out, the man he told us both to get inter a kerridge he had out in the road, and there was the young woman all curled

away in one corner a-crying; and the driver he
druv right straight to the meeting-house as ef he 'd
been there afore. So I onlocked the door and lit a
candle, and left 'em all there while I came to tell
you, sir."

"You would have done better, friend, in putting
the end of your story nearer to the beginning," said
the clergyman, a little indignantly. "We might
have relieved the discomfort and anxiety of these
poor people half an hour ago, if you had been less
diffuse in your narrative."

To this reproof John Jarvis listened in respect-
ful though puzzled silence, — a silence lasting until
the two approached a bare, bleak, uncomely edi-
fice, the universal type of the New England meeting-house of a hundred years ago. A feeble light
shone through the uncovered windows, and, pushing
open the door, Mr. Hepworth stepped inside, not
without a shiver at the deadly cold far more insup-
portable than the keen but living air without.

The bridal party (strange misnomer) were seated
in a pew near the upper end of the church, and rising, as the quick step of the clergyman sounded
hollowly up the uncarpeted aisle, they stood ready
to receive him.

Foremost was a man about thirty years of age,
tall, handsome, and of gentlemanly bearing. Behind him followed the sturdy helpmate of John
Jarvis, tenderly supporting a girlish figure with
veiled face, whose stifled sobs attested her agitation.

"Mr. Hepworth, I believe," said the stranger, in
a voice harmonizing well with his appearance.

" That is my name," said the clergyman, mildly. " Can I render you any service consistent with my duty, sir ? "

" The greatest. I wish to be married at once to this young lady. We are to sail for Europe on the morning tide. A boat now waits to convey us on board, and our passage is taken as man and wife. Our right to that position rests now with you."

" But you will surely tell me, sir, the cause of this very unusual manner of proceeding ? Are the young lady's parents aware of the step she has taken ? "

" They are not, sir," returned the stranger, firmly. " Her only parent, a father, is, on the contrary, bitterly opposed to my claims, and would force his daughter into another marriage as abhorrent to her feelings as to humanity. She is of age to decide for herself, but has not the courage to openly maintain her rights in presence of her father. She has chosen me, and no power on earth shall prevent her from becoming my wife. If you refuse to perform the ceremony, we must embark unwedded, to the scandal of all who may hereafter hear the tale, and trust to have our marriage solemnized upon the other side of the water."

" That were, indeed, a scandal ! " ejaculated the clergyman, with horror.

" And yet to that extremity shall we be driven unless you will at once make us man and wife," said the stranger, coolly, as he drew out his watch and held it in the dim light of the candles. " It is now hard upon half past one. At two we are to take boat."

Mr. Hepworth turned to the bride.

"Daughter," said he, softly, "have you considered what you do?"

"Yes, sir. I hope I shall be forgiven," sobbed the girl.

"And is it your resolve, should I decline to solemnize so strange a marriage, to follow this man across the sea unwedded, at the imminent peril of your fair fame here, and eternal happiness hereafter?" asked the minister, solemnly.

The sobs became convulsive in their strength, but presently the timid voice again whispered: —

"Yes, sir. But you will not refuse — oh, will you?"

Mr. Hepworth walked nervously up and down the open space before the pulpit, and then returning to the group said impressively: —

"I will not refuse my ministration here; for if your avowals are an earnest of your intentions, I shall, by refusal, tempt you to a deeper sin than disobedience; but I warn you both, and especially you," turning to the bridegroom, "who, as the stronger and more responsible party, should bear the greater blame, that God's blessing rests not on those who seek it while openly violating his commands; and of these, obedience to parents ranks next to obedience to himself."

"Enough, sir. We are not to be dissuaded from our purpose," replied the bridegroom, haughtily;

adding more persuasively after a momentary pause :
"and even by your own precept we are justified ;
for in choosing each other, and in resisting those
who would separate us, we feel to be obeying the
voice of God, even in opposition to that of a parent."

Mr. Hepworth to this argument opposed only a
gesture of deprecation, and after a fervent but
silent prayer, took his appropriate place, and motioned the others to range themselves before him.

" Will you uncover your face, daughter?" asked
the clergyman, kindly, as the bride showed no
inclination to raise the veil behind which she had
hitherto sheltered.   Now, however, she immediately
removed it, and the eyes of all her companions
centred upon her face, — those of Mr. Hepworth
with benevolent scrutiny, of the Jarvises with broad
curiosity, of her bridegroom with tender and sym-
pathizing love.

It was a lovely face, — pale now and disfigured
by weeping, but undeniably beautiful, and not
wanting in a latent strength such as the trials in
the new path on which she now was entering might
speedily render needful.

"Your name, my child?" asked the minister,
after a moment's attentive observation.

" Hope Murray," said the girl, faintly, a soft
color stealing into her cheek beneath the gaze of all
those eyes.

" And yours, sir ? "

" Miles Tresethen," replied the stranger, meeting
with unblenching gaze the look of severest scrutiny

with which Mr. Hepworth turned from that fair childish face to that of the man who, as he had inly decided, had tempted her to her present rebellious disobedience. And yet Mr. Hepworth's growing anger paused, and even retrograded, as he met those clear and fearless eyes, noted the noble if proud bearing of the handsome head, — came, though unconsciously, under the powerful influence of that presence.

"Judge not that ye be not judged," flashed through the clergyman's mind, and with a little sigh, he said, quietly : —

"Take each other by the right hand." Then followed the brief words of the Puritan service, and the minister gravely kissed the bride, saying, "May you be as happy, my dear, as an old man's wish can make you ; and may your fault be forgiven you as freely as I would forgive, did it rest with me to do so !"

For an instant the girl clung to his kindly hand as if he had been indeed her father, and then turned to her husband.

"We could not help it," said she, simply. "We loved each other so, and we were so unhappy."

"Good-by, sir," said Tresethen, extending his hand, and grasping warmly that of the clergyman. "Accept my thanks — our thanks, for the sacrifice you have made to-night of prejudice to necessity. Never doubt that, on sober second thought, conscience will acquit you of all wrong."

"Can you speak as boldly for yourself ?" asked Mr. Hepworth, dryly.

The bridegroom paused. The bride uplifted to his her tear-stained face.

"Before God I believe that I have done right," said Tresethen, solemnly; and the clergyman added nothing more except, "God bless you!" as he parted at the church-door with the new-married couple.

"And here's another piece of money he give me as we came down the aisle behind you and the young woman," said John Jarvis, while the minister and he stood upon the steep steps of the meeting-house, listening to the quick rattle of the wheels whirling down the stony road toward the water; "and he said I was to come right along, and take the kerridge and hosses when they left 'em (that's his servant a-driving, sir), and fetch 'em to you, and put 'em at your disposal, he said, sir."

"At my disposal, Jarvis!"

"Yes, sir. Give 'em to you, you know, sir."

"But I do not wish for them, Jarvis. I cannot take them, — indeed I will not. Go at once to the landing, and tell Mr. Tresethen that it is out of the question for me to accept his present, and ask what other disposal shall be made of the property."

Sexton Jarvis sped away, while his dame turned silently homeward, as did Mr. Hepworth, his brain whirling with the excitement of the last two hours.

As he reached the house he paused, and waited some moments without, although the rich red firelight streamed invitingly from the study window, and the night was bitterly cold. The rattle of dis-

tant wheels had reached his ear, however, and he
stood patiently waiting until John Jarvis carefully
checked the span of fine horses close beside their
reluctant owner.

"He won't take No for an answer," said the
sexton, importantly. "And when I says, says I,
''T ain't no use. The minister says he can't nor he
sha'n't take 'em;' he says, says he, 'Tell him they
are his. He may use them himself, or sell them
and give their price to the poor, but I have no
more control over them.'"

"And is he gone?" asked Mr. Hepworth,
anxiously.

"Yes, sir. There was a boat waiting at the
wharf (though the ship she belongs to must have
run in sence dark; there wa'n't none in the
harbor at dayli't down), and they was aboard when
I come, — that is, the man and his wife. The one
that druv stood holding the horses till I got there,
and then he chucked the reins inter my hand and
jumped inter the boat. The sailors pushed off, and
in a minute more I could n't hev told that there'd
ever ben sech doin's ef it had n't ben for the
hosses and kerridge. What's to be done with 'em,
sir?"

"Why, we must put them in my little stable for
to-night," said Mr. Hepworth, reluctantly. "And
if there is really no owner for them but myself, I
shall follow the suggestion of this strange young
man, and sell them for the benefit of the poor of
this parish. God knows they need relief."

Two days elapsed, and again Mr. Hepworth sat alone beside his study fire, this time in the daylight, thinking of the strange event so lately transpired, and anxiously pondering his own share therein, when a loud knock at the front door attracted his attention, and presently a stranger was ushered into the study.

This was a tall, stout man of middle life, with scowling brows, sanguine complexion, and a choleric expression, whether habitual or temporary Mr. Hepworth found it impossible to determine.

" You 're Mr. Hepworth ? " began the stranger, as soon as the door had closed behind him.

" Yes, sir. Will you sit down ? " said the clergyman, mildly.

" No, I won't. I want to know if you married my girl to that d—d scoundrel of an Englishman, who 's carried her off."

" Sir, I shall answer no questions until you remember the decent respect you owe to my cloth, if you choose to lay aside higher obligations," said the clergyman, severely.

" Well, well, beg your pardon, sir, and all that; but it 's enough to make a man swear. You have not told me yet whether you married them."

" I married Miles Tresethen and Hope Murray two nights ago, in the parish meeting-house of this town," said the minister, quietly.

" And by — Well, I 'm not going to swear, but what right had you to do so ? "

" I did so because both parties assured me that

Miss Murray was of age, that she chose to marry Mr. Tresethen in preference to any one else, and that they should certainly embark within half an hour in a vessel then awaiting them, married or unmarried. Should you have preferred so equivocal a position as that for your daughter, Mr. Murray?"

"What was the name of that vessel?" asked the angry man, waiving reply to the clergyman's question with an impatient gesture.

"I do not know, sir."

"Perdition take them! I'll have 'em yet. I'll sail to-night, — I know a ship. I'll be in England as soon as they, and I'll have her back if I kill that villain first. Disobedient jade, — worthless trollop" —

"Mr. Murray, I must request you to leave my study and my house," exclaimed the mild Hepworth, with unwonted energy, as the pure and lovely face of Hope Murray rose to his memory from amidst this sea of angry words and epithets.

"But I tell you, sir, that my life was bound up in that girl, and now she's gone. I should die if I could n't swear!" exclaimed the father, with vehement simplicity. "I had such plans for her, — I had such a match in view. She'd have been the first lady in the States in time. And now to go off with that miserable fellow, — an Englishman too!"

"What are your objections to Mr. Tresethen, may I ask? I judged him very favorably in our brief interview," said Mr. Hepworth, pitying the genuine sorrow visible through all the offensive manner of the man.

"Why, sir, his father was a Tory and a refugee. He came here a young man and made a fortune; then, when our troubles broke out, and I and others left all our own concerns and took up arms to fight for our freedom and our liberty, this miserable Englishman quietly transferred his ill-gotten gains to his own country, and skulked off after them. Then, with the devil's own luck (your pardon once more, sir), he inherited a fine estate and lived in luxury, while our brave fellows, sir, were eating their own shoes at Valley Forge, and tracking the snow with their bloody feet as they marched on without 'em. Then, when the war 's all over, and matters settled down again, back comes this fellow, this Miles, who had been left in England for his education while his father was living here, to inquire after some landed property that the old fellow could n't carry with him when he ran away, and was afraid to sell. My girl met him, sir, fell head over heels in love with him, and forgot her duty, her home, and her old father to run after him to the ends of the earth. But he sha'n't have her, — he sha'n't keep her. I told 'em both, when they came asking my consent and all that, I never would consent, — never, to my dying day, nor I won't."

"But if Mr. Miles Tresethen was educated in England, and never lived in this country at all, surely he need not share the odium of his father's desertion," suggested Mr. Hepworth.

" Well, perhaps not, but at any rate he's an Englishman, and we've had enough of Englishmen. I hate 'em, from the king upon his throne down to the meanest soldier in his army. We've all given our strength, and our hearts, and some of us our lives to getting rid of 'em, and clearing 'em out of the country, and now do you think I'm going to give my only child to one of 'em? Not I, sir. I'll have her back. I'll get her divorced. I'll undo the knot you were so foolish as to tie, sir. I'll have justice, and I'll have my girl."

And his anger having regained its full heat, temporarily checked by the calm presence of the clergyman, Mr. Murray was rushing indignantly from the room when he was stopped by his host, who, recounting briefly the incidents connected with the carriage and horses, requested that he would take them and dispose of them as he would.

But at this request the ire of the injured father reached its height; and with vehement protestations that horses, carriage, Englishman, and all, should go to a very unpleasant place before he meddled with them, he slammed out of the house, leaving Mr. Hepworth to recover at his leisure from the horrified consternation into which he had been thrown.

Out on the wild Atlantic a hunted ship flew before the storm that rushed madly after. All day and all night and all another day the trembling quarry had sped on, and now at sunset of the second day the storm seemed gathering fresh strength, as if resolved at once to end the conflict by one overpowering effort.

It was the Roebuck, the ship on which James Murray had hastily embarked in pursuit of his daughter and her English husband; and as he now at nightfall came on deck and looked anxiously about, marking the fiercer gloom of sea and sky, the disordered ship and sullen crew, he remembered, not for the first time, the warning he had received just before sailing, against trusting himself at sea with such a captain and such a crew; and, after the fashion of angry men, he cursed anew the cause of his present peril.

"If it had n't been for that d—d Englishman," said he, "I should not have been here. And where is Hope — poor child! — and if she is lost, who will be her murderer? Who but that villain that tempted her away? I 'll have his heart's-blood yet, — trust me but I will!"

"Well, Mr. Murray, what did you see on deck?" asked a husky voice, as that gentleman painfully descended the companion-ladder into the cabin.

"I saw everything except the captain," returned Murray, gruffly, casting a scowling glance at the bottle and tumbler sliding about upon the table.

"Ha, ha! that 's meant for me, eh? Well, I 'm just going up, though I don't know what in thunder to do when I get there, except what 's been done already. Won't ye have a glass, Mr. Murray?"

"No, sir!" returned the passenger, sternly.
"If we are all to be swept into eternity before
morning, as I expect, I for one will go like a man,
and not like a brute."

"H-m! Surly devil! Go on deck to get rid
of you, if nothing else," muttered the captain, as
he climbed the steep steps with more than usual
difficulty.

Mr. Murray, after watching his clumsy movements with an expression of angry disgust until he
had disappeared on deck, entered his own stateroom, changed his dress, put his papers and money
into an oilskin belt girt about his body, tied on his
excellent life-preserver, and wrapping himself in a
heavy cloak, ascended in his turn to the deck.

The hour that had elapsed since his previous
visit had wrought no material change. Perhaps
through the intense blackness of the night the mo-
notonous sweep of the wind sounded more fearfully;
perhaps the leaping waves snatched more hungrily
at their prey in the sheltering darkness; perhaps
the doomed ship groaned more audibly and intelli-
gibly; at least, these things seemed so to the passenger, who now clung to the main shrouds and threw
piercing glances hither and thither through the
night. Sheltered beneath the windward bulwark
crouched the captain with his chief mate, their
position only to be determined by their voices as
they shouted an occasional order to the men, who
sometimes sullenly obeyed, sometimes in the darkness contented themselves with muttering that it

was impossible. At last a man came staggering aft with the request, or rather demand, from his comrades for the key of the spirit-room. It was received with an oath of denial, and the man sullenly withdrew; but the demand had aroused the officers to a sense of their imminent peril, as the storm had failed to do.

The captain, rising with difficulty to his feet, began to make his way toward the hatch, intending to descend and broach the casks, well knowing, drunkard as he was, that if once the men gained access to the liquor his shadow of control over them was lost, and with it all hope for the ship and those in it. As he passed Murray, the latter said indignantly : —

" Why don't you have lanterns placed in the rigging, and send that lookout man back to his duty? He has left it to plot mutiny with his comrades there on the forecastle. We shall all be murdered next, if you don't show some authority."

To this perhaps unwise but very natural reproof the angry skipper retorted with a string of oaths and coarse abuse, bidding his passenger attend to his own concerns, and expressing a hope that, in case of mutiny, he might become the first victim.

Mr. Murray turned contemptuously from him, and again fixed his eyes and his attention upon the dense mass of blackness ahead, into which the ship was wildly plunging, trembling at every leap. Listening with ears preternaturally sharpened by

the extremity, he was aware of a new sound added
to the wild swirl of winds and waves. A heavy
rushing sound, — a hissing of the waters as they
parted perforce before some swift-advancing object, — a shrieking of the wind as it tore through
the shrouds, not only above his head but beyond
in the black unknown. Murray fixed his strain-
ing eyes upon the point whence these sounds approached. Yes, a great black mass, shapeless and
ominous as terror itself, bore down upon them, the
seething waves and shrieking wind singing jubilee
over the destruction in its path. On it came, —
there was no more doubt.

"Ship ahoy!" shouted Murray. "Helmsman!
mate! bestir yourselves! Ahoy! ahoy there!"

The wind snatched the words from his lips, rent
them to fragments, and flung them scoffingly back
upon him. It was barely that those in his own ship
heard him, and then the mate, staggering to his feet,
gazed blankly at the doom impending so closely
over them a full minute before he shouted to the
helmsman through his trumpet: —

"Port there! port, you villain! port, you dog!"

It was too late. Before the man could obey the
order fully, before the leaping ship could be put off
her course, before one tenth of that ship's crew knew
that Death had laid his hand upon their garments,
and claimed them for his own, the blow had fallen.
The unknown ship, swerving slightly, as those on
board her discovered too late the obstacle in their
path and vainly strove to evade it, came crashing

down upon the Roebuck, amidst a wild confusion
of sea and wind, of human shrieks and cries and
oaths, of splintering wood and falling masts. Then,
carried on by her fearful impetus, the stranger, cut-
ting through the doomed vessel, passed on into the
blackness, with no power, had she the inclination,
to render assistance to her victims.

Seizing a spar that mercifully would have dealt
him a death-blow, James Murray found himself
floating in the water, surrounded on every side by
drowning men and fragments of the shattered vessel. Clinging to his spar, he struggled to maintain
his head above the blinding waves that sought to
bury him while yet quick, in the grave beneath his
feet, and he succeeded.

The storm soon scattered the few survivors of the
wreck who had not at once been drowned; and
when at last the morning broke, and Murray, raising himself as well as he was able upon the spar,
looked despairingly about him, no trace remained
of ship or company, — nothing but the wild waste
of waters, stretching far away to where on the horizon line the great waves reared their crests upon
the sullen sky.

"Worse than death, — worse a thousand times!"
groaned the desolate survivor; and for a moment
he was tempted to release himself from spar and
life-preserver, and sink at once, escaping thus the
torturing hours lying between him and the almost
inevitable end. But in the powerful organization
of the man vitality was strong and deeply seated;

and after the first pang of terror at the gloomy prospect, James Murray summoned his strength, and resolved to die, if die he must, when no further efforts of his own could sustain him.

Hunger and thirst were now his greatest foes. Against the former he was fortified for a while by some bread and meat which he had placed in his pocket before coming on deck, thinking it possible that the crew might suddenly take to the boats without adequate preparation, and determining in such a case neither to be left behind, nor to die of starvation should the winds and waves allow a boat to live. But this food, saturated as it was with salt water, would only increase the fearful thirst already tormenting him, — a surer and a crueler foe to life than any hunger, — and so Murray reflected with a shudder. Still he resolved to neglect no means of preserving life, even though it must be in torture, and tying together his cravat and handkerchief, he passed them about his body, and firmly secured himself to the spar. This left both his hands at liberty, and gave him greater ease of position.

Extracting from his water-filled pocket a bit of the meat, he ate it hungrily, and could have cried at finding the bread a mere mass of saline pulp, entirely inedible. Somewhat refreshed by this slight nourishment, the lonely man looked once more about him, scanning the horizon with anxious scrutiny, if haply a white-winged vessel might be on its way to rescue him. But the only comfort that could be gathered from all the untold miles of sea and sky around and above him was the hope that the storm was over. Surely the clouds were thinner and more broken ; the rain had ceased ; the fitful wind did not so incessantly lash the waves into more furious sweeps. Toward noon a watery sun shone for a moment through rifts of sullen cloud, was overwhelmed, but struggled out again with fuller rays, and from that gained steadily upon the clouds, until at setting he flashed out a broad banner of victorious rays far across the unquiet sea, still throbbing fiercely with its late emotion.

Still no hope, no rescue for James Murray. Every hour of that December day had stolen somewhat from the vigor that upheld him. His limbs were numb, although he tried to keep the blood alive in them by active motion. His teeth chattered, his eyes grew dim, a sick dizziness at his brain made sea and sky swim before his sight; in his ears grew a drowsy song as of the sirens calling to him from beneath the waves.

" I cannot live till morning ; and oh, my child " — No anger now, only yearning love and bitterest sorrow. In that dreary trial the heart of the worldly man was learning the lessons that prosperity had never taught. Again he said : —

" I hope she will never know how her poor father died ; I hope she will be happy all her life. I wish she knew that I forgave her before I died. Poor dear, I said hard things to her that night before she left me. I would give all my slender chance of life to take them back. Why should she not choose for herself, as I did in my youth? Cruel and tyrannical! *She* did not say it, though. That poor little note she left for me had no such words as those in it. I tore it, and stamped upon the pieces before I burned them. God forgive me! Did her mother see me do that, I wonder? Fifteen years ago since Mary died, and she bade me to be father and mother both to that poor child. Have I done it? O God, let me live! Save me from this death, that I may make amends for the wrong I had sworn to do!"

He raised himself from the water as far as he might, and gazed once more on all around with a piteous earnestness such as no care for mere life had brought into that hard face.

Nothing but sea and sky, cloud and wave. Only there, on the horizon line, what is that? A wave leaping higher than its fellows? No, for it does not sink and rise as the waves do. It cannot be a ship, it is so low in the water; there are no masts to be traced on that golden background of the sunset clouds. A boat, perhaps; if so, are there men in it? Will it cross his path? Can he attract their notice?

A wild flutter of hope and desire thrills through the soul and body of the man, struggling so vehemently for life, and he begins with all the little strength at his command to swim toward the distant haven of his hope. But before he has made the least perceptible progress, before he has resolved one of all those doubts as to the nature of the object he so wildly strives to gain, heavy darkness shuts down upon him and it. It is no longer possible to distinguish the least trace of the boat, if such it was, and with a bitter groan James Murray ceases his efforts and sinks down upon the spar in listless inaction.

"It will be gone by morning," said he, "or I shall be dead."

But morning dawned, and he was not dead. Very weak and exhausted, indeed, unable to swim or to make any other motion, but still alive, still conscious of that little link holding him to this lower world, still anxious for the sunrise, that he might with his dying eyes sweep the wide horizon line before he closed them forever.

So faint and weak he was, he could not bring himself at once to make the exertion of rising on the spar that he might take that last look. It was not till the warm sunlight fell upon his face that he gathered his energies and feebly rose.

Oh, God is good! It is close upon him, drifting slowly down across his very path. No boat, indeed, but the dismasted hulk of a vessel, its bows shattered and sunk, but its stern high and safe above the water, and human figures looking down from it curiously upon him.

He raised his arm and feebly waved it; as feebly shouted a reply to the hail that met his dull ears, and then the song of the siren shut out all other sound, a thick darkness closed his eyes, and he had fainted.

An hour after, when James Murray unclosed those heavy eyes, he stared incredulously into the face bending so tenderly over him, and moved uneasily within the arms that folded themselves about him. But he could not shake off the dream.

" Hope ? " whispered he.

" Yes, dear, dearest father, it is indeed your own wicked child, to whom God has kindly given time and space to ask your forgiveness."

The father feebly closed his eyes without reply, — it was all so strange. It was so little while since he had longed to live that he might ask *her* forgiveness.

A man's voice spoke next : —

" Let me pour some more of this brandy between his lips, dearest. You should not have spoken yet of such matters."

" I could not help it, Miles. I have so longed to say it. But see, he is getting better surely ; see the color in his lips. O father dear, open your eyes once more ! "

James Murray did not resist that appeal, but opening his eyes, fixed them more lovingly upon his daughter's face than she remembered him ever to have done before.

Tears rushed into her own, but she restrained them at a look from her husband, and only stooped to kiss her father's cheek.

" It was Miles who saved you," whispered she, after a moment. " He leaped in and drew you to the vessel."

"Where is he now, — Miles?" asked Mr. Murray, feebly.

"Here. O darling father, you forgive us both, — I see that you do!" And then the tears *would* come, and did.

"And now, sir, if you are strong enough, I will take you down to the cabin and put you in a berth," said Tresethen, presently. "We have the after-part of the ship at our command, and may be very comfortable here for a long time if the fair weather holds."

"Wait a while and I'll go down myself. I'm too heavy for any one to carry."

"I think not, sir, if I may try." And the broad-shouldered young Englishman, raising his reluctant burden from the deck, carried him carefully down the steep steps, and after stripping off his wet and almost frozen clothes, placed him carefully in a berth and covered him deep with blankets.

"Now, if you will take a good long sleep, sir," said he, cheerily, "I think you'll wake up all right, and Hope will have some hot tea ready for you."

Mr. Murray did not answer, but went to sleep with a queer smile upon his lips. To think that this should be the end of all the threats and curses he had heaped upon the head of that young man!

Hope was ready with the tea, and before night her father was nearer to being "all right" than could have been expected after the severe exposure he had undergone.

The next day he was able to sit up and hear the story of the Tresethens' voyage and present position. He was not surprised at learning that this very hulk on which they now found themselves was the remains of the destroyer of the Roebuck. That shock, so fatal to the smaller vessel, was not harmless to the larger. Her bows were badly stove, and shortly after the collision a cry was raised that the ship was sinking, and must immediately be deserted. With the selfishness of terror, the crew seized upon the boats and refused to allow the passengers a place. The captain, after exerting alike uselessly his authority and his powers of persuasion, declared finally that unless the passengers were taken he himself would remain behind.

"So much the better!" cried the brutal boatswain as he pushed off the overloaded boat, which was immediately hidden by the darkness. The three, thus abandoned, sat down quietly upon the quarter-deck and waited for their death. It did not come, and in the morning they perceived that, having settled to a certain depth, the ship would sink no further, at least toward the stern. The cabin and cabin stores were thus saved to them, insuring shelter and subsistence so long as the hulk should float in its present position. A quantity of charcoal stored in an empty stateroom promised the comfort of fire, and in all, except the uncertainty of permanent safety, their situation might be as agreeable and comfortable as it had been during the first days of their voyage. But a few more hours brought yet another shock to convince them that no man may calculate in what form his last hour shall meet him.

The captain, whose great weakness was a love of gain, had mentioned several times that a great deal of money might be collected from the seamen's chests in the forecastle, if they could be reached, as the sailors had, according to custom, received their wages for the outward voyage upon the day of sailing.

The next morning after the shipwreck he had been heard to quietly leave the cabin at an early hour and ascend the companion-way. Some time after, Tresethen, going up to join him, was startled at finding only his coat lying upon the deck. The captain was never seen again; and the two survivors could only surmise that he (being a bold and skillful swimmer) had dived into the forecastle to try to recover the treasure hidden there, and had either become entangled in the wreck, or struck his head in the descent so as to stun himself. At any rate, the sea never gave up this one of its many secrets, and Tresethen and his bride remained alone, until, by almost a miracle, James Murray was brought to join them.

A week passed away, and, spite of all the perils of their position, — spite of their uncertain future, — Hope thought and said that it was the happiest week of her life. Her father, having once made up his mind to forgive and like her husband, did it so heartily that his daughter sometimes smiled merrily

at finding her own opinions and arguments peremp-
torily set aside in favor of Tresethen's, and in
noticing the honest admiration in the face of the
older man, when his new son argued eloquently and
firmly, although respectfully, with Murray's unrea-
soning prejudice against England and Englishmen.

Tresethen, too, beginning in a mere feeling of
compassion and forbearance, grew to feel a real
affection for Hope's father, — to regard him with
that complacent fondness one always feels for a
person he has won over from opposition to amity.

These pleasant days were, however, drawing to
a close. Hope, awaking one night from uneasy
dreams, was startled by hearing the plash of water
close to the edge of her berth, and putting out her
hand, dipped it into the ice-cold element stealing
so treacherously upon her sleep. Rousing hastily
her husband and father, and procuring a light,
her terrible suspicions were soon confirmed. The
wreck was settling. They must at once abandon
the cabins, and trust themselves to the shelterless
deck. Hastily gathering what food was at hand,
and snatching some clothing from the beds, the
fugitives fled from the cruel foe, steadily if slowly
pursuing them.

The first effort of both men was to shelter as
much as possible the delicate girl so dear to them ;
but when Hope was wrapped closely in shawls and
blankets, and seated between them upon the deck,
there seemed nothing more to do except to wait
resignedly, till that creeping, sliding water, whose

warning plash sounded every moment nearer, should at last reach and overwhelm them.

"What should be the cause of this sudden change?" asked Mr. Murray, breaking with an effort the painful silence.

"Captain Jones told me," said Tresethen, "the reason the vessel did not sink at once was, that he had caused a bulkhead, as nearly air-tight as he could get it, to be placed across some portion of the hold, thinking that, in case of just such a disaster as befell us, this confined body of air would, as it actually did, buoy up the stern and prevent the wreck from sinking. In the first moments after the collision he supposed that his experiment had failed, and did not mention it to us until several hours of safety had reassured him. I suppose this partition must now have given way at some point, so as slowly to admit the water. Probably it was just beneath our feet last night, while we sat so cheerfully talking over our future plans before separating for the night."

"Dreadful!" murmured Hope, hiding her face upon her husband's breast.

"Well, I don't know, daughter and son," said James Murray, after a little pause. "It does not strike me that we've been very hardly dealt with, after all. It would have been worse if I had died floating on that spar, and you had gone down when your shipmates did, and neither of us had ever said the words we have said since. It would have been worse, even if you had got safely to England and

lived out your lives, with the weight on your con-
sciences of having started wrong; while I, a poor,
miserable, lonely old man, had stayed in America
cursing and swearing at my disobedient children."

" O father! "

" Well, I did, girl, and so that Mr. Hepworth
will tell you, — would have told you, I may as well
say. No, children, I think, on the whole, Almighty
God has done full as much for us as we anyway
deserve, considering we none of us have kept
straight to the mark ; and I for one have wandered
off far enough. Now, son and daughter, don't you
agree with me that we shall all go off into eternity the happier and the better for this last week
we 've spent together ? "

" Indeed I do, sir," said Miles, solemnly ; and
Hope, sobbing on her father's neck, answered him
with quivering kisses.

" I know I have n't lived what the ministers call
a godly life," said James Murray again, after a
little thought. " But I hope I 've been sorry first
or last for all the wrong I 've done; and I 've
heard it read that such as repented were to be forgiven. I don't know yet. We all shall soon. Hope,
child, can't you say over one of those prayers I
used to hear your mother teaching you in the old
times ? "

Controlling her own emotion with a woman's
quiet strength, Hope, after a little pause, repeated
in her clear, low voice the simplest and greatest of
all petitions, the Lord's own prayer.

When she had done, and the men had muttered
Amen, no more was said for a long while.   Each
one took counsel with his own heart, and silently
set his house in order for the mighty visitor who
stood close without the door.   At last Tresethen
said, quietly : —

" The day is dawning."

All eyes turned eastward and silently watched
while the sun rose through a glory of purple and
golden clouds and came to look at them.   Presently
his light and warmth revivified their chilled frames,
and, creeping closer together, they divided the food
they had brought with them in their hasty flight.
It was not much, not more than would last one
day ; but as all thought, though none said, it was
very unlikely that another sunrise should find them
in need of earthly food.

The bright winter day passed on.   The air,
though keen, was not insupportably cold, and the
little party were well provided with wrappings of
various sorts, and exerted themselves, from time to
time, to take such exercise as the limits of the deck,
now very nearly level with the water, would allow.
But here again the waters stayed.   For what reason
they could not tell, but from an hour before sunset
the settling of the wreck was suspended, and faint
human hopes and longings came creeping back to
the three hearts that thought to have done with
them forever.

Darkness fell, and the father slept, his head
upon his daughter's lap.   She, gathered to her

husband's breast, neither spoke nor moved, and, though her blue eyes did not close, her spirit seemed far away. Tresethen, strong and manful, warded off as yet the subtle attacks of cold and hunger, watching sleeplessly the starry horizon, hoping against hope to see there the dim outline of a sail.

The long night passed, the morning broke. Hope, quietly arousing herself, drew forth the remnant of her yesterday's food and tried to slip a portion into her father's mouth that he might unconsciously swallow it. But Murray, awaking suddenly, detected the pious fraud, and smiling feebly, said : —

"No, no, child ; life is young and full of promise for you, — keep it while you may. My race is run."

'Will you not take it, father? Indeed I do not want it."

"No, Hope ; positively no."

"Then you must, Miles. You are the strongest of us all. Eat, and you may yet be saved."

"Do you think, my wife, that I would live so?" asked Tresethen, reproachfully. "What charm remains on earth for me, that I should take the morsel from your lips and watch you die of hunger in my arms? Eat this morsel yourself, my darling, if you love me ! "

"No, Miles, I cannot, — I will not. Indeed, I think it would choke me were I to attempt it."

'Then we will divide it in three parts, and each

agree to eat his own share for the sake of the others."

" I will try," said Hope, faintly; and James Murray, sitting upright, could not restrain the hungry glare of his hollow eyes as he seized the portion offered him by Tresethen. Hope — her husband's eye upon her — swallowed with difficulty her own morsel, watching in her turn Tresethen, who, making a very good pretense at eating, quietly hid his untasted food, reserving it for Hope.

Again the sun rose and looked pityingly down upon the forlorn group clinging to that sinking wreck.

The three watched it steadily.

" Hope ! Mr. Murray ! What is that ? There, close under the sun — you can hardly see it for the light ! Is it — can it be ? — it is, a sail ! "

" You 're right, boy ; it is surely a sail ! " cried the father, rising excitedly to his feet.

Hope did not speak, but her dim eyes turned to Miles with a look of unspeakable thankfulness.

It was indeed a sail, — a homeward-bound merchantman, sweeping gayly on before a strong east wind, directly in the path of the sinking hulk.

Every moment as it passed brought her nearer, and brought back life and hope to those three, so lately resigned to die.

Nearer and nearer, till the fluttering ensign of distress held aloft by Tresethen was acknowledged from her decks ; nearer and nearer, till she gracefully rounded to, and a boat was manned and lowered. Then, as it came leaping on across the waters, how those hungry eyes watched lest it should suddenly be swallowed up; lest it should not, after all, be meant for them; lest they should die some sudden death before it reached them. And then, when it was come, — when rough hands, but tender hearts, helped them aboard with many a word of pity and of wonder, — then how the truth of their safety in very deed came crowding in upon their hearts, till even Tresethen turned away his face, while Hope and Murray sobbed aloud.

All honor to that captain and that crew, Englishmen every one! All honor to the underlying good of human nature in its roughest form! How many ways it found to prove itself in the days before that merchantman dropped her anchor in Boston Harbor! How affectionately Tresethen and Murray and Hope herself grasped the hard hands of those sailors as they parted from them at the wharf! How tenderly they ever recalled their faces and their names; and how gladly, years after, they ministered to the wants of one of them who, sick and poor, sent to ask their charity!

And so Miles and Hope came home to the roof whence they had stolen awhile before; and that angry father, who had pursued them with such threats of vengeance, welcomed them there as one welcomes all that makes life dear; and when the year came round, and there was a baby to be christened, none but Mr. Hepworth should bestow

that benediction on its little head, and sanction
with his presence the merry dinner afterward
which Mr. Murray gave, as he told every one, in
honor of " My grandson, sir, Miles Tresethen,
Junior ! "